Praise For Inseverable: A Carolina Beach Novel

"Robson builds a sweet and lightly dramatic romance that deals with love, hope, and forgiveness. Well plotted with an array of personable and defined characters. Smooth flowing conversational dialogue engulfs you and draws you right into the middle of their lives." –*Smexy Books*

"Unforgettable! Callahan and Trinity will tug at your heart strings and keep you turning the pages. Inseverable is a great love story that will leave you smiling and in tears." –*USA Today* **bestselling author, Jamie K. Schmidt**

"This is, hands down, one of my favorite books of 2016 thus far… INSEVERABLE, the first book in the upcoming Carolina Beach series, is FUNNY, like really funny. Heartfelt and sweet and goofy and just plain amazing." –**Top Pick,** *The Romance Reviews*

"Call this Rom-Com on Steroids-This story has teeth and it leaves little love bites." –*Addicted to Happily Ever After*

"2016 Editor's Choice Winner…The emotion is so well grounded and layered, the characters rich and believable, the conflict complex with just the right amount of hopelessness. *Inseverable* is a beautiful romance and a story worth dedicating a weekend to." –*Grave Tells Romance*

"This is just the start of a new series by Ms. Robson, and already a favorite. I can't wait for more."
--**5 stars,** *Give Me Books*

"Equal parts sexy and funny! Cecy Robson's new book had me swooning and laughing out loud! A perfect beach read!" –*USA Today* **Bestselling Author Annie Rains**

"Absolutely loved this story! ... A great start to a new series - I'm looking forward to getting books on the rest of Trinity's friends. I see great things for all of them!" –**Sizzling Pages Romance Reviews**

"I wanted to hug this book... All the feels Robson gave me as I devoured Inseverable provided that book high I am constantly craving." –*CaffeinatedBookReviewer*

"A sexy, sweet, heart-rending story. Cecy Robson pushed every single one of my reader buttons. Loved this book!" –**Kate Meader, Author of *Playing with Fire***

"This was my first Cecy Robson read, and it will absolutely not be my last. From the minute I picked up this book, I knew I wouldn't be able to put it down. Inseverable is definitely going on my list of memorable books that I can't wait to reread." –*Reviews From the Heart*

"Already [Cecy] Robson was becoming one of my favorite authors but Inseverable sealed the deal. Inseverable shows Robson's different writing style and I couldn't get enough of this new setting and the new characters that were introduced." –*Lush Book Reviews*

BY CECY ROBSON

The Carolina Beach Novels

Inseverable
Eternal
Infinite (coming soon)

The Shattered Past Series

Once Perfect
Once Loved
Once Pure

The O'Brien Family Novels

Once Kissed
Let Me
Feel Me
Crave Me

The Weird Girls

A Curse Awakened (novella)
The Weird Girls (novella)
Sealed with a Curse
A Cursed Embrace
Of Flame and Promise
A Cursed Moon (novella)
Cursed by Destiny
A Cursed Bloodline
A Curse Unbroken
Of Flame and Light
Of Flame and Fate

ETERNAL

A Carolina Beach Novel

Cecy Robson

DEDICATION

To all the dreamers: may you land among the stars.

ACKNOWLEDGMENTS

Thank you to Nicole and Jamie, as always. One is my agent, one is my husband, and both are my friends. Nic, you believed from the moment you read. Jamie, you believed from the start. I wouldn't be anywhere without either of you.

To Kim, you started out as my assistant and became so much more. Thank you for your dedication to my success.

To Kristin, my artist and (very patient) creator of fabulous covers. No one understands my visions like you!

To my copyeditor, Gaele, who works hard, yet takes the time to enjoy my stories.

To my fellow authors and friends, Amanda Flower, Beth Vrabel, and Mary Kate SeRine. We share the good, the bad, and the sometimes *way* too ugly. Thank you for the virtual comfort food and the laughs when the tears threatened to fall.

To my readers, those who write me, interact with me on social media, those who visit me with smiles and tears in their eyes, those who know my characters as well as I do, those who speak of them as if they are as real as I believe them to be, thank you for making my publishing journey worth it all. You have my heart and gratitude.

Lastly, to my beloved children. Don't be me, be better. Take the path beside me and follow it further than I've travelled, lived, dreamed, and loved. Mommy loves you.

Chapter One
Landon

The wind picks up, brushing the gritty sand along the shore in that graceful way it only seems to do during winter. Kiawah is always bustin' at the seams in the summer, drawing tourists from as close as North Carolina to as far away as Sweden.

I take a long pull of my beer and dig my feet further into the sand. This time of year, there are two a kinds of people: the locals and the lonely. I was always the former and only mildly entertained the latter. That changed when I caught my wife blowing her manager with the same wild enthusiasm she blew me.

"Goddamn it," I mutter.

I'm not sure which part was more disturbing. Her blowing him in the kitchen, the same place we'd fucked earlier that morning, or her finishing him off while I stood there like an idiot.

I'm going to go with her finishing him off.

I can still picture her rising from her kneeling position, the front of the four-hundred-dollar blouse she insisted on buying flapping open, exposing her bare breasts with each step she took.

"It didn't mean anything, Landon," she told me, wiping her mouth with the back of her hand.

Maybe. But his teeth meant something to him. I could tell by the way he kept batting his face looking for them when the police finally pulled me off him.

The pathetic way he looked bordered on comical. Shit, the whole damn thing was comical. I might have even laughed if my heart wasn't busy joining his teeth on the floor.

Bernadette wasn't a perfect person. I knew that long before I put a ring on her finger. But I'm not either, so I thought we'd be perfect together. She needed someone to help her after the rough life she'd had. And she needed someone to take care of her, seeing how bad she still had it when we first met. I was willing to do it. Hell, I was willing to do anything for her.

Up until that moment I found her on her knees.

Call me a fool in love.

But don't make me look like one.

I push my half-empty bottle into the sand, reminding myself it's been over a year and time to move on. Sounds great in theory, but a man's pride is as important as working hard, decency, and family. That's how I was raised. That's how it should be. Bernadette, however briefly, was family. She kicked my pride almost as hard as I nailed Blaze (nice fucking name, by the way) in the jaw. All that left me to do was work hard, and damn, didn't I give that shit my all?

The wind picks up, creating swirls of bleached sand and ghosting them across the water. Mother Nature is doing her best to soothe me, gifting me with the peace and quiet I need and luring my focus to the vast ocean where the cresting waves build and crash along the shore.

Peace, I repeat in my head.

"Quiet," I say out loud.

"Trin," I mumble when my phone vibrates in my back pocket.

I pull it out, sure enough it's my baby sister Trinity. The peace and quiet on Kiawah is no match for her. "Yeah?"

"Now, Landon," she says, her South Carolina accent as thick as mine. "Is that any way to say hello?"

She doesn't wait for me to answer. "What if I was Miss Universe, calling to tell you I had the cure for global warming, and whether or not I shared it with the Environmental Protection Agency depended on how well you answered the phone? Wouldn't you feel bad for all those polar bears out there, floating on some crumbling glacier ice because you answered the phone with 'Yeah?' sounding broodier than shit, crankier than a leprechaun shoved up some poor unsuspecting bull's ass, and about as pleasant as the matador trying to coax him out—"

"What the hell does that even mean, Trin?"

"It means you should go to Becca's New Year's Eve party tomorrow night," she explains like it's obvious.

"I'm busy," I tell her.

"Doing what? Besides drinking a beer and looking out at an ocean that's not going anywhere?"

I pinch the bridge of my nose, muttering a curse when she plops down beside me.

Like me, she's barefoot. Most people wouldn't dare walk on the beach in the middle of winter. But ever since we were little, Trin and I have always loved the feel of the sand sliding beneath our feet, even in the cold.

Her jeans are rolled up like mine and she's also wearing a heavy coat. Hers is burgundy; mine is navy. I didn't bother with a hat. She did, sporting a gray beanie tight enough to keep her long black hair away from her small face. Even after having my nephew, she's still stick thin, lacking the bulky muscles keeping me warm.

She motions to my beer. "Sir, where are your manners? Aren't you going to offer me a drink? I am a lady, after all." She huffs. "Your momma raised you better than that."

I pass her the bottle. She takes a sip and makes a face. "It's warm."

"I kept rolling it in my hands," I admit. "I suppose it's hard to keep it cold that way, even in forty-degree weather."

She nods like she understands. "How long have you been out here?"

I lie. "Not long."

"How long have you been out here?"

I smirk. "A while."

"How *long* have you been out here?"

"I guess long enough."

I start to stand when her slender arms wrap around me, keeping me in place. "Landon, as your favorite and only sister on God's green earth, I owe it to you to tell you that dark, hairy, and cranky doesn't fit you." She rubs the scruff on my jaw like she's trying to swipe it off. "Lord, it's like an opossum crawled up your chest and spit out a litter of babies across your jaw."

I edge away. "Your husband has the same damn beard," I remind her.

"Oh, that's not true." She smiles and turns her attention toward the ocean, her gaze getting that dreamy look it always gets when she thinks of Callahan. "My man's beard is alpha and sexy." She makes a face. "Yours is, well, possumy." She holds out her hand. "And if that's not a word, it should be. At least when it comes to whatever the hell is laying across your face."

"Trin, if you're trying to use your charm to talk me into going to Becca's party, it's not working."

"Why? She was nice enough to invite you." She shrugs. "Besides, it's almost New Year's Eve. Time for a fresh start and a new beginning."

Her voice quiets at her last few words. She doesn't mention Bernadette. But after everything that happened, I suppose I've mentioned her enough, and so has Trin.

If hate were a super power, Trin's hate for Bernadette would have crushed the Fortress of Solitude and slapped Superman upside the head for being a little bitch. And Trin, she likes everyone.

My family is from money. It's not something I really think about, or obsess over, it's just always been there. We were taught to take care of it, add to it, but most of all be generous with it since we have so much. Maybe that's why it was easy for me to give as much as I did to Bernadette. I wanted to see her happy and maybe give her the life she always dreamed of. But where Trin and our Momma would drop a few grand setting up an auction to help raise money for the children's hospital, Bernadette would drop a few grand on herself.

My parents had insisted on an air-tight pre-nup. It pissed me off at the time, especially since they didn't insist on the same thing when Trin married Callahan. But they saw Bernadette for the gold-digger she was, not the victim I did. Love makes you blind. But it doesn't make you deaf when the woman you thought you knew accuses you of hitting her, knowing full well you'd never harm *any* woman.

It should have been an easy divorce. Sign here, initial there and then walk away. Instead, I dropped close to a hundred grand defending the abuse charges she filed against me.

"He's always been violent," she cried to the judge. "Look at what he did to my manager."

Her attorney was more than happy to present the pictures of Bernadette's manager's busted up face and put the police officers who responded on the stand. Those fine members of law enforcement admitted they hauled me off Blaze (again, nice fucking name), but were more than happy to mention Blaze's pants and drawers were around his ankles and that the missus was only partially dressed when they arrived.

"Landon," Trin says, her voice sad.

It's never a good sign when my sister grows quiet. The way she wraps her arms around mine and leans her head against my shoulder . . . Christ, the last time she did that, it was at our granddaddy Palmer's funeral.

She knows I'm remembering all I went through, and she doesn't like it one bit.

It was bad enough Bernadette accused me of abuse. But to try to make me look like a monster and get all the gossip mags talking about Landon Summers, wealthy son of Owen and Silvia Summers, accused of threatening his wife's life, and soiling the Summers name…it was more than I could take. She wasn't just messing with me. She was messing with my folks, two of the best people I know.

"She said I hit her and that it wasn't the first time," I say aloud before giving it too much thought.

"I know," Trin says. She adjusts her hold. "But Landon, anyone who knows you didn't believe her."

"But there are a lot of people who don't know me, Trin."

She sighs. "I know that, too."

The waves draw closer, but it's not until a large one breaks like an insolent slap against the shore that she speaks again. "Did she ever hit you?"

I don't bother telling her about all the shit Bernadette threw at me, including her hair dryer and the damn crystal jewelry box, nor do I mention all those dishes she'd smash when she wasn't getting her way. I don't need to. When Trin lifts her head, it's clear she knows enough.

"Landon, why didn't you say anything?"

"I couldn't do that to her."

Trin scrambles to her feet, knocking over the beer, her face pink with rage. "But she did it to you—even when it wasn't true!"

"That doesn't make it right," I say. "To be accused of something like that, it's total horseshit."

"Horseshit she was more than happy to fling your way." Her breathing becomes quick. "She didn't even blink on the stand. You saw that, right? She wanted money and she didn't care what she had to do to get it."

Which was why I spent as much as I did on the best divorce attorney in the state. Messed up childhood or not, no way was I giving her more than she was legally entitled to.

"You should have said something," she repeats.

"Anything I said would have made me look weaker than I already was." I shake my head. "Trin, when a man marries a woman who looks like Bernadette, he's supposed to keep her happy at all costs, and in every way possible. If she's fucking around on him and other men find out, they don't care that you gave her a home, more money than she needed, or that you'd protect her with your life. They assume you weren't man enough where it counted, and where it counts is in the damn bedroom."

"You're not weak." It's what she tells me, but the way she says it, I think she understands as much as she can.

I tilt the bottle, letting what little beer remains pour into the sand. "It sure didn't feel like that when I found her."

The foam dissipates, like it never was. It reminds me too much of my marriage, making me mad, bitter, and probably sad, too, despite the fact I'm tired of feeling all three.

I rise and brush the sand off my jeans.

"One drink," she says.

I do a double-take. "Now?"

She shakes her head, looking about as happy as I do. "No. Tomorrow night at Becca's. One drink, a few hellos, and you can leave." She inches up to me. "Please, Landon. Show me and everyone that you're okay." She smiles, despite the worry behind it dulling her soft brown eyes. "Even though you may not be."

The sun sets behind her, calling an end to another day. I'm ready to tell her to go home and be with her husband and child, that she's wasting her time. But Trin, she's trying, and she's the only person I've allowed in this whole year.

"It's just down the beach," she says like I don't already know. "C'mon, Landon. What could happen?"

What *could* happen? It's what I thought. The thing was, everything did.

Chapter Two
Luci

My phone buzzes, again. I don't have to steal a peek at the screen to know it's Blythe. She's been obsessively texting me for over a week now.

"You have to come to the New Year's Eve party with me, Luci," she insisted. "You *have* to. The publicist for the Carolina Cougars invited me and all the football players are supposed to be there."

It was sweet of her to think of me and to want me to go, but the party is in Kiawah, four long hours away, and very much outside my comfort zone.

I toss my phone inside my desk drawer and shut it, lifting my gaze to meet Riley's.

The hem of her short skirt skims further up her legs when she leans forward. "Are you firing me?" she demands.

Riley blinks her outrageously long lashes rather dramatically before crossing her arms over breasts greatly at odds with her double-zero figure. I'm not certain her lashes or breasts are real. From what I've noticed, every dollar she makes goes into her appearance and wardrobe. Other luxuries like food and rent are supposedly supplemented by her father, a neurosurgeon at Charlotte Central. I'm not judging her. Really, I'm not. But someone like Riley, who's always had everything yet feels entitled to more, often can't be reasoned with. Today is a prime example.

"No," I say.

"I didn't think so," she quips, narrowing her eyes.

She starts to stand, except I'm not done. "That doesn't mean you're not on probation," I add. "Nor does it mean your position is safe."

I'm not yelling or glaring. I don't have it in me to be cruel. Maybe if I did, people like Riley would think twice before mistreating me. But I've always believed in being kind. Not that anyone should mistake my kindness for timidity.

My voice is as stern as the conversation. "In the six weeks you've worked at the firm, you've arrived late almost every day."

She falls back into her chair, her annoyance clawing at the air between us. "That's a lie," she snaps.

"Watch your tone," I counter. Again, I'm not yelling. I turn my computer screen around so she can see it. "We document the arrival time of every employee who's not a member of the legal team."

"I'm a para*legal*," she tells me, her tone suggesting I'm the one out of line.

I maintain my professional demeanor, although by now it's becoming more challenging. "Which, as I've mentioned on numerous occasions, classifies you as legal support. At the time of your hire, you were informed the start time is between eight-thirty and nine a.m., sometimes earlier depending on the needs of your assigned attorney." I switch to the collection of screens. "Each square in red represents the days you've arrived after ten in the morning."

She frowns. "You can't record me like that."

"Based on the security and agreement clause you signed when you accepted the position here at Ballantyne and Bradley, we can."

"I work from home," she says.

"That's not what you were hired to do nor was it something cleared by a senior partner. I'm giving you one last warning. If you're late again, your position will be terminated."

"You're not my supervisor," she tells me.

I'm ready to beat my head against the wall. "No, your supervisor wants you fired. I'm trying to give you a chance."

"Don't bother," she says. She rips off her court I.D. and tosses it on my desk. "I quit."

I imagine this is Riley's last "F you" to me. She's never liked me and has often questioned our staff on why I hold the office manager position. "She *just* graduated from college?" I once overheard her say. "God, how old is she, thirty?"

I'm twenty-eight, not that it should matter. But since the moment we were introduced, it seems only Riley's feelings matter to Riley.

She stomps away, pausing in the doorway. "You know, Luci, maybe if you cared more about what you look like and how you dress, you'd actually have a life outside this fucking office and a reason to be late in the mornings."

"And maybe if you worked hard and committed to being a better person you'd still have a job here," I counter.

Again, there's no point in yelling. She whirls around, stopping short when she sees the two security guards waiting for her. I'd called them ahead of time in case they were needed. Riley more than proved they were. "Thank you for responding," I tell them. "Kindly escort Miss Bassett back to her desk and off the premises. Her coat and the contents of her purse are the only things she's permitted to take with her."

"Yes, Miss Luci," the first guard says.

Kee-Kee walks in front of my glass fronted office, slowing her quick steps long enough to flip Riley off. Kee-Kee is like that, which is why I've always loved her.

She slams the door shut behind her and in Riley's face. "Hey. I see you changed your mind and fired her ass."

I adjust the computer screen so it faces me and reach for Riley's file. "I didn't fire her. If you must know, she quit."

Kee-Kee is in her forties, with shoulder-length brown hair she spends a fortune on to cut and color. Between her appearance and the classic way she dresses (today a lovely navy suit), she reminds me of a younger, curvier Caroline Kennedy.

"Why the fuck did you let her quit?"

Her mouth, however, does not.

She taps her manicured nails against the armrest, something she does when she's seconds from telling someone off. Today, it's me. "You should have fired her for being a little bitch. A lazy little bitch. A lazy little bitch who liked to whore around with all the junior partners."

I hold out my palms, trying to silence her. But Kee-Kee isn't a person easily silenced. Kee is all about doing the silencing and throat-punching anyone who dares to cover her mouth.

"Did you know the last time we hit happy hour she and Jefferson went at it like wildebeests on parade following prom night?"

"I'm not sure what that means," I begin.

"It doesn't matter. What matters is she's useless and doesn't deserve to quit. You should have fired her ass. The big boss gave you the go ahead for hell's sake. Shit, even he recognized what dead weight she was and he only spoke to her twice. Didn't I tell you not to hire any millennials?"

"I'm not the one who hired her."

"Whatever," she says.

"And Mr. Ballantyne gave me no such go ahead." I shove the file into an inter-office envelope and address it to payroll. "He said it was my call and that he trusted my decision." I shrug and swivel in my seat to type the email that seals Riley's fate. "I wanted to give her a chance."

"Why?"

My fingers fly over the keyboard. "People make mistakes. Sometimes, they just need the right person to give them a chance."

"Like Mr. Ballantyne gave you a chance?" She huffs when my typing slows. "Not the same thing, Luci. You work hard, stay late, take care of everything and everyone. Riley . . . how can I put this? Riley sucks as a paralegal and pretty much as a human being. You have any idea how many other paralegals and secretaries had to pick up the slack for her?"

"I realize she's young and immature."

"She's a little shit," Kee adds. "That's what she is."

"I won't argue that," I agree.

I'm trying not to think about what she said, about how I look and how I don't take care of myself. It shouldn't have bothered me. I realize she meant to hurt me the best way she knew how. But I can't deny that at least some of what she said is true.

Managing the office has become my life, from ensuring the attorneys and staff have everything they need, to picking up the slack for those who fall behind. I eat well and run a few miles on my treadmill every other day. I just don't do more for myself than necessary.

Maybe I should.

"What's wrong?" Kee asks.

"It's nothing," I say.

"Luci, did she say something to you?" She frowns when I don't answer. "What the hell did she say to you?"

I hit the send icon and print out a hard copy. "She said that if I cared more about how I looked and dressed, I'd actually have a life outside this office."

She presses her lips and nods. "I'll give the little skank that one."

"I thought you were on my side." I stand and reach for the paperwork sliding out from the printer behind me. I'm wearing a charcoal gray pencil skirt, a light pink sweater, and a pretty floral scarf. My attire doesn't draw the eye. It's not supposed to. "And what's wrong with the way I dress? I'm professional."

"So am I, but at least men can tell that I have tits." She motions to my blouse. "The jury's still out on whether you've hit puberty. Damn it, Luci, you're thin and have never had kids. If there's a body underneath all that polyester, show it, don't hide it beneath all those layers—and what's up with all those scarves you can't seem to live without? It's forty degrees in Charlotte, not minus twenty in Buffalo."

"I thought I needed a little color." I adjust the scarf around my neck when she makes a face. "It's elegant."

Her scowl deepens. "Yeah, I'm sure all those seventy-year-old men at church get hot and bothered every time they see you strutting into a pew."

"I don't attend church."

"Then stop dressing like that's where you're headed." She thinks about it. "Or maybe you should attend. At least then I'd know you do something with your weekends."

"I do things on weekends."

"Oh, yeah?" she asks. "When was the last time you had a date?"

"October," I admit.

"You're kidding."

That's actually pretty good for me. "All right, when was your last date?"

"Last night," she replies.

"Oh," I answer.

"Why haven't you had sex since October?"

"I, um, didn't exactly have sex."

She blinks at me as if I'm speaking another language. "I don't understand. Was he cute?"

"Yes."

"Did he have a penis? Strike that. Clearly you didn't get that far. But if he was cute, that's usually good enough for me." She thinks about it. "Okay, maybe he has to be nice and employed, too. He was nice and employed, right?" At my nod she asks, "So why didn't you?"

I shove the paperwork into a manila folder and sigh. "It wasn't a good time."

"Wait." She pushes back her hair over her shoulder and knits her brow. "Are you talking about that blond guy I saw you with at *Tajos*?"

I nod, surprised she remembers. "Yes, that was him."

"What happened? He wasn't cute, he was damn hot. Nice ass, too." She drops her hand. "Did you tell him you didn't screw on the first date or some crazy shit?"

"No, even though I don't sleep around."

"I didn't say anything about sleeping. You could have kicked him out the minute you finished your orgasm."

"Kee-Kee," I mumble.

"Just tell me," she says.

No one needles me like Kee-Kee, but she's a good friend. Despite embracing her stereotypical New York City persona like a beast, she has a tremendous heart. "We were having a good time, or so I thought, until he saw his ex-girlfriend walk in with another man," I explain. "He spent the remainder of the night crying about how she broke his heart and tossing back more bourbon than should be humanly possible."

She places both palms on the desk and leans in. "Luci, for the love of God, tell me you left. No, tell me you called him an asshole loser and then left. Do *not* tell me you stayed and listened." She groans when I don't answer. "Come on, Luci. You're better than this."

I cover my face. "He was really upset—"

"Oh, hell," she says, pushing away from the desk.

"I felt bad for him." My hands slap against my lap. I know how pathetic I sound. "And then he was really drunk and I couldn't just leave him."

"So you stayed and you listened and you drove his drunk ass home, didn't you?"

I don't answer. I also don't tell her how he threw up all over the back seat of my car.

She frowns. "He puked on you, didn't he?"

"No."

"Well thank heavens for small favors—"

"He puked in my car," I mutter, coming clean.

I wait for Kee to yell at me. She simply shakes her head. "And you wonder why I took Riley the whiner's side."

"Kee-Kee!"

"Luci, your last name is Diaz not Door Mat. He trekked his dirty and sloppy feet all over you and you just let him."

"I couldn't leave him," I repeat.

"You know what your problem is?" she asks.

"I'm too nice?" I guess. It's what she and Mr. Ballantyne always tell me.

Kee shakes her head, appearing sad. "No. Your problem is you deserve more than you expect for yourself." She motions to the clock on the wall. "It's five o'clock on Thursday, the night before New Year's Eve. The building is officially closed and won't open again until Monday. Go home."

I motion to the pile of assignments on my desk, but Kee's reprimanding stare silences me. "Work can wait. The good things in life can't. They're out there, Luci. Find them and enjoy them before you lose your soul saving everyone else."

I watch her leave. For a long few moments all I do is sit and stare at the rows of cubicles laid out in front of me. One by one, the staff pile out, some hurrying to catch up with their friends, others speaking excitedly into their cell phones.

My hands shift through the stacks of projects in front of me. I need to skim through the designs the interior decorator prepared, or at the very least email her to say I'll be in touch after the holidays. I want to keep busy. I have to, even though I barely feel anything at all.

Riley's words struck a blow, but Kee-Kee's hit me harder. Kee is a real friend and real friends point out things you've ignored for too long.

It takes me a moment to gather my things. By the time I'm done, the entire floor is empty. I'm the only one on the elevator and the only one crossing the lobby. I hurry to the coffee stand when I see the workers closing down. It's early for them. But like everyone else, they appear ready to embrace the long weekend.

I put in my usual order, an egg and cheese bagel sandwich and three large waters. Belinda, the owner, moves quickly, filling my bag and another packed with bagels.

"Take them," she says when I hesitate.

If they were all for me, I'd feel bad and refuse. But she knows they're not which is why she offers. "Happy New Year, Luci," she says.

"Thank you, Miss Belinda," I reply. "Happy New Year."

I clutch the bags and hurry out, burying my face into my scarf when I push through the revolving door and the wind picks up. I step onto the busy Charlotte streets. The entire city is bustling with activity. Drivers honk their horns, irritated by the long row of cars barely crawling through traffic while pedestrians rush by, anxious to get home or to the nearest bar.

The heels of my boots click across the sidewalk in quick succession as I head toward the park, my heartbeat matching the steady rhythm. I take a deep breath and release it slowly. This is the path I both loathe and fear, and one I take almost every day. Today, however, these three blocks seem longer and more painful.

I reach the small park. During the day, mothers push strollers through the crisscrossing walkways and children play on swing sets, their little voices filling the atmosphere with laughter and the occasional cry for a snack. But once evening begins to take form, those same mothers disappear with their children, giving ample space to the tribe of people who occupy the walkways and benches, and who loiter long after the sun disappears.

It doesn't take me long to find who I'm looking for. She's sitting at a bench, waiting for me, her scraggly yellow coat too big for her thin frame. Greasy locks of curly hair stick out in knotted clumps from beneath her hat. I place the bags beside her and step away, unsure what mood I'll find her in.

"Do you have any money?" she asks, her voice deep for a woman who appears so small.

I lie, steeling a glimpse at the setting sun, the bits of light it offers pushing between the branches of the old magnolia trees. "No, Fernie, I only have food."

She shoves her hand into the largest bag, crumpling the paper with her dirty fingers. The sound is loud and bitter, reflecting her mood, but not quite muffling the encroaching sound of shuffling feet. I edge away. It seems Fernie brought friends. Like always, they appear to be the wrong kind of people and the last ones she needs.

A man with a long beard and tattered red beanie reaches Fernie first, his glassy eyes and volatile stare alerting me that he's already high and seeking more than another hit. He ignores Fernie and the bagel she attempts to hand him, unlike the other man and three other women who eagerly stretch out their palms.

"Bye, Fernie," I say. I keep the man with the red beanie within my sights without looking at him directly. As with Fernie, I'm wary of him and the people accompanying him.

Fernie doesn't glance up from the bag, nor does she bother thanking me. I'm not surprised. Fernie . . . she isn't capable of much.

"Next time bring money," she tells me.

I don't answer, hurrying away when the man in the beanie takes a step forward. My pace and heartbeat quicken when I sense him follow. I reach for the mace in my pocket.

My shoulders slump and I breathe a sigh of relief when I return to the busy walkway and a police cruiser pulls in along the curb. Two officers slide out, their attention drifting from me to somewhere behind me. Almost immediately, the steps following me cease. I glance over my shoulder in time to see the man in the red beanie inch back into the park.

I don't stop, moving ahead and away. The police officers nod in my direction. I've seen them before, usually around this time. While I welcome their presence and the safety they offer, I don't welcome what the younger patrolman has to say.

"You shouldn't be here at this hour," he mumbles as I pass.

I have to. It's the only way I'm sure my mother eats.

I don't say the words out loud, and I don't speak to anyone about Fernie. I visit her privately, hoping that one day, she'll give in and allow me to get her the help she needs.

I wipe my eyes. After a lifetime of being pushed away and abandoned by the woman who gave me life, I should be immune to the way she treats me and accustomed to the circumstances I find her in. Like the rest of my family, I should be able to turn my back and let her go.

But I can't. I never could.

I was six when she dropped me off on my grandmother's front porch. She didn't bother to knock or ring the doorbell. My grandmother wasn't expecting me and I was so certain Fernie would return, I stood on that porch waiting for her.

It wasn't until my grandmother walked out to throw away her garbage that she realized I was there. She hurried to embrace me, realizing what happened when I broke down crying.

Whether I want to be or not, I'm still that little girl, hoping for the mother Fernie never was.

I return to the building and take the elevator down to the parking deck. My phone rings as I crank the engine to my RAV 4. I hit the Blue Tooth, my hand and voice trembling as the memory of that day pokes me hard enough to sting my eyes with tears.

"Hello?"

"Luci, it's Blythe. Quit blowing me off and come to Kiawah with me."

I tug off my scarf, realizing I never responded about the party. My big plan for New Year's was a hot bath, a warm bed, and a *Stranger Things* Netflix marathon.

As pitiful as it sounds, I was looking forward to three days of doing nothing, until Riley said what she did and Kee-Kee agreed with her.

Mostly though, I think about my mother, how I constantly look for her on that bench and how there will come a day when I'll never find her.

"Luci?"

"One drink and we leave?" I ask.

Her pause is brief. "Yes," she adds quickly. "If you're not feeling it, I promise we can leave whenever you want."

"All right."

"All right what?" she asks.

"I'll go to Kiawah with you."

"Yes!" she squeals. She rattles off a storm of details, telling me she'll be at my house by nine in the morning and that this party is going to be epic.

I ease my way into the growing traffic. She's excited, her perky voice animated. I unbutton the top of my coat, wishing I could share her excitement, but more than anything wishing my life could start like I needed it to.

Chapter Three
Landon

I step into Becca's house, handing my coat to the staff member who rushes toward me.

"Thank you, ma'am," I say when she lifts it from my grasp.

The band, the Three Amigos (all five of them), blast their version of *Cake By The Ocean,* the explosion of bass pounding against the marble floor. Streamers of gold and silver fall like icicles from the ceiling, sparkling against the spinning strobe lights while waiters dressed in head-to-toe black weave through the crowd, hoisting trays covered with booze, more booze, and tiny hors d'oeuvres of shrimp and thinly sliced filet.

I'll give Becca this, she knows how to throw a party.

"Landon?" she yells from clear across the open foyer.

I offer a small wave, not expecting her to leave the group of men gathered around her with their tongues waggling. I recognize most of them, professional ballers from the Carolina Cougars. She doesn't pay them any mind, too busy pretending she doesn't notice Hale standing a few feet away.

Hale has his own entourage of admirers closing in fast; long, leggy women he finds about as interesting as Becca found those ballers. He and Becks had a bad falling out years ago, so bad neither has recovered from it, but not so bad they still don't find ways to run into each other. When you love hard, you hurt even harder, and those two . . . yeah, they ain't done hurtin' or lovin' yet.

The woman closest to Hale skims the back of his neck with her nails and whispers into his ear. He doesn't respond, too busy watching Becca and how she shakes her ass a little harder when she passes him.

"Hi, Becca," I say when she reaches me. I put an arm around her and give her a hug. After all these years, she's more family than friend. That doesn't mean I don't notice how pretty she looks.

A strapless mint dress hugs her figure. She holds out her drink and kisses my cheek. "Hi, baby," she says. "Look at you being all social." She steps back, giving me the once over. "Damn. Trin was right, you look like shit."

There's a reason she and my sister have been best friends since they tore off their diapers and went skinny dipping in the ocean.

"Still," she adds. "I'm glad you're here." She fusses with my sweater, smoothing it out. "There're a couple of ladies from the cheer squad I'd like you to meet, and some I'd like you to stay away from. Not because they're not friendly, more because they're a little *too* friendly, if you know what I mean."

She doesn't wait for me to answer, not that I could get a word in even if I tried. I edge back when she starts stroking my beard. "Oh, Lord, I'm not sure about this thing," she says.

"You don't like the beard, I get it."

"Yes, that, and the hair isn't working for me either. Goodness, Landon, when was the last time you had a decent cut?"

I'll admit it's been a while. I've always kept my hair short all around and a little long on top. The top's now long enough to brush my eyebrows, and the back, well that's grown out, too. I didn't think it looked bad, except according to Becca, I'm dead wrong and shouldn't be out in public without a paper bag covering my head.

She purses her lips like my beard physically pains her. "No, this just won't do at all. Let's get you upstairs and give you a little trim."

"No."

"It won't take long," she says, as if that's the issue. "I have a beautiful grooming set one of our sponsors gave me. High-end, expensive, it will do the trick nicely."

"The beard stays and so does the hair," I tell her. "And I'm not interested in meeting cheerleaders."

"Are you gay?"

I roll my eyes. "No, Becca."

She points at me. "Then trust me, you're going to want to meet dem cheerleaders, son."

"Where're Trin and Callahan?"

She smirks, knowing I'm trying to distract her. Becca may be blond, but she's never been dumb. "Upstairs. Hmm, come to think of it, they've been gone a long time. Must be they're working on baby number two. Shit, it's like they're twenty or something. Every time he touches her, it's like they'll burst into flames if they don't fu—"

"I'm going to stop you right there," I say.

She throws back her head, laughing. I'm not laughing. That's my baby sister she's talking about. Grown married woman or not, that's who Trin's always going to be to me.

I step away and around her. "Hey," she calls out. "What about the cheerleaders?"

"If I need to score a touchdown, I'll be sure to find them."

I follow behind a waitress hustling back into the kitchen. Becca's place is roughly ten-thousand square feet like mine. Except where my house is two-stories and wide, hers is tall with three levels. Just like I've made my money, she's made hers, snatching the public relations world by the throat and shaking it hard.

I'm near the band, who've been strategically set on the second floor overlooking the foyer. Smart. With the acoustics, they probably don't need speakers, except here they are at full volume, converting the foyer into a dance club.

Hale nods as I pass, easing away from a redhead and "the whisperer," who seem to be getting a little too close for his *and* Becca's taste. I grin, pausing to take in the show.

Becca shoves her way between the women and Hale. "Hi," she says, all Southern lady like. "I don't believe we've met. I'm Becca Shields."

The women smile the way hyenas do when a lioness tries to invade their territory. Neither say much, eyeing Becca like she's interrupting and needs to leave.

That's when the Southern lady shows her claws, all the while hanging tight to her smile. "Becca Shields," she repeats. "This is my house, my party, and my man. Keep your hands to yourself, watch your manners, or get the fuck out."

And how about that, those other women are no longer smiling. They are, however, stepping way back. Becca waits until every last hyena abandons Hale Mountain, the martini glass dangling elegantly between her fingers as if she wasn't ready to toss it aside and scratch their eyes out.

"Hale," she says, giving him a stiff nod as she turns on her heel.

He hooks his arm around her waist, and drags her to him, slamming the front of her into the front of him. If he were anyone else, I'd already have him on the ground. But like I said, there's something there neither seem ready to let go of.

Becca's breath catches, her eyes widening briefly as she meets Hale's face. "So now I'm your man? Could have fooled me, sugar."

Becca rises to her full height, her grit and fire returning. "Just trying to save you from yourself," she glances over her shoulder to where the women watch her from the corner. "And from any communicable diseases you may or may not acquire." Her gaze is rock-steady as she turns it back on him. "You're welcome."

Hale laughs, his hand sliding down her back and over her ass as he releases her slowly. The contact is brief and barely a touch, but I can feel the heat from here.

"Thanks, Becca." He loses his smile. "What would I do without you?" he asks, drawling out the words.

He walks away without another glance. That doesn't stop Becca from watching him leave. The ballers who couldn't seem to get enough of Becca's presence eye Hale closely as he passes them, the one in the front appearing seconds from taking a swing.

"Watch it boys," Hale tells the large group. "Don't start shit you can't finish."

I turn in Becca's direction when Hale disappears out the door, and the ballers don't follow. Hale's a friend and if those men had started in on him, I would have started in on them.

For a fleeting moment, I see a chink in that magnificent armor Becca keeps perfectly polished. "Damn it," she mutters, her heart appearing to sink.

I start toward her, but as quick as a snap, that peek into her vulnerability is stowed away. She beams at a couple who approaches. "Hey. So glad you could come," she says, hurrying to kiss cheeks in greeting.

Hale and Becks, they have it bad. I only hope they can work through what's keeping them down and soar off into the sunset together.

I push off the wall and bump into a man kissing his very pregnant wife. "Oh, sorry."

"It's okay," he tells me, chuckling when the woman wipes the remnants of her lipstick off his face. "Is it that bad?" he asks her.

She grimaces. "Sorry, honey," she says.

They ignore me and kiss again. I give them space and work my way to the rear of the house. Bernadette refused to kiss me in public, always worried I'd mess up her makeup. Maybe that was part of the problem. I needed a woman who cared more about loving me than loving what she looked like.

I head toward the kitchen, nodding to a few more of Trin's friends. There's Sean at the bar, just as tall and lanky as the day he turned fifteen and already slamming back shots. Some blonde I don't know jumps up and down, giggling and egging him on.

Mason stands nearby, one woman on each arm. He was always the strong silent type, built like a brick wall and about as brilliant as he is tough. He's never been chatty, but whatever comes out of his mouth works well enough.

Women love Mason. Sean, well, he's always been one toy shy of a Happy Meal, but he means well. "Damn," Sean says, wiping his mouth. "That was harder to swallow than a cow's teat." He holds out a hand. "Not that I've ever tried." He pauses. "At least not on purpose."

The blonde stops laughing.

"Hey, Landon," Sean says, waving to me.

Mason, like Hale, offers a tilt of his chin. I answer with another nod. They're good men, but I only told Trin I'd stop by. I'm not in the mood to shoot the shit.

Nor am I in the mood for some of the looks cast my way.

I don't know any of the professional players, but you'd think with them here, all those people who've known me most of my life would be somewhat distracted. Instead, there's Darlene Sotta watching me like she expects me to keel over and die.

She and the woman beside her exchange glances, whispering low. I don't know her name and I don't want to, especially after that.

"Poor thing," Ivy Lionelle mouths to her friend, her attention latched on me.

Four men who used to play ball with Hale glance at me as I pass. I keep my focus ahead. I don't like the reception I received from Darlene, Ivy, and those women they're standing with, and I don't want to hear shit one way or another from these men. As ballers in high school, they were the first to get laid. None are married, to my knowledge, which means they're still getting their fair share of dates.

Hale, Sean, and Mason took me out the moment the ink dried on my divorce papers, insisting I needed to get some, and doing their damnedest to make it happen.

They ended up getting drunk and (I shit you not) hooking up with triplets. I ended up driving their drunk asses home and pouring myself a cold one to drink alone in my living room. Although Hale's clearly into Becca, and Sean and Mason have plenty of company, I know them and my sister well enough to guess they're going to try and fix me up tonight.

Fuck that.

I step inside the large kitchen that opens up into an even larger great room where a New Year's Eve show is taking up the giant flat screen along the wall. I glance at the time at the bottom of the screen. Damn, it's only eight-thirty. Why am I so tired?

I slide into a stool at the raised counter where another bartender is mixing specialty drinks. It's a lot quieter in here which is fine by me.

"What can I get for you?" the bartender asks.

She's blonde, with hints of leftover tan like a lot of women here on Kiawah. The only difference is she's in a tight black T-shirt and pants as opposed to a tight dress. "What do you have, ma'am?"

Her lips curve at my "ma'am" remark. Even before she spoke, I knew she wasn't originally from the south. In the south, your parents are your "momma" and "daddy" no matter how old you get, and everyone is "ma'am" or "sir" regardless of age.

"You can just call me Apple, cowboy," she tells me.

I could also probably get us a hotel room by the sounds of it. "Why Apple?" I ask, ignoring the cowboy reference.

"My specialty is Appletinis." She points to all the drinks along the counter. "But tonight I'm making Jack's Grand Ball, Royal Clovers, B-52s, New York Cocktails, and Romance." She plays with her bottom lip. "But if you'd like something more like Sex on the Beach, just let me know."

"I'll take a beer, thanks."

I'm trying to be polite, and maybe I shouldn't be. Maybe I should take her up on the offer, or tell Becca that, yeah, I'd be happy to meet one of her cheerleader friends. But her offer, and all the ones I've received this year, aren't what I want. They don't mean shit.

Until I see her.

A redhead almost as tall as Becca trails in, sprinkles of freckles in all the right places peppered against her cream-colored skin. A deep green velvet dress hugs what looks like a dancer's body. I only know she dances because her figure is similar to Bernadette's, though I can't be sure this woman dances as good on the pole.

She's a gorgeous girl. There's no denying it. But she's not who my focus trains on. Behind her is a petite, slender young woman with light eyes and a pale pink strapless dress. The skirt doesn't hug her body, it flares out, skimming just above her knees.

Long brown and gold waves fall along her bare shoulders, natural curls from what I can tell, unlike the crazy amount of hairspray that must be holding her friend's spirals in place. And where her friend's skin is so fair it glows, hers is olive.

If she's wearing make-up, I don't really notice it, at least not from here. What I do notice is her angelic face.

She glances around, unsure she should be here, unlike her friend who's already making herself at home.

I lift the beer the bartender passes me and take a hard pull. I can't remember the last time a woman caught my interest. It was nice while it lasted. Maybe in another year, I'll be willing to say hi to one.

"Landon!"

"*Landon!*"

I scrunch my eyes closed when I hear not only Becca, but Trin, too.

They rush me, all enthusiastic-like. Lord, help me.

Trin gets to me first, throwing her arms around me. She's in a simple blue dress, and the only jewelry she's wearing are small stud earrings and her wedding band, but that's just Trin. "There you are. Me and Becca have been looking for you."

"I'll bet," I say.

"I couldn't get him to trim the beard," Becca interjects, like I'm not right here.

"Mmm-hmm," Trin says, nodding.

"Or the hair," Becca adds.

Trin pats her arm. "The important thing is you tried." She clears her throat, turning on me. "Becca has a few friends she wants you to meet. Isn't that right, Becca?"

"Sure is," she says. She claps her hands. "Ladies, can y'all come over here a moment? There's someone I'd like you to meet."

At once, what seems like the entire Carolina cheerleading team appears. One of them leans in close to Becca. "He's cute," she says, loud enough for me to hear.

And cue the introductions. Becca shimmies forward. "Darlins, this here is Landon Summers, engineer extraordinaire. Landon, these are my girls, Britney, Teenie, Mindy, Sandy, Chrissy, Lizzie, Brandi, Clarey, and Blythe."

"Hi," they all say, offering a well-rehearsed wave. All, but one.

The cute brunette who walked in with the redhead is off to the side, checking her phone. I almost ask Becca what her name is, but change my mind.

"Nice to meet y'all," I say. I nod for like the hundredth time since I've walked through that door and turn back to my beer.

My mind starts to wander to next week when my self-appointed mental-health break wraps up and the time to get back to work begins. Becca introduced me as an engineer, which I was and probably always will be at heart. I don't remind her I'm an attorney now. After attending law school and passing the bar two years ago, it still feels new to me, probably since this last year numbed the last few years away.

"Landon?" Trin presses her hand on my shoulder. She looks sad. I suppose I should try to smile and reassure her, but I don't manage that much.

"I only promised you I'd show and that I'd have a drink. Here I am." I tilt my bottle of beer. "And there it is."

She glances toward the great room where the cheer team has begun to work the room. "Didn't one of those ladies pique your interest?" she asks.

I almost turn to see if the little brunette is gone. Almost. Instead I answer the best way I can to explain what I'm feeling. "Trin, I need time and space. I don't want to force something that's not there. I spent three years doing that when I was married, and never want to go there again."

She smiles softly like she understands a lot more than I'm admitting to her and myself. Wasted time. That's all those years with Bernadette were. I knew something was missing. I beat myself up trying to make her happy—trying to make up for her troubled childhood and convincing myself that her past was what held us back from the life we needed and deserved. I was *convinced* that if she could just be happy, I would be, too.

It took finding her in that kitchen with her manager to see what was actually missing was love. She never loved me enough to want my happiness, no matter how hard I worked to make sure she had hers.

As I think about it and what I told Trin, I'm not sure I'm right. Time and space may not be enough. Christ, it's like the day I found Bernadette and that idiot, I lost everything, including my trust in women and belief in forever. It eats me alive even now, even as all these sexy women strut past me. They think they have a shot. They don't. Hell, how can they when I don't bother to bring a gun and load the damn bullets?

"Hey, Landon." I look up to find Callahan, tension tightening his brow. He doesn't clap my shoulder in that brotherly way we've been doing for years. His long, bulky arms immediately find Trin's waist.

That's my first clue that something's wrong. Trin senses it, too, angling around to get a better look at him. "Is it too loud for you in here, love?" she asks.

"Some," he says, the strain building along his shoulders telling us otherwise.

"Then we'll go," she says.

He doesn't reply, something in his expression widening her eyes. She lifts her hand, stroking his beard. "Baby," she says. "Can you hear me?"

The little brunette in the pale pink dress appears behind Callahan as he slowly nods. She makes her way to the other side of the raised counter, unaware of what's happening. "Hello," she says, her voice as soft as her appearance. "May I please have some water?"

The bass from the music intensifies, and from the foyer, the crowd screams, energized.

Callahan's lids fall closed and he seems to be working to breathe. "I saw Becca near the stairs . . . told her I'm taking off," he says, struggling to speak. "She told me to take a bottle of champagne."

"Okay. Let me check on the crab cakes. I just put them in the oven." She cuts herself off when she realizes Callahan may not last that much longer.

"Excuse me, do you need help?"

We turn in the direction of a small voice. The little brunette raises her hand in a way of an apology. "I'm so sorry," she says. "I don't mean to intrude. But if you need to leave, I'm happy to check on the food for you."

"That would be wonderful, thank you," Trin says. She glances at Callahan leaning against the granite counter, rubbing his eyes, the muscles along his broad back straining against the collared blue shirt he's wearing. "Wait for me outside, love. I'll be quick, I promise."

He doesn't argue, making me think he's a lot worse off. "All right."

Trin snags my arm when I start to follow. "Give him a moment, won't you?"

She knows him better than I do, so I watch him cross the great room and open the sliding glass doors leading onto the terrace. The ocean is loud in her song tonight. I can hear her over the roar of the music and the growing throng of people. He and Trin will likely walk home, in the opposite direction from my house. The walk will do him good, the ocean waves crashing along the shore a better remedy to restore the soul than any medicine I know.

"What's wrong with him?" the bartender asks.

She's not being rude, she seems concerned. "He's a war hero," I reply. It's the best way to sum it up, and the best way to honor what he's been through.

"I'm sorry," she says.

I am, too. I'm thankful for soldiers like Callahan. I just wish there was a way to ease their suffering and erase the damage of war.

The bartender gives me her back, allowing me to focus on Trin where she's whipping an orange sauce in a bowl. "It's okay, you go," the tiny brunette tells her. "I'll make sure they get done."

"Thank you. They're Becca's favorite," Trin explains. She doesn't tell her Becca's grandmother would make them every New Year's Eve, and how Trin took over the tradition when her beloved grandmother died. Knowing Trin, she wouldn't share something so personal about her friend, even if she wasn't in a rush.

Becca appears behind her with a bottle of champagne, along with Hale who's carrying a couple of coats. They talk low and fast, and move even quicker, Becca's hand tight in Hale's as she follows him out.

They pause by the doors to the terrace, waiting for Trin. Trin throws her arms around me, everything she's feeling for her husband seeping through in that tight hug. "Love you, Trin."

"Love you, too, Landon," she pauses to look at me with those same sad eyes. "Happy New Year."

She takes off, shrugging into the coat Hale handed her, Sean and Mason at her heels. Like Hale and Becca, they seem to know what's happening. These are Trin's real friends. Through thick and thin, they've always stood by her.

Banging from the kitchen has me turning in the direction of the wall oven. The brunette shoves the tin of crab cakes into the center, shiny with the sauce she basted them with.

No sooner than she sets the timer and takes off her oven mitt than Kirk Watson arrives. "Hey, sweet thing. How about you fix me a plate of food?"

How about I punch you in the head, Kirk?

I glare in his direction. She's the only non-Caucasian woman in the immediate vicinity. I'm not trying to be a dick and assume he's racist, I've just known him long enough to know that's what he is. Not to mention, she's in a cocktail dress or whatever the fuck, not dressed in a black shirt and pants like the caterers Becca hired.

Her small chin juts slightly forward. "I'm sorry, sir," she says. "I don't work here, I was just helping someone out."

Kirk is already drunk and way past horny. He leans his arm against the overhead cabinet and gives her the kind of once-over that should send her to the nearest shower to wash his filth clean. "Then how about I buy you a drink?"

"It's my understanding the drinks are free," she tells him.

He sidesteps in front of her when she tries to walk away, blocking her. "Come on, sweetie. I'm just trying to be nice."

I don't think things through. I storm in from the opposite side and from one blink to the next, I'm suddenly there.

The brunette takes a step back and into me, my presence startling her and making her jump. "Back off, Kirk. She's with me."

Maybe I shouldn't have said what I did, but Kirk's the type who doesn't know when to quit unless there's a bigger man there to make him.

Tonight, that bigger man is me. He swipes his shaved head, offering me a slick smile that turns challenging real quick. "Is that right?"

"Damn straight." I think the brunette looks up at me, but I'm too busy looking at Kirk. Yeah, he's drunk, and ready to take a swing. The protective side of me kicks in. I grasp my supposed damsel in distress by the elbow and gently guide her behind me.

His gaze trails to her briefly before returning to me. "I thought you were hard up."

"Nah," I say, not wanting to give this idiot any amount of satisfaction. "Onto bigger and better as you can see."

"Or tinier and cuter?" he offers.

"Watch your mouth," I fire back, knowing he's not complimenting her, but rather trying to rile me. "Like I said, she's with me."

I clench my fists, causing my knuckles to crack. I don't think he hears the crunch, not over the music and escalating clamor of voices. He sees me, though. Whatever he catches in my hardening features is enough to make him back down.

Smart man, at least when it comes to a fight. He knows I can take a hit, and give one a hell of a lot harder.

He grunts and slinks away, like he did me a favor by letting me off and not the other way around. I keep him in my sights. By the time he reaches the door leading out to the foyer, he perks up, likely having spotted the next woman he'll approach.

I wait until he disappears into the next room before turning back to the brunette. "Ma'am," I say, tilting my chin.

I mean to step away and back in the direction of my beer. One drink and out, right? Sounded good in theory except the moment I shift my weight to walk away, her smile holds me in place.

It's not the kind of smile that promises anything close to what the bartender offered, nor is it teasing and daring like the ones from the cheerleaders. It simply is, fragile like the first snowflakes that fall in winter, and shy like a young woman at her first dance, hoping no one notices she's not dressed like the rest.

I like what she's wearing. She looks nice to look nice, not to impress or show off. And someone as pretty as she is, doesn't need to be so shy.

Her lips are glazed in a soft pink like her dress, not overly done, just enough to give them a shine and glisten her light eyes. "Thank you," she says, quietly. "For helping me out."

"You're welcome."

I take a step in the direction of the bar, eyeing my beer like it's waiting for me to return. But the step feels unusually heavy and I think my friend the beer can wait.

I turn slowly and offer this little thing with the pretty eyes and soft smile my hand. It shouldn't seem like such a big deal or much of an effort, but it's a little of each. Maybe for both of us. "I'm Landon."

I watch her hand disappear within my grasp.

"Hi, Landon," she replies quietly. "I'm Luci."

Chapter Four
Luci

I was cold from the moment we rushed out of the car. "We don't need coats," Blythe had insisted. "The party's indoors."

The moment the brisk air smacked our faces, I started shaking and couldn't seem to stop.

But I'm not cold anymore, not with all the warmth radiating from Landon's palm.

His hand swallows mine whole. But neither my hand nor I will complain. Landon is . . . wow.

My fingers slide along his skin as he slowly releases me . I thought he was headed out and away from me, perhaps to meet some elegant socialite he was expecting. It could explain his disinterest in Blythe and all the stunning women on the cheer team. But here he is with no other woman in sight.

Except me.

Blythe told me Kiawah had a lot of wealth. I imagined pretty and classic southern homes with worn wooden siding overlooking the ocean, similar to those in coastal New England. I wasn't picturing this modern masterpiece, nor was I expecting so much flash. No wonder Blythe dressed like she did. Like the other women flouncing around, she's in a designer gown that appears spray-painted rather than zipped on, unlike the leftover bridesmaid dress I retrieved from the back of my closet.

She could have warned me. I thought she chose her dress simply to impress "the guy" the Cougars's publicist wanted her to meet.

"The guy," evidently is Landon.

"Luci?" he asks. "As in, *You Picked a Fine Time to Leave Me, Lucille?*"

I laugh a little. "No, Lucianna."

The corners of his mouth curve slightly. It's not much of a smile, but enough to add to his allure and more than enough to show me smiles don't come easy for him.

"I like that better," he says, his Southern accent outrageously thick and all-too sexy.

My shy smile widens, becoming more of a real one that maybe I'm not used to showing either.

I glance down. "Thank you."

"For liking your name?"

"For that, but mostly for talking to me." I motion around. "I don't really know anyone. I came with a friend."

"It's all right. Most of these people aren't worth noticing." He shrugs. "But maybe some are."

I think he might mean me until he averts his gaze. Perhaps he doesn't see me like I see him.

I, conversely, noticed Landon right away. He's the only man in jeans, but it's his looks and beard that caught my attention.

It's not one of those trendy beards men grow, the long ones carefully groomed to lay over clothes designed to appear earthy and casual. This is the type of beard men grow when they could care less about shaving, and even less about impressing anyone.

With dark brown hair and brown eyes, there shouldn't be anything especially gripping about him. Yet everything is, from his classically handsome features to the hint of strength and muscle lingering beneath his plain black sweater.

"Would you like to join me at the bar, Luci?"

I glance from where the bartender is smiling at a man speaking low into her ear to the great room. Blythe is cozying up to one of the football players. If he's who I think he is, he's married and she should be stepping away instead of stepping closer.

"You don't have to," he adds.

His tone gives me pause and lures my attention back to his face. He's not angry that my attention skittered briefly. The casual way in which he spoke made it clear that life will go on regardless of whether I join him.

"It's not that." I steal a glimpse at Blythe. "My friend that I came with . . ." I crinkle my nose when I realize how much I'm telling him. "She, um, was looking forward to meeting you."

His playful smile warms my cheeks. "Doesn't look that way to me." He leans in, pretending to whisper. "Between you and me, I think she's doing her best to meet Number Sixty-Nine."

My mouth pops open. "She's not really like that." It's what I claim, even though Blythe very much is.

Landon raises his brows. "You do know that's the number on his jersey." My beet red face answers for me. He smirks. "Guess not."

I cover my mouth. "Oh, God."

He bows his head, chuckling. "You don't follow football do you?"

"No, I'm afraid I don't."

"Now, how can you live in the Carolinas and not watch America's favorite pastime?"

"I'm from New Jersey," I offer apologetically.

Oh, and there's that smirk again. "Well, then I suppose you have more problems than not watching football."

"It's not as bad as people think," I counter, unable to suppress my smile.

We walk as one toward the bar. "Oh good, because I think it's pretty damn bad."

He pulls out a stool for me before taking a seat and reaching for his beer. I cross my legs. "I'll have you know there are a lot of great things about New Jersey."

He drums on the bottle, but doesn't quite take a sip. "Name one."

"We have the shore," I point out.

He makes a face. "Yeah, I've seen the show."

I laugh. "Not that shore, the rest of it. The whole Jenkin's boardwalk is pretty and fun, a great place to be a teen and hang out. Oh, and Sea Girt, Bay Head, and Stone Harbor are pieces of paradise you never want to leave."

He tilts his head toward the wall of sliding glass doors. "I don't know there, Luci. I can't imagine any place better than Kiawah."

I grin. I can sense how much he means what he says. "Have you always lived here?'

"Born and raised and hope to die here," he says. He takes a swig. "No place like home."

"If you've always lived here, how do you know there aren't better places?"

His grin takes him from a man jaded by the world, to one still hoping the world might be better than it is. "I've been everywhere," he replies. "That's how I know this is where I'll spend the remainder of my days."

"Tell me where you've been."

He frowns, as if he doesn't really believe I want to know.

"Come on," I say, motioning with my hands. "Wow me."

"Wow you?" He rubs his beard. "I don't know, that's a lot a pressure to put on a man, but I'll give it my best seeing how you were nice enough to help out my sister."

I expect to hear Switzerland and France, based on the atmosphere. I don't expect all the places he rattles off. "Vietnam, Bosnia, Thailand, Israel, Egypt, and about every country in South America."

"Not Europe?" I ask.

"I've been there, too," he says. "Iceland, Spain, Italy, Germany, Austria, Hungary, Sweden, and all of the U.K."

"But also the other places you've mentioned?" He nods. "Why?"

"My parents volunteered all over the world and thought me and my sister should volunteer with them." His focus flickers over my face as if trying to gauge my reaction. "They wanted us to see and know life outside of Kiawah."

"To show you the imperfections outside your perfect world?" I ask quietly.

He pauses with his beer at his lips. "Something like that."

In the time that follows, only silence comes, and a lot of him eyeing me when he doesn't think I'm paying attention. I'm not a person who's uncomfortable with silence. I prefer it to the noise people make when they speak words that say nothing and mean even less.

Perhaps Landon feels the same.

My focus wanders back to Blythe, who is closing in on a different player. I almost think I should take her aside and tell her not to try so hard, that it's not so bad to be alone. But I'm no longer positive that's true.

Being next to Landon is nice, even though he's not saying a word.

"You have something on your collar."

At least he wasn't.

I turn to find him pointing at my neck. "There, right there," he says.

I know he's messing with me. I don't bother to look or remind him my dress is strapless. "Are you trying to tweak my nose?"

"Yes." He shrugs when I laugh. "It always works on my nephew."

"I'm not your nephew."

The corner of his mouth curves in a way that should be illegal. "Oh, I know that."

His face reddens slightly, the color probably matching mine. "Are you trying to flirt with me?" I'm not typically so bold, but he's charming, regardless of the hesitation I sense.

He hangs on to his lopsided smile. "Yes."

"Oh." I reply so quietly, I'm not certain he hears me.

He leans in, careful to keep a respectable distance, but close enough that I can smell his cologne. It's fresh, lightly sweet, but clean and masculine. "Don't tell anyone, but it's been a long time since I flirted with a pretty lady. Toddler humor is the best I have."

"It can't be so bad if it makes me smile." I point to my mouth. "See?"

This time when he grins, the sadness and resentment I first noticed dissolve into the pool of his dark eyes, leaving an attraction he couldn't mask in his silence and one that draws me further in.

"You didn't like that idiot hitting on you in the kitchen, did you?" he asks.

I shake my head.

"Well, Miss Luci, I didn't much care for all those women Becca tried to pawn me off on, including your friend. What d'ya say we make a deal?"

I don't know what he's offering. That doesn't mean I'm not ready to say yes. "What kind of deal?"

"I'll keep the idiots off you." He points in the direction of the couch where a few men gathered collectively frown, muttering low and turning away in a huff. "And you keep the women trying to make me their sixty-nine far away from me."

I didn't realize anyone else had noticed me, but Landon did. Just as I noticed more than one gorgeous woman in an all-too gorgeous gown cast a smile his way. I offer a hand. "Deal."

He shakes it, smiling. "How about some romance?"

He chuckles when my jaw falls open and points to the purple drink the bartender is mixing. "That's the name of the drink." He holds out his hands. "But if you don't like romance . . ."

I gnaw at my bottom lip. "How about a shot of courage instead?" I turn to the bartender. "May I please have two shots of Tequila? One for me." I glance over my shoulder at Landon. "And one for my bodyguard."

~ * ~

I bat my hand as the shot burns its way down my throat. "Take a lime. Here, *here*," Landon says, passing it to me.

I pull it off one of those mini-plastic swords and suck hard. "Oh, that's strong."

He coughs into the back of his hand, laughing. "This was your idea." His tongue flicks across his lips, gathering the drops of Tequila that dripped out when we tossed back the shots and he caught the look on my face. "What do you think, one more?"

"Okay," I say, which only makes us laugh harder.

"Two more, please," he tells the bartender. He pulls out his wallet and drops what looks like a Benjamin into the tip jar. "Want a Corona to go with the shot?"

"Sure."

"Yeah?" he asks.

"Yes," I assure him. "And a bottle of water, please."

"Good call," he agrees.

The bartender nods in his direction, affirming she heard us, despite the horde of drinks she seems to be working on, and the man she can't seem to stop flirting with.

"All right, my turn to ask a question," he says. "What's the worst date you ever had?"

I blow out a sigh. We started out simple enough, favorite foods, mine, sushi, his Thai. Favorite music, both of us fist bumped when we agreed on classic rock. Landon is a die-hard Springsteen fan, but he gave me props for my love of the Eagles. Now, we're getting personal. I don't mind. Maybe this is better.

I re-cross my legs and fan the skirt around me. "All right, here's a good one. I'm sixteen and all beside myself because this cute guy from my science class wants to take me out for a slice."

"A slice?"

"Yes," I reply, wondering why he appears so perplexed. "A whole pie would have been too much."

"He took you to eat pie?" he asks, slowly.

"No, pizza," I clarify. "We call pizzas 'pies' up north."

He cocks a brow. "What's wrong?" I ask. "Did I confuse the good ol' Southern boy?"

He grins. "So now I'm a good ol' Southern boy?"

"Don't worry," I say, patting his hand. "We all can't be from Jersey."

"Well thank Christ for that," he says.

I giggle at his remark, exactly as he intends. "Okay," I continue. "So I was stressed about what to wear since I didn't have a lot. I begged my cousin to lend me something. She gave me this pretty dress with flowers on it that I absolutely loved. I was giddy and excited and for once in my teenage life, actually confident. I walked into the pizzeria with my head up, smiling when I saw him and absolutely beaming when I sat down across from him." I make a face. "That was the highlight of the story. From there, everything pretty much goes to hell."

He cracks open the bottles of water and passes me one. "Why?"

"Turns out the cousin who lent me the dress was the girl he actually wanted to date."

"Ouch," Landon responds. "How did the pie lovin' Romeo screw that up?"

"My cousin and I were at the mall when he and his friend saw us. He told his friend my cousin was hot, and his friend falsely assumed he was referring to me."

Landon lowers his bottle. "Oh."

"Mm-hmm," I say. I swallow a few gulps of water and some of the pride I lost that day. "The best part is, guess who were assigned as lab partners the following week?"

"Shit," he says. He tosses back his water, putting down the half-empty bottle on the counter a few seconds later. "Want my take on this?"

I play with the cocktail napkin in my grasp, trying to appear casual even though I'm worried about what he'll say. "I'm all ears."

He holds out a fist and counts off his fingers. "One, he's a dumbass. Two, he's a rude dumbass." He works his jaw, as if he doesn't want to admit the rest. "Three, his friend was right in thinking you were the hot one."

I cover my mouth, trying to hide my surprise and delight. "You don't even know what my cousin looks like."

His gaze locks on mine, the intensity and heat behind it causing my hand to drop away. "I don't have to," he says, adding a wink.

The deep thrum of his voice and the oh-too sizzling way he looks at me makes me fall eerily still. For a moment, I don't even breathe, waiting for him to turn away or take it back. Instead he keeps his eyes on mine, assuring me he means what he says.

"Thank you," I whisper.

"My pleasure," he replies.

The insecurities that I walked in with tumble to my feet, fading away and leaving only Landon behind. The quiet that first greeted us when we sat down returns, but rather than finding somewhere else to look, our full attention remains on each other.

Landon is ridiculously good-looking. Not in a way most would immediately notice, but in a way no one could ever forget. I should be embarrassed by the way my smile widens the longer I stare, and maybe I would be if he wasn't doing the same.

In his eyes, I see the woman in me who remains, the one who's young and whose future is yet to be determined rather than the woman who buries herself in work and stows her fears away.

The shots appear, as well as the beers. He motions to the bar with a tilt of his head. "You still feel up to it?"

This will be my second shot and my first beer. I'm feeling the effects of the first for certain, but I'm feeling the effects of Landon more. He wants to make sure I'm okay, adding more sexy points to the ones spilling across his broad shoulders. "I'm ready if you are."

"Well, then, far be it for me to tell a lady no."

I lower my gaze and I give the back of my hand a flick of my tongue, pausing when I meet Landon's gleaming stare. I think he's going to say something. Instead his tongue passes over his skin in a swirl, the motion widening my eyes.

Good. Lord.

He cocks his head. "Something wrong?"

"No," I say, or rather, whimper.

He chuckles and lifts the bottle of salt, sprinkling the crystals onto our hands. "Bottoms up?"

I clink my glass to his. "*Salud.*"

We taste the salt, slam back the shot, and suck on the lime. My face scrunches as that familiar burn rips a line of fire down to my stomach. Landon cracks up, reaching for his phone and snapping a pic.

I dab my mouth with a fresh cocktail napkin. "What are you doing?" I ask.

He taps away on his phone. "Oh, nothing. Just setting up my new wallpaper."

I gasp. "Don't you dare! I look awful."

"No, sweetheart. You look fucking adorable."

I wince. "I doubt it." I pass my fingertips over my throat. "I seriously think this last shot put hair on my chest." I tilt up my chin, exposing my throat. "Are there any hairs growing? A real friend would tell me."

I lower my head when he doesn't answer, my lips parting when I see the way he's watching me. A sense of desire I'm not familiar with reflects in his gaze. I only recognize it because it mimics the sparks firing within me.

"You don't have any hairs," he manages.

"Good," I stammer. The timer goes off in the oven, saving me by the bell, although I'm not certain I want to be saved.

He clasps my hand when I slide off the stool. It's not hard, just enough to keep me in place. "Where are you going?"

"I have to check on the crab cakes your sister made."

He starts to rise. "I'll help you."

I place my hand over his chest. Although my touch is gentle, this time I'm the one keeping him from moving. "No, I'll take care of it. Will you . . . will you save my seat?"

He turns my hand, curling it in his and lifting it to his lips to kiss. "Darlin', you don't have to worry about a thing."

It takes some effort to step away, my chest hurting from how hard I'm gushing. When I finally do, I work quickly to fill the serving plate Landon's sister left. "Ma'am, would you like these at the buffet?"

I look at the server, a young man likely in his teens. "Yes, please. But if you're able to, would you save some for the hostess? It's my understanding they're her favorite."

"Yes, ma'am. I'll set some aside."

"Thank you." I finish placing the lemon wedges when Blythe appears.

"Hi," I say.

"Can I talk to you?" she asks.

Blythe doesn't return my smile and appears upset. I glance back to Landon where he's finishing off his water. "Ah, sure."

She leads me into a small hallway. A door to a bathroom opens beside us and a young woman steps out, hurrying into a billiards room just past a large dining area.

"You look like you're having a good time," Blythe says.

Her tone seems off, and at first, I think she's angry that I'm spending time with Landon. "I'm sorry, we started talking and—"

"I met someone," she interrupts. She gives a small laugh. "Okay, that's not entirely true. I met him before, but now we're actually talking."

"That's good," I say, wondering where this is heading.

She passes me her glass of wine, taking a moment to adjust her breasts beneath her gown. "The thing is, he's here with other people. It's complicated and, well, I was wondering if you would mind if he and I went back to our hotel room."

"Wait, where am I going to stay?" Because I'm certainly not staying with them.

"There's the pull-out couch," she reminds me, referencing the suite she booked. "But I realize that may be awkward."

"You think?" I ask.

"Luci, please don't be mad."

"Blythe, you invited me. I was perfectly happy staying home."

"If you'd stayed home, you wouldn't be warming up to the man I was supposed to hang out with," she counters.

"You mean you and the entire cheer squad," I point out. She presses her lips into a firm line, appearing insulted. I continue, "Don't blame me for something you *think* I did to you. Not when you walked away from Landon and on to the next man who caught your interest."

I'm not certain what she's more bothered by, that she wasn't the only one Becca had planned to introduce Landon to, or that I was the one he chose to speak to.

She glances toward the end of the hall, where a man and woman are speaking quietly. "Look, I'm sorry," she says. "And I feel terrible about putting you on the spot. I spoke with Becca. She has a ton of space and offered you one of her bedrooms. It's upstairs, the one at the end with the dark blue linens. It's private, so you'll have the whole suite to yourself. There're toiletries and everything you might need."

I shake my head. Blythe is many things, animated, beautiful, and athletic, but not much more. I should have known she'd do this.

"It's safe here, Luci. If it wasn't, I wouldn't leave you."

She's already made her decision. There's no sense in arguing. "Fine," I say, even though it's not.

"I'll be back for you tomorrow afternoon," she adds. She knows I'm angry. Yet it's not enough to keep her from doing what she wants. "Becca says to help yourself to anything in the kitchen."

"You're leaving now?" I ask.

Guilt and maybe something else passes along her features. "He's ready."

"Then I suppose you shouldn't keep him waiting."

"Luci," she says.

I step away and into the bathroom, shutting the door a little too harshly. I wash my hands. As I dry them, I catch my reflection in the mirror.

The small amount of makeup I applied remains in place and my hair is still behaving. I'm dressed for a party and a fun time. As I think of Landon, I'm reminded that's where I am and what I'm having.

Blythe won't ruin my night, not when it's gone so well without her.

The smile that faded in her presence returns when I think about who's waiting for me. I ease out of the bathroom and return to the kitchen, but Landon is gone. So is my purse and . . .

My heart falls to my belly, only for it to quicken when a hand gingerly presses against the small of my back.

"Are you hungry?" Landon asks. He motions to the corner where a set of heavy curtains sway in the breeze. "I figured with all that we're drinking, we should get something to eat."

"That would be lovely," I say, realizing how much I mean it.

He passes me my clutch and leads me forward. A server slips out from behind a curtain with an empty tray. He nods at Landon. As he passes, Landon slips something into his palm.

"Thank you, sir," the young man tells him.

Landon winks when I look up at him. "After you," he says.

He parts the curtain, allowing me onto a small terrace surrounded by tall glass dividers that repel the wind and allow a magnificent view of the ocean. There's not much room, but what's here is enough.

A rectangular fire pit radiating with turquoise glass warms the small area, while a table and two chairs press horizontally against the dividers. To our right, people laugh from a larger, more open terrace one level down. They can't see us well and I don't really care to see them.

Our beers and two unopened bottles of water are waiting beside two empty plates. At the center of the table is a large serving dish toppling with food.

"Becca likes to eat breakfast out here when she's home," Landon says. "But she's not using it and I didn't want to waste the view."

"It's amazing," I say, taking in the splendor.

I didn't expect to see the ocean this far from the water's edge, especially at night. But with the moon as bright and as low as it is, its light spills across the waves, illuminating the water and casting a glow along the sand.

Landon pulls out my chair. "I wasn't sure what you liked, so I asked the staff to bring a little of everything." He pauses. "You're not one of those crazy vegans are you?" I laugh. "If you are, I can ask them for some of that crazy vegan food you people like to eat."

"My people like everything," I assure him, watching him take a seat in front of me.

"So do good ol' Southern boys," he replies.

We spend an outrageous amount of time talking, and even more time simply gazing at each other, smiling softly when the words don't quite come and laughing when they finally do.

It's only when Rihanna's *Love on the Brain* begins to play that Landon tears his attention away from me and back in the direction of the party. "Don't you hate it when everyone is dancing and you have no one to dance with?" he asks.

I glance down, playing with the fabric of my skirt. "I think it's worse when the wrong person asks you and you've been waiting for the right one."

"Oh, yeah?" He grins when I nod. "I suppose I should ask you before the wrong person gets a chance."

He doesn't really ask. He doesn't need to. I place my hand in his when he opens his palm.

He pulls me up and into him, wrapping his arms securely around my waist as mine circle his neck. He smiles as he gazes down into my eyes. I look into his beautiful browns, losing myself in his warm stare.

We move in unison to the beat as if we've danced a hundred times, although what I'm feeling is a slew of firsts.

The first time his hard muscles press against me.

The first whisper of his breath against my skin.

The first touch that has no inkling of innocence.

And the first stroke of desire.

His fingers drag along my back as the bass pounds deeper, his body appearing to crave more. "It's almost midnight," he murmurs against my bare shoulder.

I shudder when his lips graze over my skin, not quite touching, trailing just enough to tease. "Almost," I agree.

The allure in his voice robs me of air. "I didn't plan on having anyone to kiss."

I almost reply, but the way Landon's mouth hovers over the sweep of my neck keeps me silent, as does the way he draws an invisible line to my ear with his lips.

My heart thuds mercilessly as I wait for his next words.

"But I guess I didn't plan on you either," he adds, each word softly tortured.

His mouth feathers over mine as the song ends and the countdown to New Year's begins, opening and closing tentatively, giving me a chance to pull away.

I don't. I *can't*. Not when he feels this good and not when his large frame curls protectively around me.

Urgent voices and anxious steps echo from inside as the countdown reaches ten and people rush to find partners to kiss.

Landon and I aren't waiting. His tongue dives deep, prodding possessively.

He grips my hips, pulling me closer, turning the sweet, tentative kiss passionate and daring.

I'm no longer simply kissing him, I'm moaning.

And I'm not alone.

A rumble builds in his throat, ending in a long, dragged out groan.

My body trembles with need, responding to the rough caress of his palms along my spine.

The clock strikes twelve, people are cheering, bottles of champagne are exploding, and the waves crash harder against the shore. I barely hear them. I only hear Landon when he pulls away, his breath labored like mine, his intensity holding me in place.

"I wasn't supposed to be here," he says, his tone harsh. "I was supposed to spend the night alone."

I nod, recognizing a loneliness in him I see in myself.

"I don't want to be alone any more, not tonight. Will you come home with me?"

There's no hesitation. "Yes," I reply.

Chapter Five
Landon

I push my body against Luci, forcing her back against the wall and kissing her brutally, my straining erection poking against her hip like a branding iron and marking her as mine.

She claims me in return. Her nails drag down my back and her hips sway, rubbing me and making me harder.

"*Fuck*," I grunt against her ear.

I curse again, thinking I'm being too rough, that I need to slow down, and because I can't turn the damn alarm off!

"Sorry." I pull away from her just enough to punch the code again. This time, I get it right. You might say I'm distracted. You might also say I've never been this desperate to be with a woman in my whole damn life.

Luci is gorgeous and so sensual, I could barely keep my hands to myself the short ride back to my place.

Like I told her, I was supposed to be alone and sleep alone. Now, I'm doing neither. Now, I have this beautiful woman staring back at me, her chest rising and falling with how fast she's breathing. I think she's turned on, like me. But I need to be sure.

I rest my palm next to her head. She's wearing my coat. When she told me she didn't have one, no way in hell was I letting her walk out into the cold dressed like she was. I helped her into my coat and into my Maserati, but all I've wanted since my arms first wrapped around her was to help her out of this dress.

I'm trying be a gentleman. I swear I am, except it's hard to behave when she kisses like she can't get enough of me. I slide my lips over hers, savoring the way her mouth makes love to mine. Each pass is like a challenge that dares me to kiss her more passionately. I accept the challenge whole-heartedly, unable to resist.

My thumb grazes her plump bottom lip as I pull away. "You sure you want to do this?" I ask.

"Do what?"

I stop moving until a playful gleam warms her delicate features, amping up the already incandescent fire scorching my veins. "You want me to say it?" I ask, grinning against her mouth.

"I do," she whispers. Her thin fingers thread through my hair as she plants a kiss that robs my breath. "It will mean more if you say it."

I almost reply with, "Then let's fuck all night long." Almost. It's what I'm prepared to do and what Bernadette would want me to say. But Luci isn't Bernadette. Not even close.

My deep timbre lowers and my smile vanishes. "I want to be inside you," I say. "And spend all night making you feel good." I slip my fingers into her mouth, waiting until her lips fasten around them before pulling them out slowly.

I smirk when her gaze heats like melting jewels. "You'd like that, wouldn't you, Luci?" I dig beneath the layers of her skirt and yank the crotch of her panties away. She gasps when I find her nub and give it a few swirls. "Yeah, you would, wouldn't you?"

She stiffens at first, watching me until her lids grow heavy and her pelvis follows the motility of my fingers. It's erotic and seductive. I'm loving the way her face transforms from innocent and angelic to sexy and desperate for my touch.

I want to keep teasing, but her slick center makes me think she wants more.

My fingers slide right in. Her nails dig into my shoulders and she throws her head back. I stroke in and out, slow at first, then faster when she squirms.

I don't think she's expecting what follows, or maybe she is. It seems new to her yet something she can't get enough of. She likes where I'm taking her and I'm all in for the ride.

My hands get busy, my mouth, too, kissing the base of her throat, the weight of my body the only thing keeping her standing. I straighten when she whimpers, the bright light in my foyer allowing me to watch her face flush from pink to red. Her head falls forward and against my shoulder. "*Landon,*" she gasps, her thighs shaking against my hand when she comes.

She's not quite done when I whisk her in my arms and carry her up the stairs. My mouth seizes hers, she holds me in place, cradling my head.

God, *that mouth,* soft and sinful all at once, threatening to bring me to my knees.

I can't see where I'm headed, making it hard to manipulate the steps. It doesn't matter. My strength and Luci's sex appeal propel me to the second level and down the long hall just fine.

We crash through the double doors leading to my suite. I place her on her feet only to shove her against the wall and grind against her. She moves with me, following my lead, exposing her throat for me to kiss.

My head spins, my need for her making it hard to recall where I put the damn condoms. I break away when I remember, pulling the drawer free from my dresser in my haste and all but slumping with relief when I find that long forgotten box.

I toss it on the bed, stopping a few feet from where she waits for me against the wall. "You ready for me?" I ask.

She nods, her eyes blazing with yearning. "Yes."

That's all I need to hear. I dip my head, kissing her in long, languid motions.

I grip the lapels of my coat, peeling it off her and letting it fall in a crumpled mess on the floor as she fumbles with my belt. My tongue gets busy along her throat, teasing her skin between gentle bites while I unzip her dress.

I tug the fabric down to her waist, bending slightly to unsnap her bra and bury my face between her breasts. They're bigger than they looked, soft and full within my palms, the tips as sweet as honey.

She shudders. "Are you cold?" I ask, giving her nipple a deep suck.

"No," she stammers. "I just like what you're doing."

Her words cut off in a grunt. I rub the sweet spot over her panties just twice before sounds of lust tear from her throat and I lose my mind.

I peel off her panties between kisses. She slips out of her shoes and shoves down her skirt, giving me time to practically rip off my sweater and ditch the rest of my clothes. I glance up to find her naked. Her shoes are lying near my pants. She's shorter now without her heels, maybe five-feet and change.

That doesn't mean she's not beautiful.

Aw, hell. It's like she's photo-shopped.

In the moonlight streaming in from my floor to ceiling windows, her skin is a rich gold. Her soft breasts lift up and down as she breathes, and her large brown nipples strain to pebbled points, begging for my attention. They'll have it, but for now my focus travels to her small waist and the curve of her hips.

"*Damn*," I rasp.

Her gaze shoots to my waist. "I was thinking the same thing," she says, stumbling over her words.

She's not referring to my six-pack. Nope, not the way she swallows, hard.

"Come here," I tell her.

My voice is so harsh it comes out like a command, masking the relentless desire I have to rush her and spread her legs.

She doesn't argue, walking to me slowly, allowing me to take in the sway of her hips and how her hair gathers around her shoulders. My hands grip her ass, needing her close.

"God damn, you're beautiful," I tell her.

I attack her mouth, the force I use bending her spine. She moans like she did back at the party, as if I'm not already out of control.

I break off the kiss when she strokes my hardening length. The head is throbbing and I'm ready to ram inside of her. Already a small bead of fluid gathers along the tip. She notices, placing her finger around it and spreading the drop in a circular pattern.

"You have no idea what you're doing to me," I breathe against her skin.

I back her into my unmade bed, falling in with her.

She parts her legs, allowing me to rub against her while my mouth latches onto her nipple. I reach for the box of condoms, smacking the crumpled piece of cardboard a few times before I finally grasp one and rip it open.

Luci's hips sway beneath me, sweeping up and down on my shaft in a way that has me groaning in the best kind of agony.

I slide the condom in place, reaching between us to get in position.

Luci pushes up on her elbows, placing her hand on my chest. "Landon, wait," she says.

I immediately stop, my fingertips skimming against her cheek. "What's wrong?"

Her voice is as gentle as her smile, despite how scared she suddenly appears. "We have all night. Let's slow down. Okay?"

"You don't want me?" I ask.

She scans my face, taking a moment to gather her words. "It's because I want you that I want it to last. Give me the chance to make you feel good."

Her hand presses harder. I edge back, allowing her to guide me, fixated on the way she looks at me like she can't believe I'm real.

We kneel in front of each other, her hand skimming down the center of my chest and to my abs. Her touch and the attention she shows me keeps me in place, no matter how bad I need to hold her.

"Let me play, okay?" she asks, her voice more of a purr. "Please?"

She inches away until she's on all fours in front of me, pulling on my erection and securing her lips around it. I scrunch my face when I feel the warmth of her throat, every curse word I know streaming out of my mouth with each pass.

Her suction increases, encouraging me to pump, slow at first, then faster when she becomes more aggressive.

I glance down. Her long waves fall around her face, shielding her from me.

I want to see her. No, I *need* to see her. I gather her hair, expecting her to glance up. But regardless of what she's doing, and how good she's doing it, she remains shy, keeping her eyes closed and her head down.

Her silky hair slides through my fingers as I release it and curl forward. I give my fingers a few sucks before penetrating her folds.

Luci moans, the vibration immersed so well into her throat it stimulates the start of my release.

My palm smacks against her skin, matching her increasing speed. It becomes too much, for me and for her.

Both of us finish loudly, but neither of us succumb enough to stop our urgent movements.

I pull out of her mouth, yanking off the condom and tossing it to the side before dragging her to me.

We're all over each other, kissing, touching, and biting. My hands explore, wanting to commit her curves to memory. She returns my affections, wiggling beneath me as sounds of pleasure escape through my lips.

It doesn't take me long to get hard again, not with how hot Luci makes me. I reach for another condom, rolling it in place. Her knees fall open as I climb on top of her. Instead of kissing her, my face hovers over hers.

I want to watch her as I fill her and take in every bit of her when I thrust.

If I could just get in.

I adjust her hips and try again.

"Sorry," she says, her lashes fluttering when I rub my thick tip against her.

"Don't be," I say, lowering to nip her chin.

I push a little harder, careful not to hurt her, then toss her legs over my shoulders when I start to slide in. But she's so unbelievably tight, I'm afraid I'm killing her.

A thought occurs to me and I freeze. "Are you a virgin?" I ask.

Her face is shadowed in darkness. That doesn't mean I can't sense her blush. "No. I . . . I just don't have a lot of experience."

If I didn't think she could turn me on more, I was wrong.

She starts to apologize. I cut her off with a kiss. This one is longer, lazier, but with plenty of fervor. I like what she says and my kiss more than proves it.

I take my time stretching her, her moans demanding more with each pass. When I'm all the way in, I pull back, wanting to see her pretty face.

And damn, she doesn't disappoint.

Lust swims in her eyes, her hands slapping against the sheets when I return forward.

I do it again, each time harder and more forceful when I see how wild I drive her.

"You all right, baby?" I ask, easing off her when her spine arches.

I want to be certain this is pleasure I'm giving, not pain.

She holds me in place, her voice desperate. "Please don't stop, Landon." She gasps. "This is the best I've ever felt . . ."

Chapter Six
Luci

The winter sunlight streams through the large windows, the tiny particles in the air dancing in time with the waves roaring in the distance. I slip from beneath Landon's hold. He's fast asleep on his belly, the sheet he covered us with now a mere strip across his toned calves.

I'm not sure what time it is, I only know that it's late. After the night we spent making love, it has to be.

I grimace as I reach the edge of the bed and lower my legs onto the floor. "Making love." These are the words I use to describe what happened between us. They're likely not his, no matter how good it was.

My hair falls forward as I bow my head and sigh. Blythe should be coming for me soon. She's expecting me to be at Becca's all alone. If it weren't for Landon, that's where I would be. Instead here I am, barely having slept, my thoughts whirling over everything that happened between us.

I glance over my shoulder, watching him sleep and unable to help the soft smile that comes. He was so sweet and sexy, *perfect* in all the best ways possible.

I bite on my thumbnail, feeling nervous and giddy, and maybe a little shy.

The men I've shared a bed with have been few and on the small side. Landon isn't small in any capacity. When I first saw him naked, all I could do was gape, my awe of his body and prowess crippling me and leaving me in a well of intimidation.

It wasn't until he called me to him that I could move, his voice as seductive and addictive as his touch. Yet it's not merely his physique, nor what we did in bed that leaves me breathless. It's simply Landon, an incredible man and very unlike anyone I've ever met.

In the handful of hours we spent together at Becca's house, he was more of a gentleman than all my past lovers combined. I think most would have warned me against going home with him or tried to convince me he was playing the charmer rather than being genuine. But everything I saw showed me a man very alone in a crowd, someone who shouldn't have been at the party—not because he didn't belong— but because he didn't want to be there.

At least not at first.

Until we met.

My toes curl and relax against the slick wood floors. I'm not sure when that shift occurred, when friendly conversation turned into something more. I'm just grateful that it did. It was easy and as natural as breathing. We laughed and joked until we didn't, and took a step neither one of us had planned.

My fingertips trail over my throat, remembering what it was like to dance with him, and how that first kiss threatened to knock me to the ground.

Everything that happened was more of a dream. My smile fades. But now I'm awake in my very humble reality.

I pull the sheet around me, feeling cold, unlike when I lay in Landon's arms.

It's time to go. I know that. That doesn't mean I'm ready to leave.

I'd rather take off this way, I reason, and hang onto the memory while it's perfect and unmarred. The last thing I want is some awkward "morning after" talk, or worse yet, words of regret I'm not ready to hear.

I gather my hair, trying to remember where my panties were tossed. I find them near the nightstand and hurry to tug them on, taking a seat as I ponder where I left my phone.

"You leaving?"

I twist slowly to find Landon still on his stomach, peeking up at me. He pushes up on his forearms, the movement bulging the muscles along his arms and shoulders. "Don't tell me you just used me for sex."

I laugh, watching him edge to where I sit. He pulls my back against his chest and slides his hands across my arms until my forearms lay tucked beneath his and his long legs rest on either side of me. Traces of his cologne remain, intermixing with the erotic scent of sex and male. I take all of it in, relishing how warm his skin feels this close to mine.

He plants a kiss on my shoulder. "The third condom broke," he murmurs.

I crinkle my nose. "Yes, I know."

"And the fourth, and the fifth, too," he reminds me.

I nod. "I remember."

"It was an old box," he explains. "I should have checked the expiration date, but I didn't think about it at the time."

We didn't think about a lot of things the way we should have. He replaced each one and we just kept going, unable and unwilling to stop.

In the seconds of silence that follow, I steel myself for what may come. "Is there anything I need to worry about?" he asks.

I shake my head. "No, I've always been clean and I'm on the pill." I stiffen, my stomach churning with unease. "Is there anything I should worry about?"

He breathes a sigh of relief. "No. I'm clean, too." He pauses. "But I think you should know I'm not on the pill."

His chest rumbles against me when we laugh. I angle my head to meet his face. He rewards me with a tender kiss I wish I could hang onto forever. Our gazes lock as we break away. He strokes my face. "You sure you have to go?" he asks.

I almost say no. Yet once more reality pokes its ugly and relentless head, reminding me that my time with Landon is over. "Yes," I reply.

I can't hide the disappointment in my voice and neither can he. "All right. Let me make you breakfast and then I'll take you wherever you want to go."

"You cook?" I ask.

"Yeah, I do." He smirks. "I'm more than just good looks and a primal god of passion."

I cover my mouth, laughing as he slips out of bed. He walks across his massive suite, pausing to stretch as he reaches his bathroom, every muscle of his tall frame flexing in seamless unison.

He pauses, turning just enough to find me gaping again. "Are you staring at my ass?"

"No."

I'm lying of course, and he knows it.

He rubs his jaw. "I don't know," he says. "I'm not an expert or anything, but that's about the best example of ass staring I've ever seen."

I cover my reddening face. "Aren't you going to put some pants on?" I ask instead.

I feel him approach, his palms sliding on either side of me as he leans us back. "Darlin', I think it's a little too late to pretend we haven't seen each other naked." He nuzzles my neck. "Especially after all those mind-blowing orgasms I gave you."

The best I can do is not faint from the ungodly amount of allure spilling from his essence. "Or maybe you need reminding?" he murmurs, his thick Southern accent deliciously sexy. His finger hooks the crotch of my panties. "And now that we know we're both safe, you're on the pill, and my condoms aren't worth a damn, there might be a few more ways I can stir your memory."

My panties are down to my ankles by the time he lifts us to the center of the bed. I kick them off, wrapping my arms around him when we begin our kiss. I'm not doing much, but it's enough.

He hardens against my belly. I reach between us, wanting to touch him. I don't stroke him more than twice before he pulls away, sweeping kisses down my body. He stops only briefly to roll my nipples between his fingers before his mouth dips between my legs.

My hips jerk with his first taste. I slap my hand over my mouth, trying uselessly to quiet my grunts when his tongue circles faster. Between his sucks and frantic licks, I lose myself in a lust-filled haze, my pelvis titling back and forth to meet his lips.

"You like that?" he asks me between flicks. I crane my neck to see him. Landon isn't shy, not like me. His full focus is on my face, appearing to enjoy each moan and whimper I can't possibly contain.

I manage a nod, reaching for him and sliding my fingers through his thick hair. Something in my actions cause a change in his gaze. He gives his tongue another flick. "Don't worry, Luci," he says. "I'm not going anywhere yet."

He dips his chin, increasing his efforts. I become more vocal, the noises passing through my lips unbelievably guttural, encouraging Landon to go faster. He sucks hard, knowing I'm close, his fingers raking along my inner thighs.

My entire body jerks violently as I climax. Landon hooks the back of my knees, holding me tight and keeping me against him as I ride out the pleasure jolting through my limbs. He lifts off as I finish, allowing me to climb on top of him.

He's done a lot work to please me. It's my turn, and I have a lot to reward him for. The moment our bodies join I start to move, bouncing against him until the sound of slapping skin echoes around the room in a steady rhythm.

Landon moans, gripping my hips, the cords along his neck tightening the quicker I move. His hands slide along my stomach to my breasts, his knuckles brushing against the tips. Like last night, he can't seem to get enough of me. I feel the same, his body as intoxicating as his scent.

He pulls me down for a sultry kiss that entices me to go faster, lifting my hair as it tents around our faces. His tongue circles and his lips trace mine, making sure to get every last bit of me.

The arousing way he kisses, combined with the feel of him sliding in and out, makes me daring. "Do you like how I taste?" I ask.

His face heats and the muscles along his jaw tighten. He knows I'm not talking about our kiss. "Hell, yeah," he gasps, returning to my breasts and tugging on my nipples.

I don't stand a chance against his masculine power or the way he touches me. I bear down, stimulating my peak as a primitive roar cuts through his clamped teeth.

Lush, dark waves explode through me, making me scream. Landon flips us over, the force of his thrusts shoving us to the opposite end of the bed. I drag my short nails across his back, the relentless pounding of ecstasy almost too much and not nearly long enough.

"Fuck," he says, his head falling forward as the spasms recede. "Holy *fuck*."

We start to slide off the bed when he yanks us upward. Landon falls back on his heels as he keeps me on his lap. I almost expect us to laugh over almost tumbling off the bed. But neither of us are laughing.

Through our labored breathing, we stare at each other in shock. Perhaps like me, he can't believe what's happened or how good it was. He combs his finger through my hair, pushing my long waves over my shoulder, appearing to search for what to say.

He's not alone.

Landon doesn't seem real. None of this does. I'm not supposed to be here with this sexy man in his beautiful home, basking in more attention and kindness than a stranger could honestly show. If there's any doubt, my phone ringing near the door is a harsh reminder that this, whatever this is, is over.

I avert my gaze, knowing I have to pull away, but not quite managing. "I have to get that," I say.

Landon doesn't move, his fingers lingering over my face. I don't move either. If I do, it's like everything we shared will disappear in an instant.

I turn back to stare at his perfect features. Like me, his expression is riddled with words that don't come.

The phone stops ringing, giving us a reprieve that doesn't last. It rings again, the long dragged out tone growing more insistent.

I start to lift off him. Only it's his voice that keeps me in place. "Luci," he says.

I cup his shoulder. I shouldn't feel this miserable. We've only just met.

"It's my friend," I tell him, wishing I could say more and that he could understand why I'm feeling as much as I am. "The one I went to the party with."

His hand glides along my thigh as I slip away. I pad across the wood floor, each step I take filling me with that familiar loneliness I've felt too often in my life.

The phone stops ringing before I reach it. I bend to retrieve my small clutch buried deep in the pocket of his coat and pull out my phone. I glance over my shoulder, pausing when I realize Landon is watching me.

I offer him a small smile before scrolling through my missed calls. Two are from Blythe. I'm not surprised. I tap the icon to call her back when the phone rings in my hand and Blythe's contact information appears.

"Hello?" I answer.

"Hey, where were you?" Blythe asks.

"I couldn't get to the phone." I start plucking my clothes from the floor. "Are you on your way?" I ask, thinking how best to tell her I'm not at Becca's.

What happened between me and Landon is private. I'm not sure I want to share it with anyone. She doesn't answer. "Blythe?"

She speaks cautiously. "Luci, how do you feel about leaving tomorrow evening instead of this afternoon?"

I stop moving.

"It's not often I get to Kiawah," she adds quickly, as if that explains anything. "And I'm not sure when I'll be back."

"What are you saying?" I ask, my voice tight.

"That it's better if we head back tomorrow instead of today."

"Better for whom?" I press.

There's fumbling on the other line followed by a man's voice mumbling something I don't quite catch. "Give me a second, okay?" she whispers, to *him*.

Humiliation and anger heat my face. I already know where this is headed. I drop my clothes and storm to the bathroom, seeking privacy and positively seething over how selfish Blythe is behaving.

"I know you're mad, and I know you didn't plan on any of this," she begins. I clamp my hand over my eyes, ready to tear my hair out. "But if there's any possible way you can do this for me . . ." She sighs. "Luci," she begs when I don't respond. "It's not often I meet a man like this."

"I'll bet," I counter.

Blythe meets "the one" all the time. Each time, he takes her to bed, making empty promises and showering her with gifts. Each time he also fails to commit and, more times than not, returns to his wife.

She doesn't like me calling her out. I don't like being stranded or embarrassed or—how this is going to look to Landon!

"This would really mean a lot to me," she says.

I don't hear Landon approach, he's just suddenly there, his arms curling around my waist and pulling me to him. "Tell her you'll stay," he murmurs against my ear, passing kisses along my temple. I shudder as his tongue glides along the arc of my ear and his teeth give a tug. "And stay here with me."

"Luci?" Blythe says.

"Luci," Landon moans.

"Say we can leave tomorrow," Blythe pleads.

"Pretty please," Landon adds.

I cover my mouth, trying not to laugh. It's clear Landon can hear Blythe, but she can't hear him. It shouldn't surprise me. She's the one being loud.

I glance in the mirror. Landon meets me with a grin, a wickedly sexy glimmer lighting his eyes. He watches me as his fingers skim to my belly button and further yet.

My hand clamps over his, but his other hand is free and I'm still trying to hang onto my phone. "It would really mean a lot to me," she repeats.

"It would mean a lot to me, too," Landon agrees. He whirls me around, the kiss he greets me with almost making me drop my phone.

"Stay," he tells me quietly, his knuckles dancing along my spine. "We don't have to do anything." He laughs when I do. "Okay, maybe we'll do a little."

"Luci?" Blythe asks. "Look, I'm happy to drop off your things at Becca's if that'll help."

I return Landon's smile all the while speaking to Blythe. "No worries, I have everything I need right here."

I barely have time to disconnect before Landon lifts me, whisking me into the shower.

Chapter Seven
Landon

I cut the engine to my Tahoe 215 Deck boat in time for some
of the residual cloud cover to clear. The waves were choppy
when we first set out and I wasn't sure the weather would hold,
but the further we sped away from the shore, the more the
clouds thinned and our ride smoothed out.

The sunlight breaking through turns the lingering gray
clouds silver and sets Luci's stunning eyes aglow. They're
lavender. I thought they were light blue and only appeared
lavender because of her dress. But this morning, I have a better
view, and I swear it's a view I don't want to give up. I ease the
boat's speed and bring her to full stop.

"You okay?" I ask, as I reach into the bin for the anchor.

She turns her attention away from the horizon. "Depends.
Is this where you take all your victims?"

I pretend to give it some though. "No, I usually go a few
more miles out. It's what all the real pirates do."

She tilts her head. "So now you're a real pirate?"

"Yes, ma'am." I lunge a little deeper. "Didn't you get a
good look at my booty?"

Her laughter is as contagious as her smile, stirring my grin
as I drop anchor. I pull out the fishing rods and equipment from
the storage compartments on the starboard side, setting up

everything we'll need between the two plush fishing seats fixed to the stern.

I return to her side, not that she seems to notice.

Luci told me she'd never been on a boat unless you count the Staten Island Ferry. I told her we're not counting the ferry, not out here. But even if she hadn't told me, I would have guessed as much by the way she looks at the ocean as if it's her first time seeing it.

Her fascination with our surroundings gives me a few long moments to take her in. The coat I gave her is a heavy one, stuffed with goose feathers. She had to roll the top of the sweatpants I offered half a dozen times before they'd stay put on her tiny waist. She's in a pair of thick socks and an old pair of boat shoes Trin left behind.

The collar of the life jacket is almost up to her chin. Everything is so big and cushioned on her, she has trouble moving. But I didn't want her cold and I definitely want her safe.

She adjusts the beanie on her head, appearing to finally notice I'm right here beside her. "It's so pretty out here," she says staring out at the horizon. "I can see why you love it so much."

"What do you think of my yacht?"

"It's really nice," she says. Her hands smooth over the gunwale. "I can see you take great care of it."

I meant the yacht comment as a joke, since it's just an amped up deck boat. But Luci doesn't seem to know the difference and even if she did, she doesn't strike me as someone who complains.

She's sweet and friendly, a good-hearted kind of woman. I was starting to think they didn't exist anymore. Luci proved there are still a few out there and reminded me what a precious find they are.

When I first saw her last night I thought she was a pretty young thing. But the more time we spent together, pretty morphed into sexy damn quick and it didn't have anything to do with the booze we were drinking. We've had fun and keep having it.

I didn't want her to leave when her friend called, but I also didn't want her to think I was keeping her just to have sex. Everything's closed today, and since I hadn't planned on company, I didn't have much in my fridge except the leftover pizza I'd ordered earlier in the week and some frozen pot pies that have seen better days. We had two choices: take a chance on the pizza and pot pies or go fishing. We decided on the latter. Based on the way she's mesmerized by the waves and all the splendor, it's already worth the ride.

I offer her my hand. "Come on," I say.

She wrinkles her nose. "I don't know about this, Landon."

"What's wrong? You seemed excited back at the house."

She looks past me and to the chairs fixed on the stern. "They don't have seatbelts," she points out.

"Boats generally don't. Are you afraid you're going to fall in?"

"Yes," she admits.

"I promise I won't let you, but in the off chance you do, I also promise to save you."

Her brow crinkles as she focuses on the chair. "I'll feel bad if you have to dive in after me."

It's what she says, but she still takes my hand, allowing me to help her onto the stern and into the seat. I set the bait on her pole and cast the line. I'm not trying to show off, but I'm more than pleased by how far it soars.

Apparently, so is Lucy. "Wow," she says. "I take it you fish a great deal?"

"It's the southern boy's yoga."

Her laugh drifts into the air like a gentle breeze passing along the waves. She stops laughing when I offer her the pole. "It's okay," I tell her, "I'll talk you through everything."

She takes it hesitantly from my grip, eyeing me as I cast out my line. I plop down beside her, trying not to chuckle. She's gripping the pole with both hands, more tense than she was when she first walked into the party last night.

Damn, she's cute . . . and beautiful . . . and I should work on not gawking at her like a fool.

"Should I put on some music?" she offers. She bats at her coat, searching for her phone.

Good luck with all those layers, sweet thing. I grin, thinking it's best not to overdo the teasing. "No, the fish don't like it."

"Okay," she says. "So, what do we do?"

"We wait and hopefully snag us some dinner."

"All right." She adjusts her position in the seat, stealing a peek overboard. "You'll really save me if I fall in?"

"I will," I assure her.

"But who will save you?" she asks, appearing nervous.

I hook my arm around her shoulders and kiss the top of her head. "Don't worry about it. I used to lifeguard and was an endurance athlete for about five years."

"Of course you were," she says, smiling.

I chuckle. "Now, what's that supposed to mean?"

She purses her lips, appearing to hesitate to tell me what she's thinking. "Did anyone ever tell you you're too good to be true?"

I lose my grin real fast. Luci doesn't notice, her stare intent as she watches her line bob along the waves. "You volunteered all over the world to help those in need, you're a successful engineer who's not only attractive, but just so happens to be an endurance athlete. I swear, Landon, if you tell me you foster abandoned puppies and kittens, read to the elderly at the local senior citizen's center in your spare time, or are secretly developing the cure for cancer in your basement, it wouldn't surprise me."

"Nah, I don't have a basement."

I mean to make her laugh and move on, but she neither smiles nor laughs when she takes in my features. "What's wrong?"

"Nothing," I reply, blowing off her comment.

Her gaze dances along my face. "Something is." Her voice trails as she latches onto something, despite my efforts to keep my expression neutral. "I'm sorry, Landon, I didn't mean to offend you. I just—"

"You didn't offend me," I say, cutting her off. "I just . . . you're giving me too much credit, is all."

"No, I'm not," she adds quietly.

Her tone trickles with sadness, but I'm not sure that sadness comes from something she senses in me or something that belongs solely to her. I don't know her well enough to ask, but I want to.

"Are you happy?" I ask her.

A tiny little crease forms between her eyebrows when she frowns. She's probably wondering why I asked or assuming I'm trying to switch the focus off of me. I'll admit, she's not far off if that's what she's thinking. She takes her time answering. Not too much where the minutes pass, just long enough that I can already guess the answer.

"There are a lot of good things in my life," she replies.

"And maybe some not so good things?" I ask.

Her voice is so gentle, I barely hear it. "Yes."

"I think I know what you mean," I say.

Thinking about everything that went wrong last year often consumes me to the point I'm sure I'll go insane. More often, those memories leave me bitter, or worse yet, numb. I hate those moments and those feelings. But today, the bitterness and numbness pass me by and that overwhelming sense stays far away.

I reach for Lucy as she leans in, meeting her with a kiss that grows teasing. She laughs.

"Why are you laughing?" I ask.

"Your whiskers tickle my lips," she says, giving my beard a stroke.

"Just your lips?" I ask.

Her lids close, and her voice tightens. "Mm, maybe not just my lips," she confesses.

"No?" I kiss her again. "Then what else?"

Her cheeks redden in that way that drives me wild. "I'll leave that to your imagination," she says. She scoots back into her seat, grinning at me with a shy smile.

"Really?" I ask. "I don't know, I have a big imagination. You sure you want me to go there?"

She curls forward, the motion bunching her layers and shielding her face. "Oh, goodness," she says, shoving the heavy layers down.

I think she's annoyed, but as her face appears I catch sight of her widening smile. She settles back into her seat, content.

That's how I like her. Happy, even though like me, there are parts not to be happy about. Again, that negativity I've felt doesn't quite come, at least not here with Luci.

I recline in my seat, trying not to inundate her. I don't want her to think she's stuck having sex with me all weekend, not that I'd mind if that's what she wants to do. But I'd hate for her to think she *has* to do it.

Last night, when I entered Becca's house, staying was the last thing on my mind. Scratch that, finding someone to go home with, *that* was the last thing on my mind. But the more time I spent with Luci, the more she became what I wanted.

I'm trying not to think about how it felt to have my soapy hands pass along her breasts during our shower, how her hands slid along the tile as I pumped into her, or how she wrenched her neck to hang tight to our kiss. But I've realized it's hard not to think about Luci period.

She hangs on every word I say like it's the most important thing in the world, laughing at all the right moments, and appreciating the silence when it comes.

How is it possible I've known her less than a day? And how am I going to let her go?

I keep waiting to piss her off or for her to do something that annoys me. Hell, even the woman I married managed both the same day we met, and the second, and probably every day after that.

My thoughts wander to what should have been brunch, but turned into lunch since we spent so much time in the shower. Luci walked into the kitchen in one of my T-shirts and the sweatpants I'd given her. I was whipping up an omelet, but stopped when she strolled in.

"I'm sorry I took so long," she said, pointing behind her. "I took the staircase in the front hall. I didn't know there was another one that led directly into the kitchen." She seemed uncomfortable as she looked around, like she was somehow intruding or shouldn't be there, even though nothing was further from the truth. "You have a lovely home," she added, her voice quivering slightly.

"Thank you," I told her. For a minute I tensed, waiting for her to ask me how much money I make or how much the house cost. It's something I was asked by a lot of women when I went out on my own and started bringing them home.

Luci didn't ask. "Do you need help?" she offered instead.

"No, I'm good."

She took a seat in front of me, her attention trailing to the deck and to the ocean. "If you want, you can take a look around," I offered.

"Only if you want to show me."

"What?" I asked. Her voice was soft, but it wasn't like I hadn't heard her. I was just used to people jumping at the chance to look around.

"I said I'll look if you show me." She smiled. "But I'd rather stay here with you."

I'd rather stay here with you, I repeat in my head. If I'm being honest, it's the best damn thing she could have said.

The strong whirling sound has me jerking in her direction. "It's doing something," she says, clutching the handle as the reel spins out of control. "Landon, it's doing something."

I toss my pole onto the deck, scrambling behind her and helping her secure the reel. "Take it," she insists, trying to pass me the rod.

"Shhh," I murmur against her ear. "It's okay, you've got this."

"I really don't," she says, her voice close to a whimper.

"Yeah, you do," I assure her. "Come on, reel it in."

I guide her with my hands. It's moments like this when I press against her that I'm reminded how tiny Luci is. Even with all this padding, I sense her fragility beneath the layers and the vulnerability that teeters so close to the surface.

I suppose that's why I wrap around her like armor, trying to shield her from harm, despite the fact she's made it this far without me.

The line jerks and I lean her back. Whatever she caught is putting up a hell of a fight. I've fished ever since I was old enough to hold a pole. In fact, there's a picture of me when I was about two, perched on my father's lap with my lure in the water.

If I wanted to, I'd already have the fish in a bucket and speeding back to shore. But this is Luci's catch and her moment. I'm making sure she gets both.

"What if it's a shark?" she asks, her eyes wide as the pole bends and whatever she caught pulls harder.

"Then we're about to be eaten," I whisper.

"You're not funny!" she says when I crack up.

"Dun-dun," I sing. "Dun-dun-dun-dun."

"Landon!" she squeals, all the while laughing.

"Baby, you've got this." I should focus and reel faster. Except she's so fucking adorable, I take a moment to kiss her cheek. "Come on. That there's our dinner."

"Are you sure nothing is open?" she asks. "Chick-fil-A? Or Wendy's? A burger would be nice."

"I promise you, nothing is going to taste as good as this." I help her crank the reel harder. "Hang on. Here it comes."

Holy shit. We pull what's easily an eight-pound sea bass out of the water and onto the boat.

"Omigod. Omigod. Oh. My. *God*!" Luci is running in place, her hands shaking, unsure what to do.

I take over, lifting the fish up and hopping down to place it in the bucket. "Damn, woman," I say, taking in the size of the fish. "You sure you've never done this before?"

She stares at the bucket from her position on the stern, watching it rattle. "I caught a fish," she says like she can hardly believe it. She stumbles back in the boat, losing her footing and crashing on top of me.

She knocks us both down. I barely keep her from smacking her head. "You all right?"

Instead of answering me, she leans in and kisses me, her enthusiasm evident in the way she opens and closes her mouth. I chuckle as she pulls away. "I guess you are."

Her entire face is brighter than a collection of stars on a warm summer night and her smile as brilliant as the moon itself. "I caught a fish!" she says, beaming.

Yeah, she did. What she doesn't know is that she also captured my heart.

Chapter Eight
Luci

I search through Landon's large pantry, trying to figure out what I can use to make him a suitable dinner. I settle on a small bag of flour and a few random spices. He lifts his head as I step out. I'd taken some time to sort through the shelves. He waited for me on the stool where I'd left him, making no effort to rush me.

He's been noticeably quiet since I freaked out over catching that fish. I hope he's not having second thoughts about having me stay. In case he is, I'm giving him space.

He hurries out of his seat when he sees my arms are loaded. "No worries. I have it," I assure him.

"Are you okay? Cooking, I mean," he clarifies. "You are my guest."

I line the counter with my collection of goodies. "Of course. You cooked breakfast. Dinner is the least I can do." I offer him a small smile. "You trust me, don't you?"

"Yeah, I do," he adds quietly.

My focus drops to the large bowl he placed on the counter for me. His tone seems off, distracted. I don't know him well enough to guess what he's thinking. I don't know Landon well enough at all. What I do know is that instead of keeping me in the house with the expectation of sex, he took me out for a couple hours, making the experience that much more.

I mix breadcrumbs, salt, garlic, pepper, and dried jalapenos, then reach for a knife and slice the potatoes I washed length-wise. We spent much of the night and a good part of the morning being intimate, and although we didn't do more than kiss on the boat, I felt closer to him out on the water.

It sounds silly, even for someone like me who's always wanted someone to share forever with.

I don't know…I thought Landon and I were going somewhere, until we weren't.

The moment I finish slicing the potatoes, I coat them with olive oil and add the packet of onion soup mix I found in the pantry.

I pop open the oven and slide the potatoes across the preheated surface, feeling Landon watching me closely. He doesn't say anything until after I whisk a few eggs in a bowl and dip the first piece of fish.

"Looks like your oil is ready," he says, pointing to the large pan on the stove.

I fork a little bit of egg white into the heating oil and watch it sizzle. "You're right," I answer, smiling. I prepare a small salad while the fillets fry.

Landon quietly sets the table. I'm not sure if we're okay until I carry the food into the dining room and see that he's been busy too.

There's one place setting at the head of the table, and one right beside it. The table is large enough to accommodate twelve. Yet despite all the room only a small space separates our designated seats, showing he wants me close.

I set the food down next to a pretty plate with four votive candles placed at its center. He shrugs when I turn at his approach. "Ambiance," he says, as if that explains it.

"Thank you," I say, meaning more than just the added touch.

I step forward to return to the kitchen. His gentle grasp on my elbow keeps me in place. "Thank you for dinner," he says.

"Don't thank me until you've tasted it," I say.

My laughter cuts off when he cups my face with his hands, but it's the kiss that comes that lodges my breath.

It's slow and sultry, a kiss that hints there's more to come, and more to do, reminding me we still have a full night ahead of us.

His hands slide down my arms. They don't quite stay there, moving to my waist. I'm only wearing the borrowed T-shirt and set of boxers he lent me. His fingers disappear beneath the waistband, skimming my backside.

His caress tickles and makes me jerk. I ease away. "We should eat first," I say.

With a great deal of relief, I find him smiling. "First?" he asks. "Am I to assume you want to do something else second?"

He hangs onto his grin. I don't. "Yes," I reply, my tone and the promise within it dissolving his humor.

Between munching on snacks from his pantry and eating the frozen foods stowed away in his freezer, we could have spent the entire day having sex. It would have been fine with me. I can't get enough of him. But he switched things around in a way that both delighted and surprised me.

The boat trip on the ocean was the nectar to all the sweet Landon is. That doesn't mean I don't want another night in bed with him.

"Then I suppose we should get the meal out of the way," he says, his voice low.

"I suppose we should," I agree softly.

I return to the kitchen. He shadows me, reaching for a bottle of red wine perched on the counter. "This okay with you?"

"Whatever you want."

My hands reach for the salad and the dressing I prepared, almost dropping both when Landon grasps my hips and drags a montage of kisses along my throat.

My eyes roll into the back of my head. "What I want is you. All night," he says. "But I'll be polite and eat, even though it's you I'm dying to have another taste of."

I gasp, breathing hard. He mumbles a curse and steps away, gripping the counter with both hands. "You make it really hard to be polite," he says. "You know that?"

I start to nod and speak, but don't manage either so I force my body into action. I carry the remaining food to the table and just about run into Landon when I whip around.

"Oh, sorry," I say.

He adjusts the wine glasses in his hand, as well as the opened bottle. "Where are you off to?" he asks, his gaze sliding over me just as it had the first time I smiled at him.

"We don't have anything to drink besides wine," I respond, trying my best to keep from tackling him. "I thought I should pour us some water."

"I'll get it," he says. "You sit and relax."

"Where do you want me?"

"With your legs thrown over my shoulders," he replies, his tone matter of fact. "But since you prefer calorie eating before calorie consuming, wherever you want."

"Uh," I say, and that's about it.

I can't tell whether he sees me blush. His chuckle tells me he can. "Damn, you're sweet," he tells me.

I gush, just a little, then a little more when he winks.

My legs move although it takes some coaxing on my part. I sit off to the side, leaving the head of the table to him.

He pours the wine and returns with two tall glasses of ice water. I drink most of the water, never mind that we've collectively consumed at least a gallon between us since our return from the ocean. I fill my plate with salad and add the fish on top. Landon heads straight for the fish and chips. I watch him take his first bite, hoping he'll like it. I'm a good cook, but I've never cooked for him.

He pops a large piece of fish in his mouth, his chews slowing as if savoring every bite. "This is really good," he says. He takes another bite. "And what did you do to these potatoes?"

"I added olive oil and the soup mix," I explain.

"Well it works." He takes a sip of water. "And here I thought my mother and sister were the best cooks on Kiawah."

"I'm glad you like it."

"Who taught you how to cook?" he asks.

What should be an easy question is not and makes me squirm. "My grandmother, Mamita."

Landon doesn't notice the change in my voice. He's too busy eating, for which I'm glad. "Not your momma?" he asks.

"No."

He glances up. This time, he does notice the change in me. I busy myself slicing my fish and salad into small pieces as he waits for me to say more. "The man you paid to clean the fish, is he always there at the dock?" I ask, carefully squirting lime over my food.

My attention stays on my meal as I mix the greens and fish together. I'm trying to act casual rather than guilty. But in my world, guilt appears too often, reminding me it's never far away.

Landon takes his time answering. I'm hoping he's just chewing an extra-large bite, but I feel his stare upon me just as I felt his hands on my waist moments ago.

"For the most part," he explains. "If you can believe it, filleting fish was a job he started as a teen. He was good at it, fast. Eventually he stowed enough away to purchase the dock. He's been cleaning our catches ever since I was a kid. I've known him most of my life, and I think my father has known him most of his."

"He seems like a nice man," I add.

"Most people around here are. There are some spoiled brats who went on to have more spoiled brats, like that idiot Kirk who was bothering you. But the rest of us have a fix on them, and they're usually smart enough to stay out of our way." He rolls his eyes. "Usually."

I take a chance and glance up. "If he's so bad, why was he there?"

"He's Becca's cousin," Landon explains. "I'll bet you this whole house he wasn't invited and only showed because he felt he could."

"If that's the case, I'm surprised Becca didn't toss him out. From what Blythe says, Becca doesn't put up with anything or anyone who gives her trouble."

"That's for damn sure," he says, laughing. "Except you're forgetting Becca left with my sister and I can't be sure she came back."

I place my knife down. "Why would she leave her own party?"

"'Cause as much as Becca loves a good time and an even better party, she's smart enough to know who her real friends are." He works his jaw. "And my guess is, she knows who she needs to hang onto."

I'm not sure what he means entirely, but it's enough to make me admire Becca a little more.

"Man, this is good," he says, returning to his food. "With you doing all the hunting, maybe I should do some gathering to even things out."

I wipe my mouth. "You gathered the plates," I remind him. "And if you're so inclined you can gather them again and help me place them in the dishwasher."

He swallows and takes a sip of his wine. "I suppose I can do that. I just prefer to gather you in my arms."

No, that wasn't romantic or anything. I'm not swooning. No, absolutely not.

I poke through my food, trying to stop the smile that comes, but smiles aren't something I can help around Landon. "Do you hunt?"

"Why, Miss Luci," he says. "Are you trying to make small talk, instead of letting me talk about what I want to do to you?"

My fork hovers in the air, the piece of lettuce I gathered a mere inch from my mouth. "Maybe. But maybe I also want to know more about you."

I start eating again, feeling Landon's gaze on my warming face. I don't have to look in his direction to know he's grinning, and do I love that grin! But as much as I'm falling at his feet, I want to preserve the bit of me who isn't so easily charmed.

It's what I think I *should* think. Yet I'm so taken with this man, I'm ready to abandon this fine feast and lay in his arms.

"I don't hunt," he admits. "But I'd give it a try if I wasn't sure it'd break my mother's and sister's hearts."

"Really?" I ask.

He nods. "Not big game or trophy, that's bullshit as far as I'm concerned. But elk for sure, pheasant, that kind of thing. I like game meat and grew up eating it."

I finish another bite of food. "Do you own a gun?"

"No," he says, lifting his wine glass and giving the dark liquid a swirl. "I own several, two handguns, plus a shotgun and an assault rifle."

I stop eating. "Why?"

He blinks back at me like I'm missing the obvious. "Because it's the south and southerners love their guns."

His eyes shimmer when I laugh. "The shotgun is for skeet shooting, the guns are for personal protection when I'm out, and the two assault rifles are for anyone stupid enough to break into my home."

"You wouldn't have a problem killing someone?" I'm not judging him, and I hope that's not how I come across.

"I never said that," he says softly. "But I wouldn't hesitate to protect myself or someone I loved."

Maybe I should be afraid, considering all the weapons he owns. But as I remember how he protected me at the party, fear doesn't present itself. If anything, his willingness to look out for others endears him more to me. "I can understand that," I say.

"I take it you don't own a gun?" I shake my head. "Then I also take it you don't know how to shoot."

"Not at all," I admit.

"I'll take you—"

The manner in which he cuts himself off compels me to return to my food. I'm not sure if he was going to end the conversation with "sometime" or perhaps "the next time we see each other." He didn't mean "tomorrow." He knows I'm leaving. But maybe like me, for a brief moment, he simply forgot.

Last night flew by and today is almost gone. We returned in time to watch the sun set along his deck. It was magnificent, an artistic masterpiece come to life. It was also a reminder of how fast time is slipping from my grasp.

In the morning, the sun will rise just as quickly, the day will come faster than I'm ready for, and life will go on for both of us. Landon will continue his life here in this little piece of paradise and I'll return home to Charlotte, and in a way, to my mother, too.

I know it, and he knows it, too.

"I'm sorry," he says. "I didn't mean . . ."

My smile is forced, something that doesn't feel right in Landon's presence. "It's okay," I assure him. "I'm not offended."

"I hope not," he says, the seriousness in his voice keeping me in place. "The last thing I want is for you to think I've used you."

My finger slides across the handle of my fork as I set it down. I almost tell him that I'm the one who used him: to stir the smiles I often go without, to bring out the woman in me that I often forget I am, to push aside the loneliness that surrounds me, and to think about all the good I'm still capable of instead of the bad things that haunt me.

I don't admit as much, of course, although in a way I wish I could.

My gaze travels to the large windows across his living room and to where the ocean continues its gentle serenade. It's almost seven now, an hour or so from the time Landon and I met yesterday. Despite the brief time we've spent together, I know him better than some of the people I've worked with for years. I'm not certain why. Maybe because I've allowed him to know me, as well.

"I don't think you used me, Landon." I reach for my water. "But thank you for caring about whether or not you did."

The candles cast a glow against his dark eyes, adding an air of mystery to a gaze that already hides so much. We finish our meal in silence and in a way that breaks my heart.

Last night in the quiet we shared there were moments where we simply smiled and moments where we couldn't stop laughing. There wasn't tension, and there isn't tension now. What there is, is a sadness akin to goodbyes, the kind that lasts forever and one you don't forget.

"Would you like some more wine?" he asks when I rise.

I stack a few dishes onto my plate. "Are you having more?"

"Yeah," he says.

"Then I'll join you."

I hear him pour the wine as I pad into the kitchen, working quickly to rinse off the plates and stack them in the dishwasher. There's very little to clean. I did most of it as I cooked.

"Where's your dishwasher detergent?" I ask.

I jump when I realize he's behind me. He grabs my waist, steadying me. "Are you some kind of ninja spy?" I ask. "Is that why you have all those guns? I didn't even hear you come in."

His arms band around me, pulling me closer. "If I told you, my ninja spy oath would require me to use my Jedi mind tricks to erase your memory and make you forget everything you did and saw this weekend. You wouldn't want that, would you?"

"No."

The truth behind my words paralyze him. For the briefest moment he doesn't dare move. "I don't want to forget either," he admits.

His mouth slides over mine, the smooth taste of wine greeting me as his tongue explores. I push up on my toes, skimming my fingers through his hair. When I start to lose my balance, Landon catches me, lifting me in an embrace.

I'm barely wearing anything.

But it's too much for Landon.

His hand disappears beneath the leg of the boxers I'm wearing, smoothing across my cheek. It's time for us again, for our bodies to join and please. I know it, and I'm so ready for it.

I unsnap his jeans when he lowers me. I pull down the zipper, falling to my knees and taking the waistband of his briefs with me. He's already erect, adding to my arousal. Except, when I reach for his staff and try to place him in my mouth, he pulls away.

"Not here," he says.

I follow, unsure what he means. "Do you want to go in the bedroom?"

"No, it's not that." He shudders as my nails trail up his thighs and again when I trace circles along his backside.

"What is it?" He freezes when I lick my lips, his expression torn. "Landon," I say, barely above a whisper. "I just want to make you feel good."

He strains beneath my touch as I open my mouth wide. I start out slowly, using my tongue to massage him and gentle suction to stimulate him further. But as the muscles along his legs relax, I grow more aggressive.

My pulls are harder as I take him further in, falling into an erotic dance where only my hands and mouth participate. I want him to allow me to lead and give me this moment to please him. I need to, and I want him to need it, too.

His hands fist my hair, not enough to hurt me, but enough to prove he likes what I'm doing. His audible sounds, mere gasps at first, deepen to hungry growls. My fingertips skim the "V" of his waist. I want to steal a glimpse to make sure he's okay, and while I only intend to do it briefly, it doesn't stay that way. Not when his gaze fastens on mine.

Dark lust flares in his eyes. He's so consumed and turned on by what I'm doing, his pleasure burns into me. His breathing turns shallow and he bites down a groan. I'm not touching myself, nor is he touching more than my hair. But I'm so impassioned by how he's reacting to me, a low hum vibrates along my throat.

Landon lifts me to him into a straddle, his lips crushing over mine. He fumbles with his jeans and briefs, kicking them off. In a few strides, we're back in the dining room and on the table.

The fabric of my shorts rip as he strips me bare. I reach for his shirt, managing to pull it off him half a second before his mouth disappears between my thighs. My palms press against the cool granite slab as I lean back, the lower half of my body wriggling as Landon lets loose.

I'm trying to move the remaining items from dinner aside. But all the licks, sucks, and movements of his fingers, blind me to anything except him. I manage to slide the plate of votives away in time for my orgasm to hit.

The force is so sudden and deliciously brutal, my legs jerk out of control. "God, I'm sorry," I stammer, when I knock his shoulder.

He doesn't notice, burying his face deeper.

This time, I'm the one cursing and gasping, trying to hang onto any bit of composure left in his presence. I want to beg him for it, to take me now and not stop. But all I manage to say is his name. For him, it's more than enough.

He lifts up, hooking my knees and hauling me against his muscular body. We manage a brief kiss. But when the thick ridge of his erection presses against me, we don't manage much more. My fingers link behind his neck while his hands clamp over my hips.

Each thrust is hard and fast, our gazes radiating and fusing with rapture. My head falls back as that familiar tension builds in my core. Landon cups the base of my skull, tipping my head to face him.

His jaw is clamped so forcibly, it's hard for him to speak. "Don't turn away from me," he says, his voice carnal. "I want to watch what I do to you."

He gets his wish as jolts of energy fire every cell in my body. I start to finish only for Landon to pump faster, sprawling us across the table, his mouth dipping to worship every inch of my skin.

I knock over a dish when he throws my legs over his shoulders. The dark, sensual edge to his features is so erotic, I lose myself in the moment and slip my hand between my legs.

"Oh, *fuck*," Landon says, bowing his head to watch. It's the last thing he says before the grunts from his release echo across the room.

Chapter Nine
Landon

We're lying on my sectional, facing the long row of flames dancing across the slick marble fireplace. Since I moved in, I think I've turned this thing on just once, and that time was to make sure the sucker worked. It's cold outside, and except for the blanket tucked around us, Luci and I are naked. I can't think of a better reason to have a fire going than this.

My knuckles run along her arm, her skin and the tiny hairs along them smooth like satin. "Can I tell you something?"

She lifts her head from my shoulder. We've been quiet like we were during dinner. I didn't like that quiet between us. It reminded me of this great ride I was on when I was a kid, the Amazing Adventures of Spiderman at Universal Studios. I never wanted that ride to end and was having the time of my life, until the exit sign came into view and I knew it was time to get off.

This quiet I do like. It's comfortable and tender, reminding me the ride isn't exactly over yet, and here's this lovely woman smiling up at me and showing me there's a lot more left to enjoy.

"You can tell me anything," she answers her voice vanishing into the air.

I know she means it and I don't hold back, at least partly. "I'm feeling very manly right now."

She laughs and takes sip of her wine. "Really?"

"Hell, yeah," I say. "I'm ready to sprout more chest hair, wrestle a gator, and maybe chop some wood, pausing only to flex as you look on adoringly."

She covers her mouth with the tips of her fingers in that delicate way of hers to keep from laughing. "Should I clap when you flex or do you prefer I faint from your ultra-manliness?"

"Oh, baby. I want it all." I kiss her mouth, taking my time. She tastes good with me all over her. I can even pick up traces of my cologne along her skin.

I wasn't going to wear any today until we slipped out of the shower and she pointed to the bottle on my bathroom counter.

"Is this what you wore last night?" she asked.

I was toweling off and doing a piss-poor job of pretending to not stare at the way the water dripped from her hair and along her naked body. "Yeah."

"May I?"

I nodded although I wasn't sure what she wanted. She could have asked me for anything and I would have said yes. She splashed a little cologne on her fingers and swiped it in small zigzags down my chest. But it's the way she leaned in and inhaled that made me freeze.

She lowered her lashes, releasing a very satisfied sigh when she was done. "Yes, that was it," she'd said.

Remembering stirs my grin as I kiss her, just like it had then.

"More," she whispers when we come up for air. I chuckle and press another small kiss against a mouth I can't seem to get enough of.

"More kissing, or more of what we've been doing?" I ask.

She makes a little noise, not quite a sigh, not quite a moan, just enough to let me know she's doing some remembering of her own. "Maybe both?"

Her small nails tease my lower abs, causing the muscles to twitch. It tickles and I'm not even that ticklish, but Luci seems to have the right touch. I curl her fingers around mine, and kiss her hand. "I'd like that," I admit. "But I need a little more time for the latter."

Who the hell am I fooling? I should need a lot of time considering how much sex we've had. The table turned out to be a fun place to be. I have no idea how I'm going to have my family over for Thanksgiving after the way we defiled that thing.

I bent Luci over during the second round. She liked it, calling out my name, driving me wild. When I carried her to the couch, I thought we'd fall sleep the minute I covered us with a blanket. But it's like we both got a second wind, and that wind brought with it another round of pleasure.

It's almost one in morning. I'm tired, spent, but I don't want to sleep. Sleep will make the morning come faster and bring on the afternoon just as quick. I don't want Luci to go. I'm ready to offer to buy her a first-class ticket back to Jersey if she'll stay with me a few more days.

The thing is, I don't have a few more days. I have a ton of interviews lined up in Charlotte and have to spend most this week locking up and moving into my new place. Besides, sexcapades with Luci is the last thing I want, even though on the surface, it looks like this is all it's been.

Maybe with another woman, everything we shared and did would be just physical. But being with Luci, whose soul is so tender I feel it every time she smiles, everything feels like more.

Shit. I *want* more.

"What's wrong?" she asks. She passes her hand along my scraggly beard, her fingers skipping along my throat until it rests against my chest.

"I'm thinking we might need more wine."

I reach for the bottle on the table behind us, topping off her glass and then filling mine. I'm not sure why I lie. Oh, wait, I do. Because the last time I had really great sex with a woman I spent the weekend naked with, I mistook lust for love and married her.

It wasn't right away. Bernadette played her cards well, making sure I was the one pursuing her, begging for her company, and promising her a life away from the abuse and drugs she grew up with, and from that stupid pole she danced on.

What a fucking *idiot* I was. My frat brothers from M.I.T. were visiting and wanted to hit that gentleman's club in Charleston. I went as a joke, and became the joke once Bernadette saw all the bills I was dropping to make sure my friends had a good time. I might as well have been wearing a T-shirt that said "Future Sugar Daddy" on it, since it was obvious I was worth a lot of money.

It's like traveling around the world and seeing all the damaged and broken people worked against me, rather than for me, making me a mark and Bernadette the arrow that hit me dead center. When I heard about her troubled life, about her drunk father who used to beat her, and how she was the only one in her family who hadn't ended up in jail or addicted, I though, oh, yeah, I can save her. I could make her life better. And I would have if she didn't turn my life into an abyss of agony I barely crawled away from.

Bernadette started off friendly enough, keeping a respectable distance, dropping just enough hints about her past to let me know how much she suffered. She made me hunger for her, until I was obsessed with making her mine and rescuing her from a life no one should ever endure.

I thought I'd hit the jackpot. Here was this beautiful woman so lost until I found her. I realized too late all I'd hit was a jackpot straight to hell.

Luci kisses me again. "What is it?" she asks. "You seem upset."

"Just tired."

She returns to stroking my beard. "Do you want to go to bed?"

"No."

She laughs a little and adjusts the white fleece blanket around us. "Okay, so just rest. We don't have to talk."

No, we don't. That's one of the great things about Luci.

Luci says all the right things and does the right ones, too, except so did Bernadette. I don't want to compare the two. They're sweet vs. sin. An angel against the devil. But Bernadette took a while to show her horns and even longer to spear me through the heart with her pitchfork. Is it a wonder that same bruised heart is warning me?

"Tell me something about you," I say before I give it too much thought. "Something weird."

"Something . . . *weird*?" She laughs. "Are you serious?"

Damn that laugh and cuteness, too. "Yeah." The more I think about it, the more it sounds like a good idea. "But it has to be odd or bizarre, something that will send me running."

"You want me to send you running?"

She should be insulted by what I'm asking. Instead, she simply grins. "All right. If you insist."

She gives it some thought. I'm waiting for something good, like she has a collection of rocks that she stoned her ex-boyfriend with, before tossing his broken body down a flight of steps and laughing like a psycho when he tried to skulk away to safety. Yeah, that's it. This woman can't possibly be this nice.

"I like monkeys."

Okay. Maybe I'm wrong.

"Monkeys," I repeat. She nods. "What kind?"

"All primates, really. But especially chimpanzees and mountain gorillas. Silverbacks to be specific."

"Silverbacks," I say.

"They're found in the Congo, Uganda, and Rwanda," she adds. "I want to go there one day, just to see them in the wild." She averts her gaze, growing bashful. "I know it sounds silly."

"I don't think it does."

"Then why are you looking at me like that?" she asks.

"'Cause you're fucking adorable," I remind her. "Most women I meet want to go to Paris to see the Eiffel Tower, tour all the trendy shops, and take in the museums."

"I'd like that, too," she says. "I just want to see gorillas more."

"I get it. But why not play it safe and go to the *Louvre?* Have that croissant as you walk through *le Jardin du Luxembourg.*" Her eyebrows lift at how I pronounce the French words without a trace of my southern drawl. I'm not trying to show off, but I'm also not going to pretend I haven't been there or speak enough French to get around. "The Congo, hell, most parts of Africa are filled with unrest. You're risking a lot by going there versus the places governed more closely."

Her head falls back to rest against my shoulder. "Last night, you mentioned all the places you've visited that weren't so glamorous."

I brush a kiss along her crown. "That was to help. My parents acquired good guides and better people to ensure we were protected and received safe passage through the more worrisome areas. You're talking about vacationing. For that, there are other places, *safer* places you can enjoy without risking your life."

"I know, but it's a dream I have."

She probably thinks I can't picture her trekking through the dense jungle. If so, she's wrong. I can already see her, winning over some giant gorilla as easily as she won me over.

"Why primates?" I ask. I want to keep her talking and know that I'm listening. I also want her to understand I only mean to keep her safe.

She shrugs, appearing embarrassed by sharing as much as she did.

"Please tell me," I say. "You may want to know me, but I want to know you, too."

To my relief, she smiles and explains. "My grandmother gave me a stuffed chimpanzee toy when I went to live her." Her voice fades and she pauses, the worry reflected in her features alerting me she told me more than she wanted to say.

"Your grandmother raised you?" This is the second time she's led me to believe her grandmother was her mother. I should be polite and allow her to brush it aside like she did the first time, but I can't. I need to make sure she made it out okay.

"Yes," she admits.

"Why?"

"My parents weren't able to," she answers quickly.

The hurt in her voice is as obvious as the sudden sadness that appears in her pretty stare. "I'm sorry," I say, because I am and because I shouldn't have pushed. Even a fool can see it still causes her pain.

"It happens," she says. Her focus falls to her glass as she takes another sip. "Anyway, I became attached to the toy and rarely went anywhere without him. I'd watch nature shows with him and learned all I could about primates."

"Him?" I tickle her nose with mine. "And what was said monkey's name?"

"Jo-Jo."

"Awesome," I say, nodding.

She laughs. "You don't mean that."

"Maybe I don't, but it beats Chimpy or Bananas like I probably would have named him."

"You would have been more creative than that," she says.

"You're right. I would have picked something unique and manly, too."

"I'd expect no less," she offers casually. "Maybe Killer Bananas."

"Or Kick-ass Chimpy," I agree. "I'd probably make him go all King Kong, set up a city of Legos and fleeing Barbies, and make him destroy it to the ground."

"You owned Barbies?"

"Nah. My sister did. Killer Bananas would have stomped Ken to bits. After ripping my G.I. Joe's legs off, Ken deserved as much. Bastard."

She throws back her head, laughing and spilling wine against her chest. "Oh, no," she says.

Being the gentleman I am, I lick every last drop up with my tongue. She releases a small moan when I trace a small circle near her breast.

I want to climb on top of her. I want to do a lot of things. Except I want her to know this has been more than just sex, at least to me.

I slip out from beneath the blanket and walk down the hall. "Where are you going?"

"Bathroom." It's true, but once I'm done I head into the small guestroom and fetch my guitar.

I return to the sectional and plop down on the corner. Luci stills. "You play the guitar?"

My fingers fiddle with the strings to warm up. "Yes, ma'am, and sing."

"Of course you do. Of course." She bows her head and shakes it, causing all those loose and messy curls to slide along her shoulders.

I don't think too much about how it felt to fist all that hair when she fell to her knees in front of me, or how I'm the one who messed it up further when I bent her over. I have a job to do: to give this beautiful woman with the wild and sexy mane the last bit of me I can allow.

Singing and playing is personal for me, not something I do much around anyone but family. Except I want to do it for Luci. After slapping me awake and reminding me there's still a lot of life left in me, and more passion than I ever gave myself credit for, it's the least I can do, and maybe the best way I can tell her goodbye.

God knows I don't have it in me to say it any other way.

My memory scrolls through the list of songs I know by heart. Most are love songs, country ballads filled with too much pain, and even more dripping with promises of a forever I'm not sure I believe in any more.

There are a few I can really belt out, and too many I connect with and feel down to my bones. Except I'm already feeling too much around Luci. I can't give my heart away so easily. Not this soon, and probably never again.

Once bitten, twice shy, and my ex made sure to take plenty of bites.

"You like classic rock, right?" I ask.

She nods and holds out a hand. "Are you going to sprout wings now or during?"

I tighten a loose string, chuckling. "What's that supposed to mean?"

"Oh, nothing. I'm only expecting you to have a voice of an angel." She points. "No, pressure, though."

"No wings," I assure her. "But angels might appear for the chorus. And they might be naked. Not as good looking as me, but naked all the same."

"Oh, Landon," she says. "There you go being all modest again."

"Prepare to be wowed," I add, hoping to stay true to my words. "Again."

She places her wine on the table behind her and scoots forward.

"You ready?" I ask. "Oh, wait." I tug down the sheet around her breasts.

She pulls it back up. "What are you doing?"

"Looking for inspiration, woman. It's what all good musicians do."

I'm laughing almost as hard as she is, and have to start the first few chords to *Southern Cross* several times before I settle in and fall into a natural rhythm, allowing the words and the melody I know so well from years of practice, and even more years of loving this timeless song to come.

The pitch is perfect for my deep voice and Luci's smile is all the encouragement I need to relax. But as I sing the first line, her smile fades, and without meaning to, my soul anchors to each word.

The first few lyrics are innocent enough. That doesn't mean each string I pluck and each syllable flowing like honey through my lips doesn't carry the weight I suddenly feel. By the time I reach the chorus I know I'm done for, even though I never intended to be.

"*I have been around the world,*" I sing. "*Lookin' for that woman girl.*"

I glance down at the start of the next verse. I don't think I'll be able to finish the chorus while looking at her, but it's like right then, I have to. "*Who knows love can endure . . . . .*"

The song becomes more than just pretty notes attached to a fair enough voice. It becomes that goodbye I intend, and one I no longer think my heart can say.

I force myself to finish, thrumming the few last strings and keeping my head down as the final note vibrates along my fingers.

At first I think I'm reliving the breakup and ultimate goodbye I shared with Bernadette. But in this moment, nothing of Bernadette comes. I can't picture her, even though every tiny crease and minute wrinkle should be ingrained in my memory. I don't hear her voice, neither the soft one she used when she wanted something from me, nor the one laced with fury when the accusations came and the harsh words meant to hurt followed.

Bernadette is gone.

Only Luci remains.

I wish I could smile. But the many smiles I had in Luci's presence fail to appear. I look up. She seems ready to cry. I'm ready to . . . Lord, I don't know what I'm ready for.

She glances down at her hands. "Landon," she says.

I shake my head. It feels heavy, just like the air around us, quieting her voice and mine.

"Don't."

It's what I say, even though I'm not sure what I'm telling her.

Don't cry?

Don't pity me?

Or shit, don't fucking tell me goodbye?

Whatever I don't want her to say or do, I can't stop myself from feeling it.

I place my guitar on the floor and lean into her, my hands cupping her face. Her hands palm over mine, slender fingers stroking lightly. For a long while, neither of us move beyond that, everything I want to say lodging deep inside me where I think it belongs.

I'm not sure she'll welcome my kiss, but she does.

She also welcomes what follows when I climb on top of her.

Chapter Ten
Luci

We watched the sun rise from our spot in the living room before returning to his bed and falling asleep. After a few hours, Landon surprised me with breakfast in bed. He was sweet and greeted me with an even sweeter smile. But smiles are coming harder for me. It's almost time to leave him.

He stirs beneath me, rousing me from sleep. "Shit," he mutters. "Oh, sorry," he adds when my eyelids flutter open.

"What's wrong?" I ask.

"It's almost four."

I push up from where I'm lying on his chest. "We missed the day."

"Yeah. We did."

He doesn't sound happy. I know how he feels, or at least, I wish I did.

Last night, when he played me that song, all the sadness I first noticed in him intensified. I heard it in his voice as he sang each word and sensed it in the melody. Each note and lyric spoke as if he were mourning a tremendous loss. I mourned, too. But it wasn't over a goodbye I never had the chance to say or a death that came too soon.

It was Landon, and his impending absence from my life.

He didn't have to play or sing for me to win me over. He already has. His beautiful tribute yet another reminder of how amazing he is.

I wanted to tell him that I'd like to stay in touch and that perhaps we can meet up again. I wanted to tell him I really like him. As hard as it is for me to open up and spill my vulnerability like pearls from a shattered necklace, I was ready to. Until he stopped me.

I may have been ready to say a lot of things, but Landon wasn't ready to hear them.

When he held my face and stared into my eyes, I thought maybe he'd ask me to stay one more night. I thought . . . I thought he'd offer another opportunity to see him.

When he didn't, I didn't push. As much as I like him, I don't want to be that woman begging for his number and constantly checking my phone hoping he calls.

I slip out of bed and lift my phone from the nightstand. Blythe hasn't called or texted to tell me when she'll be by. That doesn't mean she won't. For all I know, she's already on her way.

I walk into the bathroom, feeling Landon's attention trail me. If I were more confident, I'd strut to the bathroom. Yet while I feel comfortable being naked around him, I keep my head slightly lowered and take careful steps.

The water takes a moment to warm as I wash my face, my mind sorting through how long I might have slept, and how much more I need to sleep to make up for this weekend.

It shouldn't matter. Every moment of rest I missed was worth it. Whether he calls me or not, Landon was worth it all.

I take my time to freshen up. I'm almost done brushing my teeth with the spare toothbrush Landon gave me when he walks in.

The gray sweatpants he wears hang low on his hips, exposing the "V" in his waist I took my time to know. He crosses his arms, bulging the muscles along his arms and chest as he leans against the wall. "Do you want to go swimming?"

I lower the towel I used to pat my mouth. "In the ocean?" I ask slowly.

He chuckles. "No, in my pool." He disappears into the walk-in closet and returns with a towel draped along his shoulders and a thick cotton robe. "Here," he says, offering me the robe. "As much as I like what I see, it's only about fifty degrees outside, too cold for you to go out like that."

I take the robe, but don't quite put it on. "You're serious?"

"I am," he says. "You have a beautiful body."

My hand clasps over my eyes and I shake my head when he laughs. "I mean about swimming in January."

He lifts his toothbrush and adds paste. "January in the south is different than January in Jersey," he reminds me.

He bends over the sink and brushes his teeth. When he finishes, and I'm still standing there with five pounds of terrycloth pressed against me.

"Come on, trust me," he says, tickling my chin.

It's only because I do that I slip into the robe and wrap it around myself. It's huge. Based on how it dangles just above my toes and the twinkle in Landon's eyes, I must look ridiculous.

"Ready?" he asks.

I shove my phone into the deep pocket. "Not even a little bit," I confess.

It's true, although when he offers me his hand, I gladly take it.

We walk hand and hand to the living room like a real couple with no cares and no real place to go. It's only when we reach the doors leading out to his massive terrace that he releases me.

Like Becca's house, clear glass partitions surround the perimeter, providing an unobstructed view of the ocean. He punches a code into what I mistook for an alarm system. To my shock, the floor of the terrace begins to withdraw.

Steam rises as the top of a large rectangular pool comes into view.

"It's heated," Landon explains.

"I can see that," I reply.

I guessed Landon was well-off based on the tips he was dropping at the party. My suspicions were confirmed when he drove me home in his Maserati. And any lingering doubts were squelched when we arrived at his home. But this . . . I'll admit I'm intimidated.

He hits a few more buttons that turn on the patio heaters. They're unlike the big, bulky ones found outside restaurants. These are sophisticated, like ornate artwork that blend in with the terrace and add another air of elegance.

"You won't notice the cold in the water. I swear you won't," he insists. "The heat lamps help a great deal. You'll only feel cold once you step out of the pool, and even then, only if you linger too long."

"Mm."

His hands skim along my hip. "What's wrong?"

The best way to describe how I feel is inferior. It's not an emotion that typically strikes me, nor is it something he's intentionally made me feel. Yet here I am struggling with how to get past it.

"I wasn't expecting this," I manage.

He shrugs, the gesture almost apologetic. "I've been a swimmer all my life. It's my go-to form of exercise. When I was looking for a house, a pool was one of my must-have items. This place was my favorite based on the location, but the ground wasn't suitable for digging. The terrace was my only option and worked out better than I planned. Now, I can swim all year."

"It's beautiful," I assure him. I don't want him embarrassed for having everything he does, or somehow feel shame.

"So are we swimming?"

I make a face. "I guess we are."

"All right then." He opens the door, his towel landing near the edge of the pool when he tosses it. Like a seasoned Chippendale, he loses his sweats and dives in.

I stand by the door with my jaw hanging open.

Have I mentioned Landon has an ass Adonis would kill Zeus to spank?

He swims across the length and back. If Michael Phelps were here, he'd say, "Hey, we have an opening on our Olympic team, care to join us?"

Landon comes up for air, a stream of water gliding in a perfect line when he flicks his hair. He folds his arms along the edge, beads of water dripping down his beard and bare skin.

God, help me. The image before me resembles a high-end ad rather than real life. I'm almost tempted to fetch his cologne and place it beside him.

"Are you coming?"

"Um," I say.

He cocks his head as if unsure why I'm standing there gaping. If he listens closely, perhaps he can hear my lady parts pounding out of control.

"Come on, baby," he says. "Let's have a little fun."

Before you have to leave, he doesn't add.

I creep out, only to run when the cold deck floor and the surrounding air sends chills shooting through my spinal cord. I hunker down at the ledge and dip my legs.

Landon swims up to me.

"So *hot*," I say, wiggling my toes.

"Thank you," he tells me.

I laugh, meeting the playful sparkle in his eyes. "I meant the water."

He presses a kiss to my knee. "I set it that way. Otherwise my muscles would cramp up. Can't have that, can we?"

"Oh, no, big boy."

His throaty laugh makes me smile. I kick my legs back and forth, allowing the water to dispel the last of my nervousness.

His wet hands slide up my thighs. "Jump in before you get cold."

I glance down the length of pool. The shallow end seems to be on the opposite side. "How deep is it?"

"Does it matter?"

"Yes," I reply. "I can't swim."

"It's ten feet," he admits.

A strong wind sweeps in, causing the partitions to rattle. While I don't feel it yet, I'm worried I will. I curl forward. "I'll go in over there," I say, pointing to the end.

He lifts partially up and unfastens the belt on my robe. "It's okay, I've got you."

"Landon, I don't know."

"Baby, you have nothing to worry about. I was a lifeguard, remember? Watched out for people in the water for years."

"You saved elderly people, didn't you? And children?"

"Once or twice." He pauses. "Okay, maybe a few times."

My shoulders slump. "I should have guessed."

"What's the big deal? The waters around here can get rough following a storm."

"What's the big deal? Seriously, Landon? You saved the lives of elderly people and children. Anything else?"

He thinks about it. "I saved a dolphin snagged in a net once, but that was more of a team effort."

I sigh, because it beats swooning. "Could you be any more perfect?"

He quiets and shakes his head. I think I offended him and reach to touch him, smoothing the long hair away from his brow. "I'm sorry for thinking you're perfect." I smile when he raises his head. "I just can't help myself."

He rubs the water from his beard. "The only thing that's perfect is this water, and the only way to make it better is for you to be in here with me. Jump in. I'll take care of you."

"All right."

I shiver when I pull off the robe, careful to place it and my phone away from the ledge. Landon lifts his hands when I position myself closer. I take them and . . . plunge all the way to the bottom.

Strong arms wrap around my waist, shooting me up to the surface. I break through the water, coughing and choking.

Landon laughs.

That's right, totally and completely cracks up.

I can't see him, only hear him, the heavy wet hair draped over my face making it hard to make anything out.

I grip his shoulders when he tries to set me down. He laughs harder, lifting me again and bouncing us in place. Somehow, I manage to push enough of my hair away to see we're at the other end of the pool.

"I thought you had me," I gripe.

"I didn't expect you to drop like a stone," he admits, unable to stop laughing. "I figured you'd at least doggie-paddle enough to help me keep you afloat."

"What part of *I can't swim* didn't you understand?"

"I thought you were a Jersey shore girl. That's what you told me."

"I did not. I said I went to the shore."

He adjusts my legs so I straddle him. "So all those beautiful beaches you claimed you saw, and all those times you visited, you never actually went in the water?" He chuckles when I shake my head. "Then why did you go?"

"For the boardwalk and a tan."

"The boardwalk and a tan," he repeats, slowly, a great deal of humor reflecting in his face.

My hands wrangle with the moppy mess my hair has become. "I'll admit, it wasn't the best place to learn to swim."

"I'll bet all the pollution and garbage made it tough," he agrees thoughtfully.

"The beaches were very clean, I assure you." I pull at the strands of my hair, trying to settle them. "The waves were often harsh and I was too scared to go in past my waist."

"I see," he says, even though he clearly doesn't.

Oh, and neither can I. I give up on my hair. "Could you hold me a second?"

I don't wait for him to answer, pinching my nose and arching backward into the water, allowing it to slick my hair back.

I do a double-take when I find Landon gawking. "What's wrong?"

"Nothing. Everything's fine. But if you don't mind, could you do that again?"

"Slick my hair back?" I ask, even though I know what he means.

"Sure, that, and tease me with your erect and tantalizing nipples." He shrugs. "A real lady would."

I laugh and wrap my arms around him. "What else would a real lady do?"

He smiles softly. "Let me kiss her like I want to."

If I'm planning a good comeback, it doesn't quite come. What does is his kiss. His lips are moist from the water, silky and lush. Steam rises around us, adding a romantic ambiance I've never experienced, and one I doubt I'll have again.

He adjusts his hold, opening and closing his mouth, his tongue exploring as he moves us across the pool. "You took your pill today, right?"

He must have noticed the small box on the nightstand. "Yes," I assure him quietly.

Water isn't a lubricant, no matter what you hear. It takes Landon a moment to enter me, and when he does, it's like an intimate union we've gone too long without. We hang tight to each other as we reach the center and his thrusts begin.

No matter how good it feels, our eager and lust-filled sounds are no match for the increasing howls of the wind batting against the glass dividers or the force of the crashing of waves demanding attention. It's okay, in a way, each cry from nature permits and encourages us to be loud. There's no muffling, there's no holding back, both of us losing ourselves to our passion.

He slows his movements as we finish. His lips, so carefully fastened around the tip of my breast, return to my mouth, claiming me as tenderly as he had when our kiss first began.

I love kissing Landon, he never disappoints. And I love the way he commits so fully to pleasing me every time we make love.

I stroke his face when he pulls away, gasping when I see how wrinkled my hands are. "Maybe we should go inside?"

He kisses my cheek. "If you want. But let me show you something first." He groans when he separates us. I'll admit, I do too. Not because it hurts. But because this is a closeness that's hard to let go of.

For a few long breaths, he simply looks at me, taking a moment to kiss me again before adjusting his hold and carrying me in his arms. We drift to the deep end. He turns me carefully, making sure I grab the ledge before releasing me and pushing up on his elbows.

"There," he says, pointing to the ocean. "This is the reason I bought this house."

From this spot, all I see is an endless sea and sky. The sun isn't overwhelmingly bright, not like it is during summer. Yet it's enough to stream thousands of sparkles across the water. They cast a spotlight on an ocean filled with the dreams and laughter of generations of people smart enough to enjoy its splendor.

I rest my chin against my forearms, my spirit lifting as I take in its beauty. "Why do you love it so much?"

"It's a great view," he says.

I smile, but don't look at him. "Why do you love it so much?" I ask again.

For the longest time, he doesn't answer. "It's eternal," he finally says. "Not everything is, not everything that matters anyway, but the ocean always will be."

I can't argue with that.

He slips his arm around me. "Are you hungry?" he asks.

"A little bit. I was thinking I can make some fish stew with the leftover steaks we have."

He strokes my skin with his knuckles. "You can do that?"

"It won't be perfect," I confess. "But I can make do with what you have, so hopefully it will be good enough."

"I'd like that."

His smile vanishes when my cell phone rings. I already know who it is and so does he.

I pull myself out of the pool and hurry to the other side. The hot water and the heat lamps keep the bite of winter from nipping my skin long enough to dry my hands and gather the robe against me. The phone stops ringing, but I catch the contact information flashing across the screen. As I suspected, I'd missed Blythe's call.

I don't bother to call her back. Instead I slip on the robe and plunge my feet into the water.

Landon swims toward me. There's so much I want to say and thank him for. But the one thing I don't want to say is goodbye.

I can't be the first woman Landon has spent the weekend naked with. No, he's too attractive, funny, and absurdly smart. And with that tender heart beating beneath all those looks and charm, he's impossible to resist.

He hops out of the pool, a cascade of water dripping down his back and legs. He reaches for his towel, drying off quickly when my phone rings again.

My focus stays on Landon as he yanks on his sweatpants. "Hello?"

"Hey," Blythe says. "I'm checking out. I should be at Becca's in about half an hour."

She sounds annoyed. I suppose the man she met wasn't so different after all. I turn back toward the pool. "You're leaving now?" I ask, my thoughts returning to the intimacy Landon and I shared moments ago.

"Yes," she says, her voice irritated. "Didn't I just say that?"

I'm taken aback by her tone, and so is Landon. He sits beside me, frowning. I don't have to guess he heard Blythe.

"Fine," I say, unable to disguise how offended I am by her behavior. "But I'm not at Becca's."

Her pause is so dramatic, I'm not sure she's still on the line. "Then where are you?"

I stiffen, not wanting to disclose anything private, especially with her being as rude as she is.

Landon holds out his hand. "May I?"

I hesitate, unsure what he'll say, not that it stops me from passing him the phone.

"Luci, where are you?" Blythe snaps.

"She's with me," Landon answers, his voice just as terse. "This is Landon Summers. I'm at 16 Ocean Course Drive, seven houses down past Becca's, sea side. Got it?"

"Yes," Blythe stammers.

"Good," he says. "Drive slow."

I take his hand when he offers it and allow him to pull me up, huddling into the robe as we hurry back into the house. He shuts the sliding glass doors behind us and returns my phone. I drop it back into my pocket, watching him as he works the buttons on his control.

"Can I borrow your hair dryer?"

He keeps his back to me, his fingers moving fast. "You don't have to ask, Luci. Take and use whatever you need."

"Thank you," I say.

He seems upset and it's the last thing I want. "She's not normally like that," I offer.

"You could have fooled me, based on how she's treated you."

He lowers his head when I wrap my arms around his waist and kiss the spot between his shoulder blades. "It's okay," I say.

"No. It's not."

He's right. Blythe has been awful this trip. But I don't want to insult her. I don't have a lot of time and need to hurry. That doesn't stop me from pressing my cheek against his back and taking a moment to feel him against me.

His skin is warm. My hair is soaked and cold, yet he doesn't appear to mind. "She hasn't been a good friend this weekend," I admit. "But it's because of her that I met you, and for that I'll always be grateful."

My eyes sting when he doesn't respond to my words or my touch. "Do you want me to run a hot bath for you?" I offer.

He shakes his head slowly, yet still won't look at me. My hands slip from his waist. "Okay," I say. "I better get dressed."

I cross the living room and head toward the rear staircase, certain he's angry and that he needs space.

"Luci?" His deep tenor stops me at the bottom of the stairs. But it's that heartbreaking way he regards me that keeps me from moving. "Remember that first night, when I asked you about the worst date you ever had, and you told me about meeting that guy at the pizza parlor?" I nod, although I'm unsure where he's headed. "Mine was this one . . . because it has to end."

My fingers slide along the slick wood of the banister. I swallow hard. "I think I know what you mean," I say.

I start up the steps carefully, not wanting him to see the tears that fall.

Chapter Eleven
Landon

It takes me a long few minutes to move, and even longer to figure out why the hell I can't. Damn, I'm pissed.

Pissed that it's time for Luci to go.

Pissed at her friend for talking to her like she did.

Pissed that I finally met someone worth talking to and she lives in New Jersey.

Fucking *New Jersey*.

In the *fucking* north!

How the hell does an area known for its bad attitude produce someone as sweet as her?

Probably because not everyone there is an asshole, dumbass.

I jog up the steps, stopping in the second-floor laundry room where her dress from the party hangs on a hook. I have a sanitizing option on my dryer and used it to clean her dress. It's not as nice as dry cleaning. But when I told her I'd cleaned it for her, and washed her panties and bra, she seemed grateful.

There's a lot I don't know about Luci, but I can't shake the feeling that as nice as she is to everyone, that niceness isn't extended back.

I mean, all I did was clean her dress. To her, it's as if I'd done a lot more.

I lift her beige panties and bra from the drying rack. They don't match. The color of the panties are a little darker than the bra. It's obvious it's not a set she bought together. I check the tags, almost kicking myself for being so nosey.

As I suspected, it's not Victoria's Secret or anything that suggests she bought them at a fancy store. I wonder if it's because she can't afford to, which leads me to wonder how much she struggles. But wondering does nothing to lift my mood. If anything, it worsens it.

I walk back to my suite. She didn't bother closing the doors leading into the bedroom, or the one to the bathroom. It shouldn't seem like such a big deal, except that it is. My ex-wife not only closed the doors, she often locked them, claiming she needed her privacy. I know now she just needed to get away from me.

Luci wants me close. She doesn't want to hide away or distance herself. She proved it with these open doors and by the way she held me downstairs, even when I couldn't bring myself to look at her.

The hair dryer is blasting away. I can hear it from here. I find her with her head to the side, fluffing her long waves. Her small purse lays open on the bathroom vanity beside her lip gloss, her phone, and mine. Even from here, I can see the small box of birth control pills inside, and what looks like a credit card and a few bills.

She shuts off the hairdryer when she sees me. "Thank you," she says, smiling when she sees I'm carrying her clothes. "I hadn't thought about what to wear."

Probably since the only thing she's worn are my clothes, when we bothered with clothes at all.

I hang the items on the hook behind the door without a word. God forbid I act like a human being and speak. Nope. The educated man has officially left the building and left the Neanderthal in charge. It's a wonder I don't scrape my knuckles against the tile when I step into the shower.

My hands make quick work of washing my hair and body, and my eyes make better work of watching Luci. There's lots I want to tell her, but even less that comes. So instead of fixating on why I'm struggling to find my words, I focus on her.

Her wavy hair looks tussled and full, not like the long, smooth curls I first saw when we met. I like this look better, mostly because it reminds me of all the time we've spent together. There was no need for fancy clothes or carefully styled hair. There was just a need to be us, and that's exactly what were.

I step out of the shower and towel off. By the time I slip out of my closet, dressed in jeans and a long T-shirt, she's done with her hair and sliding into her panties.

"Here," I say, when she reaches for her bra. "Allow me."

It's not like she can't put the damn thing on herself. But I only have a few minutes left with her, and I want to help her any way I can.

She doesn't argue, passing me her strapless bra and lifting her hair as she turns. I hook it in place then carefully adjust her breasts within the cups. She shudders. I'm not trying to seduce her, at least not this time, but the way she responds to my touch . . . shit, it does more to me than I intend.

I close the small space between us. "Is it tight enough?"

She adjusts her hold over her long hair. "It feels a little loose. Could you tighten it as far as it will go, please?"

I do as she asks, hooking my finger around the edge when I'm done to flatten the elastic against her skin.

"Thank you." She slips on her high-heels. I hadn't noticed them until now. She's taller, but still so small compared to me.

Using great care, she steps into her dress, careful not to let the fabric catch on her shoes. She sweeps her hair over her shoulder so it lays in front and gathers the dress around her breasts.

"Would you mind helping me with my zipper?" she asks.

Like I'd say no. Like I wouldn't use this last moment to feel close to her.

I pinch the tiny zipper and pull up slowly. As I reach the top, it takes everything in me to let go.

She shoves the lip gloss into her purse and lifts her phone, keeping her chin lowered long after she snaps her purse closed.

"I should wait in the foyer," she says. "Blythe won't be much longer."

"Do you want a coat to take with you?"

Her smile and the gentleness behind it cements me in place. "No, I brought one down with me. I'll be all right getting to the car."

I place my hands on my hips and nod. "All right."

When all I do is stare at the floor, Luci stretches up on her toes and kisses my cheek. "Thank you, Landon," she whispers. "For everything."

The sound of her heels clicking against the bathroom floor echoes along the silver glossed tile. She reaches the door leading to the hall and goes further yet, and all I do is stand there.

Son of bitch.

I snatch my phone and stomp forward, moving fast. I catch up to Luci where the hall overlooks the foyer. Giant windows provide a generous view of the front yard and the lush wooded landscaping that conceals the house from the main road. Next to the ocean, it's my favorite view. This time, I barely see it.

"Luci, wait."

She tilts her chin. "What's wrong?"

What's wrong is I've obviously lost the ability to speak.

"Landon?" she asks, moving forward when I stand there like a flaming imbecile. "Are you all right, sweetie?"

Sweetie. She had to go and call me that.

My mind wrestles with too much to say while my mouth struggles to keep up. "I know people. Powerful people. You hear what I'm saying?"

She blinks back at me, then glances around, stunned. "Oh, my God. You're in the *Mafia*?"

"What—*no.*" I clasp her elbow when she tries to back away. "What I mean is, if you're ever in trouble, I can help you."

Her terror eases (thank heaven for small favors), but her confusion remains, because why the hell wouldn't it? "Why would I be in trouble?" she asks.

"I . . ." Shit, this is coming out all wrong.

Her hand falls on my shoulder. "You don't have to worry. I took my birth control on time."

I pinch the bridge of my nose, muttering a curse. "That's not what I mean. Look, I'm trying to tell you that if you ever need anything, money, a car, a place to live, I can help you."

My family always wanted me to run for office. They often told me I had a gift for telling people exactly what they wanted to hear and saying it in the best way they needed to hear it. Based on what's shooting out of my mouth, I don't think Luci would agree.

"Landon, I have a job." She scans my face, likely wondering how she went home with Alex Libby and woke up next to Forrest Gump. "It's a good job," she says as if I don't believe her. "I own my own condo and have a car. The only reason Blythe drove is because she was the one who invited me."

"I'm not saying you're poor."

"Good," she replies. "Because I'm not. I do well, probably not as well as most people you know, but I'm independent and able to provide for myself."

No, I didn't come across as elitist. Nope, not at all. "That's not what I meant," I mutter, wishing I could kick my own ass.

"Then why do think you need to take care of me?"

What am I supposed to say to that? Because you're not dripping with diamonds and probably bought your panties at Target. Shit, I buy my own damn briefs at Target!

"I just want to make sure you'll be okay," I manage.

At first, the way her gaze softens, I think she's going to cry. But then she smiles in a way that melts my heart and reminds me why I don't want her to go.

"I'll be okay," she answers gently. "Don't worry about me."

But I will, and that's part of the problem.

"Take my number, all right?" I spill my digits. "If you're ever in Kiawah or . . ." I bite out another curse. "Just know you can call me whenever you want."

Considering everything I said came out in all the wrong ways, she smiles. "All right." She adds my number, a small blush spreading across her cheeks as she taps the screen.

My hand buzzes, announcing a text. I grin when I read it.

It's me, Luci.

"I don't know a lot of people," she says. "And I'm not in the Mafia. But if I can ever help you, please know you can call me, too." She steps back and lifts her phone.

"What are you doing?"

"Taking your picture so I'll have it in my contacts." She shrugs. "It's something I do."

The flash goes off, the corners of her lips tugging upward when she sees the shot. She turns her hand and shows me the screen. It's not a bad picture, even though I wasn't ready for it. But it's good enough for Luci, so it's more than good enough for me.

"Nice," she says.

I fiddle with my phone, adding her to my contacts. She brushes a strand of her hair behind her ear, suddenly shy. "I'm a mess right now, but if you'd like, I can send you a picture of me later."

"Nah, I already have one."

I lift the phone, showing her the pic I took of her following the tequila shot.

I crack up when her mouth fall opens. She doesn't look bad. She's adorable and sexy and manages both just fine.

"You can't use that picture," she insists.

"Oh, yes, I can," I assure her.

I catch her in my arms when she launches herself on me, keeping my phone up and away from her. She drops her purse and her phone, our laughter fading as my gaze melts into hers.

Her friend is almost here. She's probably already pulled onto the street. It doesn't stop me from kissing Luci.

Nor does it keep us from turning that kiss into a whole lot more.

Our hands wander, mine down her back, hers against my chest. But when I cup her breasts, she quickly unsnaps my jeans.

All at once, it's like an alarm goes off in my head, announcing that our time is up and making us desperate.

My hand slips beneath her skirt, yanking down her panties as her hands disappear inside my jeans. I don't think about anything, and maybe she doesn't either. I simply react to her touch and the fire tearing through my veins. I whirl her around, gripping her waist and plunging inside her in one hard stroke.

Her slick center welcomes me, her head snapping back and her body clamping down like a vice. She gasps, clutching the banister. I'm not gasping, not when her core grips me like it does. I'm swearing and just about crawling out of my skin with how good she feels and how bad I want her.

My fingers trail around her throat to cup her jaw, turning her enough to continue our kiss. I don't want to stop kissing her, needing her, *God damn it*, wanting her!

I pull back and ram forward, repeating the motion. Each time I withdraw, I return to her with more force, my hips crashing against her ass. She whimpers, coming undone, her fervent gaze staying on me as I continue that slow, intoxicating rhythm.

My arm bands around her waist, keeping her steady as I tug off her dress and bra just enough to tease her breasts.

I'm not supposed to come this way. I'm supposed to go full speed ahead until she screams with pleasure, and my strokes in and out stir my release. But between the way her body grips me, and the way her face flushes as she peaks, I don't stand a chance.

I finish filling her as the doorbell rings.

"Shit." I pull out and lift her away from the view of the large windows. I doubt her friend saw or heard anything, but that's not why I'm cursing.

The doorbell rings again as Luci yanks up her panties and I fumble with my jeans. She doesn't say anything, not this time, too focused on adjusting her breasts beneath her bra and pulling up the front of her dress.

"I have to go," she says, not bothering to look at me.

A gentleman would help her pick up her phone and purse, not simply stand by as she retrieves both. I'm not a gentleman, not then. I'm the miserable bastard who knows his time with this amazing woman is up. I want to say something funny, to hear her laugh one more time, or at least flash me that tender smile. Except for humor to come, you need a smile of your own, and I'm not certain how I'll find mine without Luci.

I follow her down the stairs as her phone rings. "Luci, are you there?"

Her friend isn't as bitchy, which I'm glad about. That doesn't mean I'm glad in general. "I'll be right out," Luci tells her and immediately disconnects.

"Baby, wait."

It's not the first time I called her "baby" this weekend. In theory, it shouldn't give either of us pause, except that it does. Blame it on the way I say it, or feel it, or how much it bothers me that it's the last time I'll get to call her that.

I open the downstairs closet and shove my feet into a pair of sneakers, then pull out my leather jacket and drape it around her shoulders. "It's cold," I say. "At least wear it to the car."

She doesn't argue or try to convince me not to walk her out.

Good. I wouldn't listen anyway.

The horizon has already begun to swallow the sun, dropping the temperature fast. I want to hold her hand and I do, her fingers linking with mine as naturally as if we've known each other forever.

Except it hasn't been forever. It's been two days, not nearly long enough to feel what I'm feeling and way too fast to jump into something after spending a year losing myself.

Her friend is sitting in her car. The way she's parked on the circular drive gives her a good view as we bounce down the stone steps. Her eyes widen when she sees us, maybe because we're holding hands or because Luci's wearing my coat. Either way she doesn't seem happy, for me or for Luci, showing me once more she's the kind of friend Luci could do without.

I'm not sure what she sees in my expression and I don't care, my focus returning to Luci and where it wants to stay.

We walk around the front of the car. Luci opens the passenger side door where her friend has placed her coat. She tosses her phone and her purse on the seat and turns to me.

"I guess this is goodbye," she says.

Yeah. Guess it is.

My fingers trail across her cheeks to gently hold her jaw. "Remember what I said. If you ever need anything, call me."

She tries to smile, her fingers brushing over my wrists. "It was so great to meet you, Landon."

I smile, more because I have to and because I hate how miserable we seem. "The pleasure was all mine, Luci."

This time when we kiss, all the innocence I feel within her finds its way across her warm skin. The way her mouth feathers across mine is more delicate and maybe a little lonely, too.

She withdraws slowly, shrugging out of my coat and offering it to me before slipping inside.

I step back, giving the car room to pull away. She offers a small wave as she disappears out of view.

I'm not sure how long I wait there before turning around and heading back inside alone.

Chapter Twelve
Luci

"Luci, when the hell is the contractor going to start on the floor?" Jefferson tosses a file across his desk and motions around him. "This office is too fucking small and I can't get anything done with all the noise."

I don't bother to look when he points toward the rows of cubicles behind me. "A few more weeks," I reply. "Mr. Ballantyne asked for a redesign and it's taking longer than expected."

He frowns. "What kind of redesign?"

"One you'll like," I answer earnestly. "It will offer two junior partners corner offices and expand the size of the other remaining offices significantly."

He perks right up. "I'm getting a corner office?"

"I never said that," I respond, offering a small smile. "That decision falls on the senior partners."

"But you'll put in a good word for me. Right, baby?"

I'm not your baby. "Jefferson, I never said that either." I flip through the stack of papers in my hand and pass him his benefits package.

"What's this?"

"Stock options. Mr. Ballantyne is looking to expand the firm's portfolio. Let me know which investments you prefer by Friday at the latest."

I start to walk away, but he stops me at the door. "It's the new year," he reminds me.

Two weeks and two days into the New Year to be exact, and fourteen days since I last saw Landon. I waited until the day after I arrived home to text him. I didn't want to appear needy.

"Good," he wrote back and . . . that was all.

"Luci?"

"I'm sorry, did you say something?"

I always listen to what everyone has to say, even Jefferson, who frequently complains and more often than not flexes his ego. But as my thoughts returned to Landon, all I noticed was Jefferson's mouth opening and closing. Nothing he said registered.

He frowns. "I said it's been almost two years since I've known you."

I adjust the remaining folders against my chest. "That sounds about right," I agree, unsure where he's going.

"So will you?"

"Will I what?" I ask.

He laughs as if I must be joking. "Will you go out with me?"

Okay, this time I'm certain I misheard. "On a *date*?"

When Jefferson started working here, every single woman wanted to date him. Everyone but me. Where they saw an assertive and dashing attorney on his way to take on the world, I saw an arrogant young man who'd mow down anyone who stood in his way.

"Uh, *yeah*," he says. "When I first asked you out, you said no because you didn't know me." He smiles, seemingly pleased with himself. "Now you do. How about dinner?"

"I'm sorry," I reply, still in shock. "But I'm seeing someone."

He regards me as if he doesn't believe me. Probably because it's a lie. I hook my thumb in the direction of the busy floor. "I have to see a few more attorneys before the meeting. I'll see you later, okay?"

"Sure," he says, his voice trailing off.

I'm not certain why I lied to Jefferson. As much as he can be extremely off-putting, a simple no would have sufficed. That doesn't mean I don't wish I was seeing someone, or more specifically, Landon.

The more days that pass, the more the weekend I spent with him becomes a dream. I begin to doubt how great he was, dismissing our time together as simply physical and nothing more.

He's probably already met someone else, a new woman to warm his bed and sing beautiful melodies to.

My pace slows. I don't want to think about him looking at someone else the way he looked at me. But I can't ignore his lack of contact or how easily he forgot me.

I'm almost to the next attorney's office when Kee-Kee storms forward, her face red with anger.

"Luci, you need to hire me a secretary who actually wants to be here."

I sigh when the frantic typing slows and the noise in the room cuts by half. "Kee-Kee, Liza just started," I say, speaking quietly. "Give her a chance to figure things out."

"*No.*"

The reason Kee and I are friends is that I've never been afraid to stand up to her, albeit in my own patient way, and because of it, I earned her respect. "You're not being fair and you know it."

"This isn't about being fair or unfair, Luc. It's about needing someone who knows what she's doing. Adelle is retiring in two months."

"I know. Which is why you need to give Liza a chance," I say. "It will give Adelle two months to train her and get her acclimated to your likes and dislikes."

She crosses her arms. "Are you saying I'm difficult to work with?"

"Yes."

She glares, as she often does. "Fine, but if she doesn't work out, it's on your ass."

"It always is, Kee-Kee."

She mutters something I don't quite hear and storms away.

"You're due in court in twenty minutes," I call after her.

"Your mother's due in court in twenty minutes," she fires back. She whips around, pointing at me in a way that makes the closest interns jet away. "We're going out for drinks after work on Thursday and don't tell me no."

I don't, but I likely will. I walk into the next attorney's office and place a post-it note on the folder when I find that she's not there. I want to let her know to see me when she returns. It should be a simple task, but it takes me a moment to scribble my words.

Kee-Kee doesn't know anything about my mother. If she did, she wouldn't have said what she did. I know this, but the reminder of Fernie and her situation is yet another reason why my time with Landon was more fantasy than real life.

It took me several days to find Fernie this last time. I was terrified she was dead. When I finally saw her, I was so relieved, I almost ran to her. But it's who I found her with that made me keep my distance.

She was speaking to a man parked alongside the curb through his passenger side window. I couldn't hear them, but the conversation was clear enough. She opened the door and slipped inside. I walked away when they drove off. I didn't want to think about what she was doing, but those awful thoughts came anyway.

I was little the first time I saw her drive away with a stranger. I remember telling Mamita about it, knowing something was wrong. I didn't know why she cried until the next day, when she told my uncle and he called my mother a whore.

Whore. It's such an ugly word.

But to understand what it means, and when it pertains to your mother, is a lot worse.

"Luci, I can't get the copier to work."

Cherie is another new secretary. I stop beside her and tap the buttons on the touch screen. "You have to clear the last job before starting a new project." I point to the large icon. "Consider this your safety zone. It lists your options and erases the last command. When in doubt, just hit this icon."

"Oh," she says. "Thank you. I never knew that."

"You're welcome."

My office phone starts ringing before I finish closing my door. I reach over the collection of projects waiting for me and lift the receiver. "Luci Diaz," I say.

"Hey, it's Blythe."

I walk around the desk and take a seat. Blythe and I barely spoke the entire ride home from Kiawah. "Look," she says. "I know you're mad—and you have every right to be—but I don't want to fight with you."

I don't want to fight with her either. That doesn't mean I'll ever be able to trust her. I've never come first with her, and she more than proved it the night of the party.

"A few of the girls and I have been invited to a player's house this Friday. Do you want to come?"

My first instinct is to say yes, hoping to see Landon. But I don't think he's friends with any of the players, and even if he is, I don't want to chase someone who doesn't want to be caught.

"That's not a good idea."

"Because of me, or because of Landon Summers?"

I rub my eyes, well aware she's fishing for information.

"Becca was asking about you and him," she adds when I remain silent.

I sit up. "Why?"

"She didn't say, and I didn't have much to tell her."

I suppose she's trying to make me feel bad. Yet as much as I want to spill my soul over Landon, I won't do it with Blythe.

"Think about it, Luci. It could be a lot of fun. It won't just be players who will be there, but the marketing staff and some of the agents."

"I'm not going to another party with you," I say.

I don't think she expected me to be so honest, but I won't pretend with Blythe.

"So we're not friends anymore?" she asks.

"I didn't say that," I clarify, hating how sad she seems. "I just have a lot going on."

She waits for several beats and asks, "You're not going to tell me what happened with him, are you?"

It was the same question she asked when we pulled out of Landon's driveway. I answer exactly how I did then, which is why we barely spoke during the ride home. "No," I reply.

"Well, I guess I'll see you around." Her tone is stiff, assuring me this is the last time she'll call and my last opportunity to tell her what she wants to know. "Bye, Luci."

"Goodbye, Blythe."

I hang up the phone, once more wishing my life could be different than it is . . . and brighter with Landon's smile.

Chapter Thirteen
Landon

"Hey, Landon."

Duncan waves from across the large foyer, marching toward me like he has all the time in the world and smiling like he's doing me a big favor by meeting me.

There are two things I remember him telling me during the interview process: One, the pro bono position they hired me for was to make the firm look charitable instead of the high-priced, high-rolling, money-making machine it is. The second was that his third wife is expecting his fourth kid.

The pro bono work doesn't rattle me, bring it. I'm not looking for fame and fortune, nor am I afraid to work hard. The three wives and four kids, that's a different story. *That's* my worst nightmare.

A string of Bernadettes, one after the other, and kids I can't keep track of because they live in different homes, no thanks. Or should I say, *fuck that*. From what Duncan admitted, his last divorce was just as bad as the first, and already he thinks the current one won't work out either. "She was different when we were dating," he told me. "The minute I put a ring on her finger, she turned."

Sure she did.

His gaze passes along my Brooks Brothers suit, appearing amused. His problem, not mine. If I'm representing the underprivileged, I'm leaving the Armani at home. And if he's going to support all those kids *and* their mothers, maybe he should look at hocking that Panerai watch he's more than happy to flash me.

Damn, if I was Duncan, I wouldn't be grinning. I'd be begging God to put me out of my misery. He's the "Love is Bullshit Posterchild," and I'm a moron for even thinking I had it.

He holds out his hand. "Good to see you."

"Duncan," I say, giving him a nod. I motion to the stand at the other end of the foyer. "Want some coffee?"

"No, we have people for that." He reaches into his pocket and hands me my I.D. "This will give you access to the building and garage even if you stay after hours. There are a lot of perks to working here, and you'll get to experience them during your first few weeks. That'll change once the judge starts assigning you cases." He huffs. "I've seen the list of shit being considered. You'll be lucky if you get out of here by midnight if you get some of dem' immigration cases."

"I figured, but I'm ready," I assure him.

I walk beside him to the security desk. "With the kind of people you'll be dealing with, you better be," he says, not bothering to censor his remarks.

I was raised to give back so I'm not fazed by "the kind of people" I may or may not deal with. And since I was also raised to be polite, I don't call Duncan out for being an asshole. It's only my first day. I'm sure I'll get plenty more opportunities.

After a brief introduction to the security staff, we head to the elevators.

"God," he says, when we step inside. "I wouldn't be caught dead doing what you're doing. I worked for Legal Aide in New Jersey right out of law school. I had drug addicts, prostitutes, and don't get me started on those D.V. victims. Worst six months of my life."

"I'm sure it was," I agree. Hey, for someone like him, it probably was. "But don't pay those people who needed you any mind, Duncan. You're making the big bills now."

"Damn right," he agrees, my insult completely flying over his head.

What an idiot. Out of habit, I go to scratch my beard. Smooth skin greets the pad of my fingers, reminding me that it and my long hair are gone.

"So why do it?"

"Why do what?" I don't even blink. "Work pro bono? Because it's the right thing to do."

Apparently the right thing is a concept completely lost to Duncan. "You graduated at the top of your class from Duke. You could have applied for an associate's position—hell, for a junior partner slot based on your connections and litigation experience—and you would have got it! Instead, you volunteered for *this*."

It's almost the exact same thing he said to me during the first of my three interviews. "It's the right thing to do," I repeat. I don't bother to tell him I don't need the extra cash or remind him the partners are giving me a generous salary just to make them look good. Someone like Duncan is always too busy looking at the dollars he can make rather than the people he can help.

"Better you than me," he says, reaffirming that in his world, pro bono work is pure bullshit.

He hits the button to the elevator again, even though it's already lit. "Damn thing always takes forever when I'm in a rush." He eyes me closely. "You single?"

"Yes, sir."

He huffs. "Good. You're better off. Although I should warn you, you might not be once word gets out around the office. Just try to avoid dipping your pen in the company ink. That gets messy and the last thing you want is drama."

"You don't have to worry about that," I assure him.

He makes a face. "I said the same thing and she became my second wife."

"Nice," I say, stepping into the elevator.

When we reach the tenth floor, the doors open, revealing pristine cherry paneling and more marble tile. A receptionist with dark hair glances up, the firm's name in large gold letters shining behind her.

"Good morning, Duncan," she offers brightly, her attention skipping my way.

"Cynthia, how's my girl?"

It seems Duncan is already lining up wife number four. "This is Landon Summers, our new associate," he tells her.

I switch the briefcase to my other side and offer her my hand. "Nice to meet you, Cynthia."

"Nice to meet you, too, Mr. Summers."

"You can just call me Landon, ma'am," I offer, resuming my pace when Duncan marches forward.

I don't bother to see if she smiles or says anything back. She's a pretty young woman. But nowhere near as beautiful as Luci.

Luci . . . hell, didn't I screw that up.

She texted me to tell me she arrived home safely. How did I respond? "Good."

Even though it was a damn lie.

It wasn't *good* she'd left, or that we didn't make plans to see each other again. I know I could have picked a better choice of words, but nothing seemed right at the time.

"I miss you" was too soon, even though that's how I felt.

My house . . . shit, it didn't seem so big and empty with her around. But once she left, all that space grew wider, leaving me in the middle with no real place to go.

Her text to me would have been the perfect opportunity to start a conversation, maybe even face-time with her. Instead there was nothing but silence on both ends.

Every night since then, I've wanted to call her and make sure she's okay. Except every night came and went, leaving only doubts and too many regrets.

You don't know someone after two days, I told myself. *It's impossible*, I insisted. *It can't lead you to any place real*. These are the things I kept repeating over and over, and ultimately why I haven't called her.

That doesn't mean I haven't thought about her every night I fell asleep without her or that I didn't reach for her when I woke.

I should stop thinking about her. The way her hair fell around her shoulders, her smile, and how easily my smile came in her presence.

Problem is, I can't.

Duncan cuts a right down the center row of cubicles, leading me to an office that's all wall to wall glass. "All the new guys get these."

It comes out like an apology, but I don't care. Like I said, I'm here to work. "You'll get new furniture," he says. "And our office manager will assign you an assistant."

I place my briefcase on the desk. There's not a lot to the small space, but I don't need much. The desk, file cabinet, and two chairs is plenty.

"Don't get too comfortable," he says. "We have a breakfast meeting."

"Now?" I ask.

"Yeah, this way."

He leads me down a long hall. The same fishbowl offices lay to our right while a sea of cubicles line the left. A few women walk toward us, some doing double-takes when they see me and more taking the time to watch me pass.

A few years ago, I would have welcomed the stares that lingered and the smiles that had nothing to do with being friendly and everything to do with being more. Now, all I want is to be left alone to do my job.

It's what's best for now. But I hate the thought. As much as I don't want to be Duncan with too many wives who mean nothing and a slew of kids who mean less, I also don't want to become that bitter, lonely old man, pissed that life went on without him.

I do my best to be cordial when another pair of women stop what they're doing to watch me.

"Are we late?" I ask Duncan, noting how much faster he moves when we reach the far end of the office.

"It's not that. It's just that the senior partners will be there and it's best you arrive before instead of after them."

"True," I agree.

The door he throws open is heavy and the large boardroom we enter is immense. A rectangular table, wide enough to seat about twenty, overlooks the city skyline to our right. Every chair is occupied by men and women dressed in suits, except for the five empty seats on the end.

Everyone quiets when they see us.

"Oh, it's just Duncan," a man dressed in Armani mutters.

"Fuck off, Jefferson," Duncan tells him, scowling.

Most of the male attorneys laugh. The women roll their eyes. I suppose the men enjoy the ball-busting and the women are tired of the show. I don't bother laughing, even though it's clear that's what the testosterone generators are expected to do. Hey, I'll be the first to admit attorneys have egos. But egos are like trolls. No need to feed them.

Duncan introduces me to everyone except Jefferson, making their dislike for each other all the more obvious. Still, I offer him my hand before taking a seat beside Duncan.

We're shooting the shit when the big boss comes in. I'm the first to stand, meeting the senior partner with grin and a firm handshake.

He nods, ignoring everyone else. "Landon, welcome aboard."

"Thank you, Mr. Ballantyne. I'm glad to be here, sir."

He sits at the head of the table. I resume my place by the window. "We ready to start?" he asks the woman at the far end.

"Not yet, sir. We're waiting for Luci. She has all the materials."

The name gives me pause. I chalk it up to a coincidence, although I can't ignore the feelings that name stirs, feelings I'm better off forgetting than dwelling on.

The door flies open and in walks a tall woman in a red suit, her shoulder-length dark hair skimming just past her shoulders. I relax a little. "Luci," I presume.

"I thought you were supposed to be in court," Mr. Ballantyne barks at her.

She tosses a folder on the desk in front of him, a very satisfied grin splaying across her face. "I would be if we didn't just settle," she sings. She turns to the cluster of attorneys gathered at the table. "Seven figures. Read 'em and weep, bitches."

"Language," Mr. Ballantyne mutters, not bothering to glance up.

Everyone falls perfectly still as Mr. Ballantyne flips through the folder and reads the letter. "Well done," he tells her. "Well done, indeed."

She glances around, seemingly pleased with herself. Jealousy, dense enough to slice through with a machete, thickens the air and widens her smile. She pauses when she sees me. "And you are?" she demands.

"Landon Summers. I'm the new pro bono attorney."

She shakes my hand when I offer it, giving me the once-over. "Kee-Kee Washington. Good to meet you."

I release her hand slowly. So, not Luci . . .

I lean back in my chair, wishing I could kick this nagging feeling and my own ass while I'm at it. It was two days of companionship and hot sex, I remind myself. Nothing more.

I've repeated the same thing like a mantra every night I've gone to sleep without Luci, wondering if she's okay and wishing she was with me.

"I have a case before Judge Mizan this afternoon," Jefferson says to me. "If you want, you can tag along. Get to know the clerks, some of the staff, that sort of thing."

"Yeah, sure," I say, ignoring the glare Duncan casts his way. "Do you know where I get my parking pass?"

Jefferson smiles. "Oh, yeah, Luci will totally hook you up."

Luci.

Again.

I roll my shoulders, trying to shake what I'm feeling.

"Kee, did you see Luci out there?" the woman at the far end asks.

Kee-Kee huffs. "No. She's probably fending off the mob that surrounds her every time she leaves her office. Between them"—she motions irritably around the table—"and all of you, my girl can't get a break." She turns to Mr. Ballantyne. "Sir, I'd like to talk to you about giving Luci one of the corner offices down here when we move upstairs. If anyone deserves it, it's her."

The room of suits collectively mumbles, agreeing for the first time since I sat down. Mr. Ballantyne nods as if it's already a done deal.

I loosen my collar, feeling suddenly hot.

I'm hoping this Luci woman is old, real old, the kind of old that's going to pat me on the head every time she passes me—the kind I shouldn't be interested in.

"Who's Luci?" I ask Duncan, unable to stop myself and hoping whatever he says will calm me the hell down.

Jefferson cuts him off. "Our office manager and go-to for just about everything. You're going to fucking love her."

"Language," Mr. Ballantyne repeats, not bothering to glance up.

"I'll call her," Kee-Kee says, reaching for her phone when the room quiets. A phone rings right behind the door. "Luci, get in here, will you?"

"I'm trying," a quiet and *very familiar* voice answers.

I straighten in my seat.

No way.

The door pops open. All I see is part of a leg belonging to a very petite body. I go perfectly still.

No *way.*

The person at the door, the one who can't possibly be Luci because that Luci lives in New Jersey, speaks quietly to another woman just outside the room. The other person is agitated. Luci is not, calmly talking and reassuring her.

No *fucking* way.

My heartbeat grinds to a halt when Luci, *the Luci*, walks in. The hair I tangled between my fingers when she went down on me is pulled up in a messy bun held together by a pencil. Maybe this shouldn't be my first thought and maybe it shouldn't be my second either. But I am a man and that's exactly what happened.

Instead of a cocktail dress, she's in a long, shapely brown skirt and silky white blouse. Her arms are stacked with folders, and still she greets the room with a warm smile.

"Luci."

"Luc!"

"'Bout damn time."

Almost everyone is saying something to tease and reach her. Everyone is happy to see her.

Everyone but me.

What *the hell*?

"Hi, everyone," she says. "I apologize for being late." She drops the stack in her arms at the opposite end of the table, moving toward me when the people at the end start shooting the folders down the line.

"Luci," a woman asks. "What's going on with the new hire?"

"I've scheduled you to meet her tomorrow morning before your eleven o'clock appointment," Luci replies, using that same sweet voice she used when she offered to cook me dinner. "She's a highly qualified secretary with years of experience in tax law."

"Wait," Kee-Kee says. "Why does Sharon get the highly qualified and I get Liza?"

Luci pauses, barely blinking. "Liza will be fine, Kee. Sharon needed someone with a specific area of knowledge, hence her candidate's more advanced qualifications."

"Luc, I need to talk you about the stock options," Jefferson calls out.

"That's fine," she replies, scrolling through her iPad. "Does four work?"

"Anything for you," he tells her, *winking*.

She's almost to me. I wait for something, some sort of recognition, apology—*something* to explain why she's here, in Charlotte, the same place I'm supposed to work for the next year.

She doesn't so much as glance my way, her focus on Mr. Ballantyne as she nears my end of the table. "My apologies, sir," she tells him, fussing with the scarf around her neck. "There were a few issues that needed my attention."

"Don't worry, Luci," he says. His expression is relaxed and he appears to calm in her presence. "If you would, I'd like you to meet our pro bono associate."

She turns, her olive skin and light eyes radiant, and her presence just as magnetic as it was the first time we met. "Hello," she says, smiling politely. "I'm Luci."

At first, I think she's blowing me off. Until it becomes perfectly clear she doesn't recognize me. Frustration punctures my chest as I wrestle with how to play this.

Except I'm done playing games and I'll be damned if I pretend to be someone I'm not.

I rise, offering her my hand almost at the same time a spark of recognition goes off beneath that mound of hair. "Landon Summers, charmed."

Her eyes fly open and her hand doesn't quite make it to mine. She jerks her head in Mr. Ballantyne's direction and then back at me.

"No," she says

And that's about it.

"Something wrong, Luci?" he asks.

"This . . ." she says, struggling to find the right words to describe what "this" is.

"Luci, what's going on?" Kee-Kee asks.

I think Kee-Kee is looking at me. I think everyone is looking at me. But my eyes are on Luci and that's where they stay.

"*You're* the new associate?" she stammers.

It's not really a question, more like a "holy shit" response. Hell, that makes two of us, because what the unfathomable fuck is happening here?

Duncan nudges me as I take a seat, oblivious to anything that's happening. "Luci's going to take care of all your needs," he says.

She already has, I don't bother to add.

"Do you know each other?" Kee-Kee asks.

If her reddening face doesn't answer that question, mine for sure does.

"Oh," some asshole a few seats down says, dragging out the word.

Well, I'll say this, I know how to make a lasting first impression.

Chapter Fourteen
Luci

The second the meeting is adjourned, I leave. Oh, I'm sorry, leave is not quite the word I'm searching for.

I run back to my office like my butt is on fire and Landon just squirted me with gasoline.

While standing naked.

Holding a sign saying he saw *me* naked.

I clutch my chest. He saw me naked.

And now he works here.

"Luci?" Tara calls. "Is now a good time to talk to you about switching cubicles?"

"Not at all," I say sprinting past her.

I fall with my back against the door when I slam it shut. Sweat drips down my spine in tiny rivers.

"Oh, God."

"Oh . . . God."

"Oh, *God.*"

It's the only thing I can think to say. This was supposed to be a better year. After last year, it had to get better. I mean, isn't that how life is supposed to work? Isn't there some kind of balance in the world, good on one side to even the scales and keep all the bad tipping the other side from spilling onto the floor?

I walk slowly to my desk and collapse in my chair. I'm supposed to meet the designer in another hour and start the process of revamping the new floor. I'm supposed to meet with Mr. Ballantyne about the staff office party. I'm supposed to do my job!

I stare, simply stare at the mountain of work I have waiting for me.

It's not so bad. Staring beats screaming, and crying, and curling into a ball, and . . .

Oh, my God. I'm in hysterics. I'm actually losing my mind.

The door flies open and in walks Kee-Kee, her dark hair almost as wild as her eyes. "You fucked him, didn't you?"

I straighten, batting my hands and trying to shush her when the rows of paralegals and secretaries slow their typing and glance up as one.

She whips around. "Don't you people have work to do?" she demands, immediately causing the typing and hustle to resume full speed ahead.

Kee doesn't wait for me to answer or for an invitation. Of course not, why would she? She's not embarrassed.

She didn't have the new attorney go down on her *four times*!

I cover my eyes. She also didn't have Landon sing to her, or dance with her, or teach her how to fish.

He did all those things to me and with me, and now he's here.

She lowers herself in the seat closest to me, crossing her legs like a real lady, and speaking like she's not. "He has a big dick, doesn't he?"

"Kee-Kee!"

She hooks a thumb behind her. "I can tell by the way he walks, there's no hiding a package like that."

"I never—"

"All right," she says, holding out her hands. "You don't have to give me the dirty details, but a real friend would so I'm kind of expecting them. So I'm asking as a real friend, did he bend you over and pull your hair?"

My voice is more of a squeak. "I'm not having this discussion with you."

I wish I could lie and tell her no. But it's more than obvious Landon and I had sex. That doesn't mean I'm spilling the facts how he and I, I mean how we, and—

Oh, *God*. We had sex.

Kee smiles. "Your face is really red," she says, as if I don't already know. "It was that good, wasn't it?"

I wring my hands. "Kee, I'm begging you. Don't tell anyone."

"Pfft. Don't worry about it, only the people who need to know will know. Now tell me everything so I can know it."

"No," I insist.

"Luci, I thought we were friends."

"We are friends," I assure her.

"Then I don't need to remind you that real friends tell their other real friends everything. Including how you got the hot guy to fuck you on a raft while going downstream."

I blink back at her. "There wasn't a raft and we didn't—"

She throws her hands up. "I'm talking about me. I was twenty-two. Sven was twenty-six."

"Who is Sven?"

"The river guide at camp Kenobi." She bites down on her bottom lip. "Let's just say he liked to be paddled."

If she weren't one of the top lawyers in the south, I'd have her committed. "So because you told me about Sven, I should tell you about— I'm mean, admit to . . ."

I can't even get the words out.

Kee shakes her head. "My point is, I'm not twenty-two anymore, there's no Sven, and I only have you and Landon."

"You . . ." I latch onto something she said. "Wait, didn't you just go out with someone the other week?"

"Yeah, but we didn't have sex." She gives me a sly grin. "Unlike you and Landon."

I place my palms on the desk and lean in. "There is no me and Landon. Do you understand?"

"I understand that I've blown out three vibrators in two years," she tells me flatly. "Now, tell me everything so I can believe there's still hope for me and so I don't have to freeze the five eggs I have left."

"*No.*"

The door flies open and in walks Mr. Ballantyne. "Luci, what the hell is all this talk about a staff holiday party. The holidays are over, thank Christ."

Oh, yes, the party! Because I'm in the mood for one now.

I reach for my notes. "Sir, the support staff and paralegals were given generous bonuses as per your request, but they never had a formal celebration to thank them for their hard work and contribution to the success of Ballantyne and Bradley."

"So?" he asks.

"So due to the settlement in Brown vs. The City of Charlotte—"

"Which I secured," Kee-Kee reminds me.

"And the sums obtained," I agree, speaking quickly. "I think it would be a nice thing to do to thank the staff. I have secured a very nice dinner package from Sullivan's—"

"We already ate there," he says.

"Yes, sir. You, me, Kee-Kee, and the rest of the attorneys. The remainder of your employees, however, were not present at the dinner and feel spurned."

He makes a face. "Spurned?"

"Yes, sir. The large majority of your employees put in extra hours every day. I think a nice dinner would be good for morale and would ensure continued devotion and loyalty."

He looks at me, exactly as he did all those years ago when I was a teen and down on my luck. Like then, he picks up on a lot more than I'm saying.

He crosses his arms. "Is this what you want?"

When he doesn't ask me how much it's going to cost, I know he's giving in. I smile, probably the same way I did all those years ago when he offered to help me. "Yes, sir, I think it would be a nice thing for your employees."

"Okay, Luci. If this is what you want, make it happen."

"Thank you, sir." I stand to shake his hand. "It's the right thing to do."

He pulls his hand out of mine and looks down at his palm. "You sick? You're sweating like it's August."

I wipe my hand on my skirt. "No, I'm fine."

He looks over a Kee. She shrugs. "She's just nervous because she and Landon had relations," she says, adding finger quotes over the final word just in case she wasn't clear enough.

"*Relations*?" Mr. Ballantyne barks.

Jefferson pokes his head in. "No, shit," he says.

Of course, Landon is standing right behind him. Of course.

My body temperature shouldn't be this high. It's unnatural and likely life-threatening.

Mr. Ballantyne's chin jerks between me and Landon, whose face is probably as red as mine. "You slept with *him*?" he asks, pointing.

"Yes, she did," Kee answers for me.

"I . . ."

"When the hell did this happen?" Mr. Ballantyne asks.

"I . . ." I say again.

"He just got here," Mr. Ballantyne bellows.

"Sir, I assure you it's not what you think," Landon begins.

"Was it in the break room?" Mr. Ballantyne whirls on me. "God damn it, that's where I drink my coffee."

"Wait a minute, wait a minute," Jefferson interrupts, ignoring Landon and my attempts to assure Mr. Ballantyne we didn't have sex in the break room. "You spent the night with him, but won't let me take you to dinner?"

"Way to make it all about you," Kee snaps at him.

I'm ready to apologize to God for whatever I did to deserve this.

Evidently God is too busy watching the show.

"I'm just saying," Jefferson begins. "I've asked you out, what? At least five times. Each time you've shot me down."

"That's because no one wants to go out with you, Jefferson. Even me, and I haven't had sex with a real person in two years."

"I'm a catch," Jefferson insists.

"No, you're an asshole," Kee clarifies. "An asshole who doesn't call the psycho women he bangs so said psycho women show up looking for him."

"Once," Jefferson says, growing defensive. Kee looks at him. "Okay, twice, but she and her kid left when I asked."

"He's only been here two minutes," Mr. Ballantyne says, unable to get past the concept. "In my day, it took a lot longer than that."

"Mr. Ballantyne," Landon says, the severity in his tone stopping everyone in place. "Luci and I met prior to today." His focus trains on me, locking me in place. "I assure you, I didn't realize she worked here. Regardless, we will only conduct ourselves in a professional manner."

Mr. Ballantyne has his back to me. I can't see his face, but I know him well enough to realize he isn't happy. He jabs his finger out. "Fine," he says. "But just so you know, if things don't work out, you go, she stays." He turns back to me. "Use the company card for dinner, keep it under ten grand."

I lower my chin and push aside the strand of hair that escaped my bun. "Yes, sir."

I don't look up until he storms out. Heaven forbid Kee and Jefferson follow. Kee raises her brows, waiting for all the slutty details about my time with Landon.

Jefferson grins. His attention bouncing between me and Landon. "God damn," he says, evidently having the time of his life.

"Get out," I say.

He frowns. "What? I'm only saying—"

"I know what you're saying, Jefferson. And I'm telling you, get out."

He flashes another smile, but leaves, pausing to give Landon a playful knock on his shoulder. "Good job, dude. You wouldn't *believe* how many of us have tried to get with Luci."

If he's trying to help, he doesn't.

"I believe it," Landon tells him, his gaze drifting my way.

I'm not sure what he's thinking. But I can't ignore how angry and put-off he seemed during the meeting. I kept my head down the entire time, trying not to look at him, all while dying on the inside.

He's here.

I thought I'd never see him again and now, *he's here*.

I do a double-take when Kee doesn't move. "Kee-Kee!"

"What?" She rolls her eyes. "Fine, we'll finish our talk over drinks."

She walks off, pausing by the door long enough to fire a glare at every gawking member of Ballantyne and Bradley. They resume their work at warp speed. She nods, satisfied, and shuts the door, leaving me alone with Landon.

Chapter Fifteen
Landon

This is a fucking nightmare. That's what this is. A nightmare where the lay of New Year's past appears in a silky blouse and a long figure-hugging skirt.

Luci looks entirely different than she did two weeks ago. She's not the woman I'm out on the boat with, nor the one I'm singing to. She's not even the woman I'm climbing on top of, whose warm skin presses against mine and whose arms wrap around me, afraid I'll let go.

Here in Charlotte, there's more to her. More sadness, as near as I can figure. But that doesn't make sense. This is her home, although that's not what she'd claimed.

I'll admit, when the shock of finding her here wore off, I was *pissed*. Pissed that she lied and that she was just another woman working me over to see what she could get out of me.

I couldn't get past the lying and spent most of the meeting fuming. What else had she lied about? How she felt?

The thought gave me pause. She hadn't told me how she felt, not really. And maybe I interpreted more than was there.

I also couldn't justify *how* I'd been used. She never asked me for money and she hasn't so much as called or sent me a text. The other thing is, I couldn't discount the way she looked when I offered to help her if she were ever in trouble. She seemed confused and in a way, offended.

Being the jaded man I am, I concluded she was playing me and biding her time until the moment was right to sink her teeth in. Except the longer that meeting went on, the more I picked up on that fragility I first sensed in her. It lingered and warred with the humiliation flushing her skin pink.

Even now that fragility pokes through, demanding my attention and respect. If I'm being honest, it makes me want to hold her and maybe kiss her, too. But this isn't my house, and by the way she shrinks inward, she doesn't want me anywhere near her.

Shit. Luci *is* different here, another woman I've yet to know and very unlike the woman who'd throw her head back when she laughed and who couldn't get enough of me.

I cross my arms over my chest. If you asked me this morning which Luci I preferred, I would have said the one who wore my T-shirt and boxers. In those clothes, she was mine and nothing else mattered.

Now, fuck me, everything does.

She glances around as if unsure where to look. "Did you need something?" she asks, her voice more of a stutter than that tender way she spoke when we were alone.

I push off the wall. "Mr. Ballantyne told me to stop in and see you. Said you'd change out my furniture. I'm also supposed to get my parking pass for court from you."

"I see," she replies, sounding only partially relieved. "Please have a seat."

She motions to the chair that crazy Kee-Kee sat in, doing all she can to avoid eye contact with me. I lower myself as she types away on her computer. "Are you looking for sleek and modern or do you prefer a classic style similar to Mr. Ballantyne's office?"

She's been to my place and helped christen a few rooms in my house. She knows what I have and what I like in every way possible. "I'm more into modern furniture."

My husky tone gives away what I'm thinking, including how hard we went at it over the "modern" dining room set.

Her typing slows to a stop and she shoots me a sideway glance. The tension between us couldn't be worse and neither could this situation.

I need to make it right. God damn, I owe her that much. Even if she did lie.

"There's no rush," I say. "I have everything I need at the moment."

She stares at her computer screen in the same way some people stare out a window, more for something to do rather than to see what's there. "We're restructuring the floors to accommodate the growing firm. Most of the furniture, including what's in your office, is being donated to the local YMCA and church."

She averts her gaze and lifts her phone, tapping her nails against the desk. They're not long and polished like Kee-Kee's. They're short, neat, and clean, just enough to prick and turn me on when they grip my bare shoulders and trail down my back.

I rub my face, wishing I hadn't gone there.

Her brows knit slightly as she glances in my direction, her face lighting up when it appears someone answers the other line. "Claudio?" she says in the Spanish way it's supposed to be pronounced. "It's Luci. I need to decorate another office . . . Yes, for an associate . . . Do you have any new pieces you can email me? . . . Modern please . . . Thank you, Claudio."

She returns the receiver to the charger. "Made to order furniture?" I ask. She nods. "Sounds pricey."

She laughs a little, the familiar sound easing some of the tension. "It's actually cheaper," she explains. "Industrial furniture is marked up between two-hundred to four-hundred percent the moment it's labeled as 'office furniture'. Mr. Ballantyne likes high quality at a good price. Claudio provides both." Her fingers fly across the keyboard. "I'll email you your choices in addition to the new pieces Claudio has designed. Make your selection and feel free to change out the hardware if it's not to your liking. I'll take care of the rest."

Her voice quiets as she reaches into the drawer and pulls out an electronic key card. She knows she's making small talk, just like she knows I'm doing the same damn thing. "This will give you access to the parking deck directly across from the courthouse. The spaces are numbered according to the number on the bottom. If for some reason there is a car parked in your spot, let the attendant know and he or she will provide you with alternative parking within the same garage."

She slides the card across her desk, leaving it for me to pick up. It doesn't seem right for her not to want to touch me, not after all we shared.

"Luci," I begin.

I don't think she's going to react or maybe I do and don't want to see it.

She covers her face with her hands. When she drops them away and looks at me, it's as if all that strain between us now rests on her shoulders. "What are you doing here, Landon? You told me you were an engineer."

I frown, noting she thinks *I'm* the one lying. "I was and technically still am. I went to M.I.T., developed a robotics program, and sold it to the military. After that I was bored and went to law school."

"You were bored?" she asks like she doesn't believe me.

"That's right."

"So you went to law school?"

I shouldn't smile, but despite this shit situation and my struggle with who Luci really is, here it is, widening the longer I fix on her face.

"I like a challenge," I admit. My smile morphs into a smirk at the sight of her blush.

"I graduated at the top of my class," I add when she doesn't say anything.

"Of course you did," she says.

Her reply makes me laugh. "What about you?" I ask.

"What about me?" she replies, growing quiet.

It's not like she doesn't know what I'm asking. It's more like she finds it hard to believe I genuinely want to know. It's similar to how she acted when we first met, hours before I all but begged her to come with me.

"What did you go to school for?" I clarify.

"Accounting and office administration." She glances down, the row of thick lashes shadowing her lavender eyes. "I graduated last spring and plan to take my CPA exam in the fall."

"You're a recent grad?" I hold out a hand when her eyes widen. "I'm not judging you, but you did tell me you're twenty-eight."

My last few words come out harsher than I intend. Maybe because I'm wondering whether she lied about that too.

"I am twenty-eight," she replies slowly. "I had a late start in school."

"Why?"

She tilts her head. "What do you mean?"

"Why did you wait so long to go to school?"

"I thought you weren't judging me," she adds, her voice all but vanishing.

"I'm not. I just want to know more about you." I also want to believe she didn't lie. Call me a fool, but . . . never mind, just call me a fool.

"You want to know more about me," she repeats.

I don't answer. I've told her as much before. Maybe she remembers. If so, why does it add to her sadness rather than soothe it?

"I quit high school young and obtained my G.E.D. so I could work."

No, I'm not an asshole or anything. "Why didn't you tell me?"

"It's not something you really brag about," she adds.

"You should. You finished," I point out.

Her cheeks brighten to pink. "There you go again," she says.

"Making you blush?" I offer.

"Being kind," she says instead.

My sordid past with Bernadette warns me to stay mad and keep alert—that Luci isn't that amazing woman I couldn't stop looking at or touching. In fact, it insists I should call her out on her lies. But in those few words, I'm reminded why I can't.

Luci hasn't had an easy life. I suspected as much, but now I know.

I'm not sure she'll say more, but she does, revealing a little more of herself despite her embarrassment.

"Mr. Ballantyne used to frequent the diner where I waitressed. He liked how I worked and how I took care of things when they went wrong. More than once, he told me I was wasting my talent. I thought he was just being nice until he offered me a job."

"This job?" I ask.

"No, he started me off as an administrative assistant to the office manager. But the more I did and learned, the more responsibility she gave me. I didn't realize she was planning on retiring or that she was grooming me to take over. When the time came for her to make a formal announcement, she recommended me for the job and Mr. Ballantyne agreed." She gives a little shrug, just enough that the strands of hair that escaped her bun stroke her shoulder. "His only reservation was that I lacked the degree, so he offered to pay for my education."

"He seems like a generous man," I add when she quiets.

"He is, Landon." She pauses. "And because of it, I never want him to question my work ethic or regret hiring me."

I'm not an idiot, I know where she's going with this. "He made it clear I'd get the axe over you, so I don't think you have anything to worry about."

"There's a lot I worry about," she says, her tone trickling with the same sadness I've always felt.

I nod like I understand, even though it's obvious there's still a lot I don't know. In the quiet that follows, I think I should leave and give her some room to breathe. Instead I stay and ask her what's bugging me. "You told me you live in New Jersey."

It's not the question I intend, rather the accusation I don't mean it to be.

A tiny line forms between her brows. "No, I didn't."

"Yeah, you did," I counter.

She should grow defensive. I would. Instead there's that delicate smile that hooked me the first time. "I said I was *from* New Jersey. I never told you I still lived there."

I still, feeling more like an ass than I did before, and maybe some relief, too. "So you weren't lying?"

She tilts her chin, appearing confused. "Why would I lie to you?"

Yeah. Why would she, you bitter bastard?

The corners of her mouth lift. "You told me you lived in Kiawah," she reminds me.

I take it it's her turn to call me out. I chuckle, though maybe I shouldn't. "No, I said I was born and raised in Kiawah, and I was."

"So that's not your house?" she questions.

"No, that is my house," I say. "I bought it after my divorce."

Shock riddles her small features. For all I assumed things I shouldn't have, she assumed things too, like that I've never been married. "I suppose I should have mentioned that," I offer. "Guess I'm not too good to be true after all."

The sympathy that plays in her voice is like a song, gentle like a mist yet strong enough to keep me from moving. "I don't know about that," she says.

I don't know what she's thinking. I only know there are million thoughts racing through her head, just as they're doing in mine. "There are probably a lot of things we should have mentioned," she adds. "It's just that everything that happened . . ."

I shake my head. "Don't," I say.

"Don't what?"

I meet her square in the face. "Don't tell me that it shouldn't have happened, because I'm damn glad that it did."

"I was going to say that everything that happened doesn't usually happen to me."

She bites down on her bottom lip and I all but stop breathing, remembering what it was like to hold this woman in my arms.

"I don't go home with men I don't know," she explains. "And I do everything I can to avoid leaving the wrong impression. Do you understand what I'm saying?"

"I do. You don't have to worry about me," I assure her. "Just keep those thoughts of me naked off your mind and we'll be just fine."

I rise as her jaw slacks open. I start to walk out, only to stop at the door and glance back at her. "Oh, and if you could stop staring at my ass, I'd greatly appreciate it."

She whips around, startled.

I walk out the door and head to my office, a smile I've gone too long without splaying across my lips.

Chapter Sixteen
Luci

It's late and I'm just now headed home. I press the button to the elevator. I was hoping I could bring Fernie a few things before I went home. But it's already dark outside and I can't risk going to the park alone.

That group of people I first saw her with a few weeks ago never appear to leave her side. And the way they look at me is odd. As if they're expecting more than food.

During the day, I've seen them around town, alternating where they panhandle money for drugs. Most people in the area offer them money. I want to yell at them at them to stop, that if they want to help, to give them food or clothes. Of course, I don't. I don't want to cause a scene or appear heartless. They don't recognize that Fernie and her friends are addicts, and all they're doing are providing my mother and her friends their next fix.

The elevator door dings open just as footsteps echo behind me. I press the button to hold the door and keep the elevator in place.

Landon appears, his red tie poking through the collar of his coat and his grin firmly in place. "Well, look who we have here," he says.

I scrunch my eyes closed, groaning. "Why, Miss Luci, you don't seem happy to see me."

He's teasing me and doing a good job. If I'm being honest, I'm *always* happy to see him. I'm just not certain where we go from here. In Kiawah, I was that one night, or rather, two-night stand. I didn't have to worry about coming clean about Fernie or my past. Here, it's as if I have to work harder to hide it and I hate it.

Landon has worked here for two weeks. He doesn't call or text or ask me out. That doesn't mean he doesn't stop by my office several times a day to make me blush and yes, to make me want him, too.

It starts off innocently enough, a request for office supplies, questions regarding the reimbursement policy, or other matters that pertain to my position. But it always ends with flirting. Lots and lots of flirting until my face is hot enough to boil a pan of water.

I adjust the scarf around my neck as he hits the button to the parking garage.

"Are they still there?" he asks, pretending to whisper.

My hand releases my scarf slowly. I already know where he's headed.

He rests his back against the wall beside me. "The hickies," he clarifies. "I must apologize, Miss Luci. I didn't mean to leave you as many as I did. But you gave me no choice, not with how crazy you were driving me when you—"

The elevator stops and the doors open. "Ma'am," Landon says, when a woman in scrubs steps on.

"Good evening," she replies. I recognize her as the nurse who works in the cardiologist's office on the seventh floor. "How y'all doing?"

"Fine, thank you," we both say.

Landon keeps chatting with her. I keep my eyes ahead, determined to focus on our blurred reflections against the doors rather than the hickies. I fail, of course, but who can blame me?

The last few that faded were the most memorable. One, near the swerve of my neck, and another on my inner thigh. But it was the one just above my right nipple that kept me up at night, not because it hurt, but because it's the one I remember most graphically. How is a woman supposed to sleep with visions of Landon Summers thrusting hard against her?

"Something wrong, Luci?" he asks. "You look a little warm."

I narrow my eyes only to find him grinning. The nurse, being a nurse, turns around and places the back of her hand against my forehead. "You do feel hot," she says, totally and unfairly taking Landon's side. "You should go straight to bed."

"I've been telling her that all week," Landon interjects, making my already heating skin scorch.

"You should listen to him," she tells me.

"You should," Landon agrees.

It's taking all I can not to stomp my feet.

The woman steps off at the first level. "Y'all have a good night," she says.

"Good night," I stammer, unlike Landon who has no problem speaking.

The elevator zooms down. "Was that necessary?" I ask.

"Which part?" he asks. "The part where you should go to bed, or the part where it might be dangerous to sleep alone in your condition."

"I don't have a condition," I say.

"Oh, I don't know about that," he tells me. "That there was a professional in the healthcare field. If she's telling you to go to bed with me . . ."

"She said nothing of the sort," I interject.

"Who are we to argue?" he adds, ignoring me. He huffs. "Hell, that woman might have just saved your life."

I'm trying not to grin and doing a terrible job. Somehow, I manage to compose myself as we reach the parking deck.

Landon nudges me. "You really have to stop doing that," he says.

"Doing what?" I ask, knowing he's baiting me.

He leans into me. "Undressing me with your eyes. It's getting embarrassing for the both of us."

Another blush heats my face and spreads farther down. "Landon," I say. "I'm not undressing you with my eyes."

He frowns, following me as we step out. "Why not?"

"I . . ." God, he's cute.

"I mean, I'm pretty muscular. You women like that kind of thing, don't you?" He doesn't wait for me to answer, much less deny it, because no, I'm not blind and why would I? "And you seemed to like how I flexed and moved." He dances his brows. "You remember my moves, don't you, Luci?"

"Stop *it*," I tell him.

"Stop what? Whispering sweet nothings in your ear?"

"Landon," I warn.

"Calling you out for all that ass-ogling you're doing?"

"I don't ogle." Much.

"You can't mean stop making you blush?" he offers.

"Yes, that too," I say, my body responding in turn.

"Or are you referring to me giving you more hickies?'

I turn around slowly. "You want to give me hickies?"

"Oh, hell, yeah," he replies like it's obvious.

"I don't want to jump back in bed with you," I tell him. It's true, to a point.

I still dream about the way he touched me and how it felt to sleep against his chest. I still dream about a lot of things when it comes to Landon, including how he held me when we first danced and how he made me laugh like no one else. But that was Kiawah. In Kiawah, I didn't have Fernie and all the issues that surround her.

Landon is from a good, stable family. I'm not. I never have been. Mamita did her best, but the little she saved for retirement wasn't enough for two people and she hadn't expected to raise another child.

More times than not, we went without. That's not something Landon can say. Oh, certainly, he's experienced his share of poverty through the eyes of those he and his family helped. But I don't want to be someone he feels he needs to save, and I never want to be someone he pities.

As kind as Landon is, Fernie and her condition aren't issues I want him aware of. The day he offered me money, he meant well. But I couldn't help feeling that I'd come across as weak and helpless.

I don't want or need to be rescued.

I just want to be loved.

"What if I'm asking for more?" he questions.

"Pardon?"

If I was an attorney, I'd ask the judge to find that smirk guilty. "I said what if I'm asking for more than just sex? I mean, not that I'm asking for sex."

"You're not?" I give him the once-over. "You could have fooled me."

He nods, appearing to think matters through. "I mean sex would be nice. You seemed to like it fair enough and it was okay for me too."

"Oh, good," I say. "I was worried when you took out your knitting supplies that you weren't enjoying it."

"You have to admit, that doily came out nice."

We both laugh. I may not be the most confident woman in the world, and I may have my share of insecurities, but I know we made each other feel good. I know because every inch of his skin is ingrained in my memory.

"So what do you think about the non-sex and the something more?"

I stop beside my car. "As in a date?"

"Yeah."

"You want to date me?" I ask, barely getting the words out.

"Why wouldn't I? Knitting time aside, we had fun."

"We did," I admit before I can stop myself. "But I wasn't planning on anything."

"Anything serious you mean?"

I shift my weight. "I wasn't planning on anything at all."

"Do you think I was?"

This time, I'm the one smiling. "Then why did you have an entire squad of cheerleaders batting their pretty eyelashes and lining up to meet you?"

I adjust the strap on my purse, lifting my chin when Landon strokes it lightly. "Why do *you* think I did?"

I might have been laughing just now, but that humor is long gone. "Because you're gorgeous and they would be fools not to want you."

"Is that what you think?"

"It's what I know, Landon."

My comment makes him smile. I miss his beard and almost reach up to pass my fingers along his smooth skin. "I almost hate to tell you you're wrong, but I will," he says, closely scrutinizing my response. "I made the decision to move and work in Charlotte a few months back. Becca and my family didn't want me in a city where I barely knew anyone. That's where the cheerleaders come in." He grins. "If I met one and things didn't work out, no big deal. It's not like they'd be working directly under me, unlike you," he adds with a wink.

I almost release a sigh, since yes, Landon Summers is that sexy.

"My family thinks I'm lonely," he admits. He waits and says, "And they're right."

I tilt my head. "You don't have to be."

"Oh, I know," he says, looking straight at me. "You don't have to be either."

I glance down. "I mean you really don't. Any woman would go home with you. All you have to do is ask."

"Maybe," he says. "But you're forgetting, you're the one I asked on New Year's, and you're the one I'm asking now."

"I'm not forgetting," I add quietly, that sense of misery I often feel gathering like a ball at the pit of my stomach. "My point is, being with someone or not is a choice for you."

"But not for you?" he asks.

I can't look at him when I answer. "This isn't a good time in my life to be with someone. I wish it could be, but it's not."

"Why?" he asks, no longer smiling.

"It's just not," I reply, hoping he doesn't push.

For a long few minutes he simply watches me. I expect him to be angry and walk away. But there's a reason he's occupied my every thought, and again he doesn't disappoint.

His arm slinks around my waist, pulling me to him. I follow his lead, my gaze seared to his. There's no hesitation. I'd follow Landon to hell and back.

My eyes close as his lips brush against mine. It's barely a kiss and more of a whisper, yet I feel it down to my soul.

"We had a lot of sex," he murmurs against my mouth. "And I fucking loved it."

My heart stops.

He stills as if he can read my thoughts, the ones that tell him how much I loved it too and how good it felt every time his hands wandered and his tongue explored. Every caress, every thrust is like a memory my body can't forget. It lives within me, driving me mad.

This morning, I woke from the movements of my writhing body and the thrusts of my hips, lifting to meet his.

But he wasn't there.

He is now.

His voice lowers, gathering a husky edge. "But when I say I want more, I mean it. Let me take you to dinner or a movie. Hell, let me take you to both. We don't have to spend the night and maybe that's better."

"Landon, I don't know."

His soft lips grazing over my mouth silence my barely there words. "Luci, I didn't realize how lonely I was until I met you. You helped me to see it and you helped erase all the bad that came with it." He swallows hard. "It took everything I had to let you go."

I expect one of those kisses that leaves me breathless, like the first one he gave me, the ones that followed in bed, and the one where we said goodbye.

Instead his warm mouth sweeps over my crown. "Think about it," he says. "You have time and I'll be waiting."

He releases me slowly, which is good. I would have fallen over otherwise. He steps back, giving me ample room to slip inside my car. I suppose I should say goodnight, and maybe he should, too. But I shut my door without a word and carefully ease out of my spot.

Landon watches me pull away, oblivious to how hard my heart is beating as a result of his words and gentle caress.

I turn onto the ramp that leads to the street level. I want to whip around, invite him to dinner at my home. I want to do a lot of things right now, like tell him how hard it is to leave him, and how I wish he hadn't let me go.

Yet when I reach the light at the next block, I realize I can't. A woman in a brown coat crosses the street, gripping the small wire cart she's pulling. She's the same woman I've seen Fernie with. She's also a harsh reminder why I can't be with Landon.

He doesn't have a Fernie is his life. I do, and as long as I can, I have to take care of her.

The street she heads toward is a side street, more desolate and away from prying eyes.

Although I'm scared, I take a chance and follow. This street isn't too far from the park. I pull against the curb, checking on the box of supplies I keep on the passenger side floor while I wait for her to catch up, careful to watch my surroundings.

My box is relatively full. Every time I go shopping, I pick up items to keep in my car in case I pass Fernie on the way to work or back. But it's been a while since I've found Fernie while driving, and I'm cautious about how much I carry into work.

I fill a grocery bag with a few bottles of water, a small tube of toothpaste and toothbrush, and a few packages of snacks.

The woman starts to pass me on the opposite side of the street by the time my bag is halfway full. "Excuse me, ma'am? Ma'am?"

I have to yell a few times before I catch her attention. She pauses and I'm not sure she can see me, not with how dark this street is. I stiffen when she crosses the street, placing my car in gear and edging out slightly in case I have to make a quick getaway.

"Hi," I say when she reaches the window. "Are you on your way to see Fernie?"

"Fernanda," I clarify when she doesn't answer.

She presses her mouth in a tight line, her dark eyes eyeing my supplies. "Would you give this to her?" I ask. "There's plenty for the both of you."

It's only when she nods that I lower the window enough to pass her the bag. "Thank you," she says, tying the bag and adding it to her cart.

An oncoming car slows when the driver sees her, allowing her to pass. I'm not sure if this woman plans to give Fernie anything or keep it all to herself. But she has a story, too, just like my mother and just like me.

I wait until the traffic clears and pull onto the road, shame burning its way through me. I wish that's not what it was, but after living with an emotion this strong all my life, it's as familiar as the lines and ridges across my hands.

When I was little, I associated shame with anger and regret. Anger that it wasn't my mother who walked me to school and regret that I wasn't enough to keep her.

I wasn't even enough to have her miss me. If she called, it wasn't to ask how I was. It was to guilt my grandmother into giving her money.

"Where's your mom?" the kids would ask me.

"She's away," was my answer in grade school.

"She's sick," became my reply years later.

"She's not coming back," was what my family finally convinced me to say.

Yes, shame is something I've experienced most of my life. But it's not something I ever learned to live with.

My eyes sting as I pull onto Johnston Road. I'm tired, God, so tired of hurting and worrying, but most of all carrying this shame.

I don't cry often when it comes to Fernie. After so many years of doing as much, I simply can't.

But today the tears come. Only this time, they fall for Landon.

I envy him. I wish I came from the kind of family who is gentle with each other and does more good than harm. Instead, I'm taking care of a woman who doesn't acknowledge me as her daughter and who wouldn't think twice about hurting me if it meant getting what she wants.

The first time I tried to coax her into my car was one of my worst moments with Fernie. She seemed to be listening and agreeable to getting help. The more I spoke about the treatment center, the more she appeared to relax. I told her I'd pay for it and not to worry. I told her she was going to be okay.

We were only about a mile or so away when something changed in her demeanor and she lashed out, hitting me hard. I hadn't quite maneuvered my car to the side when she leapt out, taking my purse and leaving me with a busted lip. I was only seventeen. But she didn't care.

That didn't mean I didn't care about her.

My phone rings when I pull onto Providence Road. I hit the Bluetooth. "Hello?"

"Hey," Landon says. "Have you thought about it?"

For once I'm glad he's not beside me. If he were, he'd see my tears fall.

"Luci?" he asks. "You okay?"

"I'm really tired, Landon," I reply, each syllable releasing in a quiver. "And this is really a bad time."

At first I think he disconnected. But when that familiar voice with the tremendous empathy responds, I know he again heard more than I intended. "All right, baby," he says. "Just remember, when you're ready, I'll be waiting."

He disconnects. I wipe my eyes, worried I'll never be ready.

Chapter Seventeen
Landon

I meant it when I told Mr. Ballantyne I'd keep it professional, and I'm not trying to be a dick. But with Luci so close, professionalism took a step down and skipped happily away, leaving me to step up and get to know this sweet thing a whole lot better.

"Knock, knock," I say.

She glances up from her desk. As always, it's littered with neat piles of papers that never seem to get smaller, regardless of how late she stays.

"Hi." Her attention shifts from the letter she's skimming through to the bags in my arms. "What's this?"

"Lunch."

"For me?" she asks.

"Yeah, but I bought a lot." I shrug. "I was hoping some of the Jersey's rubbed off and enough southern hospitality has sunk in so not only will you thank me for being a gentleman and buying you lunch, but insist that I join you."

She nibbles on her bottom lip just as she does when she thinks she shouldn't give in, except in the end she always does. Good. It gives me hope we still have a chance.

I think I should tell her how crazy it drives me, in all the right ways, of course. But then she might stop doing it and we can't have that, can't we, y'all?

"Thank you for being a gentleman." She clears a spot on her desk. "But I must insist you join me."

"You sure?" I hold out a hand. "Far be it for me to impose."

She laughs, appearing shy. I don't remember her being this shy around me back when we were alone at my place and the rest of the world seemed so far away. But here the world is front and center, appearing to drive us apart, although I don't understand why.

Her job is important. I get it. Except there has to be more.

"Do I smell Asian?" she asks.

"Why, Miss Luci, that's quite an impressive nose you have there." I pass her a small white container packed with noodles. "Right there is the best Pad Thai this side of Charlotte. Your favorite, right?"

She reaches for the box and the pair of wooden chopsticks I dig out from the bag. "I do love it. But if memory serves, it's your favorite," she reminds me.

"True," I agree, opening the lid to my crispy duck. "But if I'm buying you lunch, I think it's fair I buy something I like, too."

"It was very nice of you," she says, her voice growing quiet as if she's worried she's said too much. She places her food down and removes her scarf, folding it carefully and placing it on the shelf behind her. I want to tease her and ask her about the hickies I know now are long gone. But I promised myself I wouldn't push her and wait until she's ready. I'm just hoping she'll be ready for me sooner rather than later.

The other week, when I called, I laid on the charm, hoping to make her laugh and coax her into dating me. But the way her voice splintered just about broke my heart. She has a lot on her plate and I can't help thinking she handles too much on her own.

The work in the office keeps her busy. The attorneys, staff, *everyone* are always wanting and needing a piece of her. She takes it all in stride, putting out fires, offering support and assistance. No wonder so many people like her. But it's what goes on when she leaves that concerns me.

If you're going to be a boyfriend, be a friend first. It's what my mother always said. I didn't pay much attention to it, until my sister Trinity started dating. It opened my eyes to how much women need a friend in those they entrust their hearts to. The thing is, it doesn't always work in reverse. Some people aren't worth giving your heart or your friendship to. My ex proved that. Luci, though, I don't know, I'm hoping I can be that friend she needs, as well as that something more.

The light casting through her window engulfs her in ethereal light. She's wearing a black turtleneck that hugs her figure and a hound's tooth black and white skirt. She typically dresses in pastels that soften her further and bring out her eyes and the highlights in her hair. But the black brings out the sexy, even though that's probably not her intent.

She sits, careful not to make direct eye contact. It's something she does a lot around me. I wonder if she's scared I might pick up on something she doesn't want me to see. That doesn't mean I don't want to have a look.

"How's the Loreno case going?" she asks.

I finish swallowing a bite of my food. Being who she is, she uncaps a bottle of water and passes it to me before I ask. I take a sip and set it down on her desk. "You heard about that?"

"I don't involve myself in a lot of the cases," she explains. "But every now and then some pique my interest."

"You're checking up on me?"

"Maybe."

I cock a brow, surprised she'd admit as much. "Maybe?"

She laughs. "I wanted to make sure you were transitioning well into your new role. And if you weren't, I wanted to see if I could help."

"Even if you don't have Mafia ties?"

She covers her mouth with a napkin. "I'm sorry about that. But the way you phrased your words could have been better." She clears her throat, her light voice deepening in an attempt to mimic mine and her words drawing out to match my thick southern drawl.

"I know people," she says. "Powerful people." She's nowhere close to how I sound, but her attempt is damn cute.

"Luke, I am your father," I add.

"What's that supposed to mean?" she asks.

"It means you sound more like a Southern Darth Vader than anything like me.'"

"Forgive me. I don't possess the vocal chords or the chest hair to sound like you." Her expression pinches as if she went somewhere she can't come back from. "I didn't mean . . ." she begins.

"Mean what?" I point at my chest with my chopsticks. "You weren't referring to the soldiers lying along the muscular field, were you?"

She holds up a hand. "I really didn't mean to go there," she stammers.

"Go where?" I tease. There she goes again, thinking about me naked and maybe how her palm would rest against my "soldiers." I want to ask her how it felt to have me so close. But I'm trying to be good, even though sometimes, like now, it's damn near impossible.

"Luci?" One of the secretaries pokes her head in, her face lighting up when she sees me. "Oh, hi, Mr. Summers. I didn't mean to interrupt."

"Hey." I think she's apologizing to Luci, but her attention stays on me. I return to my food. I think her name is Tiffany or maybe it's Cindy.

"Can I help you, Coral?" Luci asks.

Hmm, wrong on both counts.

"Hey, Luci," she says, evidently forgetting Luci is still present. "I was wondering about the office party."

I search through the bag when I remember I ordered an appetizer we've yet to start on.

"What about it?" Luci asks.

"I was just hoping you'd give us more details."

Luci pauses. "I sent an office-wide email explaining the time, who would be there, and what we're offering. I could send it again."

"I have it," she says. "I wasn't sure if there would be more to it, like a gift exchange."

Shit. I don't know Cora or whatever her name is, but I know she's lying.

I think Luci knows, too. She replies politely, like always, showing patience most of the higher ups lack. "Since we're so far away from the holidays, we didn't want the staff to feel obliged to buy gifts. If you feel they'd like one, you can certainly post it—"

"That's not necessary," she says, cutting her off. "I'll see you later. Bye, Mr. Summers."

"Bye," I say. I pass the tin of stuffed shrimp. "Would you like one?"

My focus turns to where Luci is staring behind me. Cora is leaning over a cubicle whispering to a woman. The other woman looks up when she sees us watching her. Cora stops speaking, her eyes widening before she straightens.

Luci is already to her feet. Cora starts to walk away. "Excuse me, Coral, Tricia, I'd like a word with both of you." She positions herself between the women, her voice soft but loud enough for me and those in the immediate area to hear. "I think this might be a good time to remind you that office gossip is greatly discouraged."

"I wasn't gossiping," she quickly answers.

Man, Cora, Coral or whoever she is can't lie worth a damn.

"If so, you have nothing to worry about. Otherwise, I think you should consider how seriously you take your job and how you'd like your coworkers to perceive you." She turns and heads back to the office.

"Sorry, Luci," the other woman calls after her, but not before casting Coral a nasty glare.

Luci shuts her door as she walks in, her steps slowing. "Are you okay with the door closed?" she asks.

"Whatever you want." I grin. "I trust you to keep your hands to yourself."

About me giving her space, I'm trying. But she is beautiful and I am human.

I place a couple of the shrimp on the lid to the tin, focusing on what I'm doing rather than greeting the blush that no doubt comes. I pass her the food, grinning like a fool when I catch traces of her heated cheeks.

"A lot of the people who work here are really great," she tells me.

"Hmm," I say, finishing off another bite.

"Unfortunately, we have had some issues and I like to stop them before they start." She waits for me to answer.

I keep chewing. This is some good duck.

"A few years ago, one of our attorneys became involved with his personal assistant. It was fine at first and turned serious rather quickly. It also didn't take long for those emotions to fade and for something decent to become ugly." She shudders. "Very ugly."

I take a few gulps of water. "Are you talking about Duncan and wife number two?"

"You heard about that?"

"Straight from the horse's mouth about all the mares he's had in the stable."

She sighs. "Did he happen to mention one of the mares tried to sue us when he ventured into another pasture?"

I chuckle. "Nope. But I'm not surprised."

"What saved us was that she no longer worked here," she explains. "With the amount Duncan brings in, she didn't feel she had to work."

"She was probably right," I agree. "Nothing against her."

"Right," she adds slowly. "But since that day we've encouraged employees to be cautious with whom they interact and how they treat others." She fiddles with her chopsticks and adds, "I'm not sure what Coral said, but I was afraid she was leaving Tricia with the wrong impression of you, and possibly misinterpreting your presence in my office."

"Oh, yeah?" I slide my water bottle away from the edge of the desk. "And what sort of impression do you think she was misinterpreting?"

I'll admit I'm playing with and twisting her words. Same way I'll admit I like the way she's fighting that smile.

Never mind. There it is.

I turn around, pretending to look behind me, not that I really bother. "Shit. You think she thinks we're a thing?"

"It's possible . . ."

"Mmm."

"I take it you agree?" she asks.

I finish my food. "No, I just really like this crispy duck."

I wink when she laughs.

If I'm being honest, I hope Coral tells the whole office there's something between us. The "did you know they slept together" train is slowly coming to a stop and I'd rather keep it going. Not to be a douche, but too many men have asked me how I snagged her, not just because they're nosy bastards, but because they want to have her, too. I don't bother to share the details, just like I don't hesitate to tell them to go home to their wives.

"You're not worried about me, are you?" I smirk when she averts her gaze. "Here I thought you were only concerned about your reputation."

For the first time in too long, she meets me square in the face, her pretty gaze softening and reminding me just how much I like this woman and how real she is. "You're a good person, Landon. I think it's only fair people know it, too."

"How can you tell?" My voice quiets. "You don't even know me."

It's what I say, although I think the same thing about her.

She pokes at food with her chopsticks. "I know enough," she answers almost silently.

Yeah, and has seen even more.

"What about you?" I ask when she quiets. "Aren't you worried about your reputation being in here with the likes of me?"

I swear that lovely face is going to split me in two. "I'll be okay." Her smile fades. "But with you being single, and with so many young women working here, be careful, okay?"

I'm not sure if she's jealous. I'm hoping she is. She's seen a few of the women approach me to chat. I'm polite, don't get me wrong, and I'm also as friendly as I can be. The thing is, they don't stand a chance. No one does, not with how I feel the more I get to know Luci.

"You don't have to worry about me being with anyone else," I answer truthfully.

What looks like relief seems to relax her shoulders. She knows what I mean. Just to be sure, I add another wink. It's not really flirting. If it was, I'd pull her in for a kiss. Hey, if the staff wants to talk about us, let's give them something juicy to talk about.

We polish off our entire feast a few minutes later. She gathers the containers and puts them in the bag as I chug the last of my water. "Thank you, it was delicious," she says. "I don't usually have lunch, so it was a real treat."

"You don't?"

She shakes her head. "My responsibilities usually keep me from eating."

"Then where were you all last week?"

"What?" she asks.

"Every time I drove back from court, I saw you walking outside. I figured you were headed somewhere to eat."

"I run errands during lunch time," she says.

I raise my eyebrows. Like Coral, Luci isn't much of a liar. "All right," I say, not knowing exactly why she feels the need to lie.

My tone alerts her that I don't believe her. Her gaze falls to her desk. "Speaking of errands, I have to head out. Thank you, again." She tosses the bag in the garbage and reaches for her coat. "My treat next time."

As easy as that, the tension I feel dissolves. "And when will next time be?"

"Tomorrow?" she offers.

I make a face. "Can't. I have Federal Court in the afternoon and I have to stop by Dania Loreno's place in the morning."

She pauses in the middle of buttoning her coat. "What are the chances you'll be able to keep her in the country?"

I huff. "With everything happening in the world, not good. But I'm going to try, even if it means a plea for asylum."

She lifts her purse slowly. "On what grounds?"

I stretch out my arms. "She left Ecuador with her kids to escape an abusive ex, counting on those damn coyotes to get her across the border. She and her girls didn't make it here unscathed and she's worked herself to the bone to give them everything they wouldn't have in her country. Her husband never got over her leaving him. If she's sent back, she's as good as dead, and so are her daughters. I don't care what I have to do, but she's not going back there on my watch."

I'm prepared to send my client and her daughters to Canada if I have to. Luci probably knows it. But that's not something that needs announcing. I like Luci too much to burden her with information the partners may not approve of.

"Hopefully it won't come to that," she says.

"Hopefully," I agree.

I start to follow her to the elevators. "Where are you going?" she asks.

"I'm walking you out. It's what real men do. Besides flex and buy women lunch, I mean."

She doesn't laugh like I want her to, putting my good humor immediately to sleep. "Oh, you don't have to," she says. "Like I mentioned, this is my time to run errands."

I cock my head, not sure why she seems so nervous.

Hmm. Maybe nervous isn't the best word. More like troubled.

I pause at the end of the hall, thinking I'm crowding her. "All right. I'll see you when you get back."

"Yes, I'll see you then." She heads out, her pace fast. She seems to catch herself and slows, taking a moment to glance over her shoulder. "Thank you. It was nice spending time with you."

"You're welcome," I say.

My smile returns at the sight of hers. But it's the way she regards me that stays with me long after the elevator doors close behind her. She's so gentle in her mannerisms and the way she seems to take on the world.

I turn toward my office, bent on reviewing my case before the Federal Court. As a die-hard perfectionist by nature, I need to prepare and do right by Dania and her girls.

It's going to be a rough and tumble case, and it's going to keep me late tonight. When I think about how late, I reason a boost of caffeine might help.

I swing back around and head for the elevators. My phone buzzes as I step inside. Elenora, Dania's oldest daughter sent me a text.

Mr. Summer. Will you be able to help my mama?

I shake my head, unable to grasp the kind of hell this kid is going through.

I'm going to do my best and take care of things. I promise, I text back.

I want to tell her not to worry. To just be a kid and let the adults handle the rest. But a kid like Elenora doesn't have that luxury. She, like many in her situation, can't just run outside and play. They're constantly looking over their shoulders, well aware they're not safe and don't quite belong.

The elevator reaches the ground floor as I hit send.

My mind is on Dania and her family as I step into the large foyer. I pocket my phone, grinning when I see Luci at the coffee stand. I march forward, hoping I can pay for her coffee. But instead of coffee, she hefts a large paper bag in her arms and rushes away.

She seems tense. But what confuses me is where she's headed with all that food. We just had lunch.

I wander toward the counter, looking at Luci as she pushes through the clear glass doors. "Hi, Mr. Landon," the woman behind the counter says. "Would you like the usual?"

"Yes, thank you, Belinda." I stop her before she can really start. "On second thought, no. I'll be right back."

She slides the large paper cup back in place, eyeing me like I've lost my damn mind, probably because I just might have. With more determination than reason, I take off after Luci.

The way my feet strike the marble tile is an indication of how fast I'm moving. I force myself to slow, stopping in front of the building as I step through the revolving doors. I glance to the right and down the long street. There's no sight of Luci.

"What the hell are you doing?" I mutter to myself.

My first mistake was stepping out here. My second is turning left in time to see Luci disappear around the corner. I realize I'm being an idiot and possibly a stalker as I hurry after her, making what has to be mistake number three.

Okay, maybe mistake and stalker are strong words. Something isn't right. Forget that we both ate a ton during lunch and forget that she's carrying enough food to feed a small army. To make myself appear less like a freak, forget that this doesn't appear to be a regular errand.

She tensed, becoming uncomfortable when I asked where she was headed. And for some bizarre reason, she also tried to lie her way out of it.

Luci is the go to for everything in the office, her duties extending past any office manager tasks I've ever seen. But those tasks are handled within the confines of the building. If she's in some kind of trouble, I want to help her. And if she's doing something she shouldn't be doing for the firm, I want to stop her.

Shit. What is it with my need to protect her and make sure she's safe?

I do a double-take when I catch sight of the lavender wool coat she's wearing.

She crosses the street and heads toward the park. "Luci," I call out.

I curse when I don't quite make the light and Charlotte traffic drives full speed ahead. She didn't hear me. At least I don't think she did. Rather than yelling again, I watch her disappear into the park.

The minute the crosswalk sign lights up, I jog across. February in Charlotte is milder than up north, but it's still a brisk forty degrees. If I wasn't moving as fast as I am, I'd feel winter's bite a hell of a lot more.

I follow the walkway Luci took, catching up to a few women pushing strollers. They turn toward the playground where about twenty kids are running around near the swings. Another woman trails them, holding the hand of a toddler who's gripping a lollipop for all he's worth. She smiles when I nod in her direction. The kid smiles back, his sticky and red-smeared face making me laugh.

Kids were something I always figured I'd have. My ex didn't want them and since I wanted her, I started to accept they weren't in my future. But it's like every time I'm around my nephew Cal, I'm reminded of why I wanted them to begin with.

Under the best circumstances, children aren't jaded to how cruel life can be. They have hope that the world is okay, and that it remains a place they can laugh and play in. It's something we all need to keep believing, even when we're old and gray.

I make a mental note to call Trin later, hoping maybe to face-time with Cal, Jr. He may not be my son, but for now, he's the closest thing I have and carries enough hope for the both of us.

The park is busy, mostly filled with mothers and their babies. I catch a few fathers, one adjusting his daughter's bunny hat, another pretending to be a bear chasing after his giggling son. That was always my dad, getting dirty right along with me and Trin while our mother giggled and set out our food.

If it weren't for my need to make sure Luci is okay, I'd stop to take in all the parents fussing over their kids and how the sunlight trickles against the dogwoods starting to blossom.

But then I see her, continuing to hurry along.

I follow, surprised she's not sitting on a bench, watching the children play. It's closer to her nature, at least the side I've seen.

She walks to the end of the park, searching from left to right, the tension I sensed earlier just as evident as before. I start to close in when she latches onto something, her shoulders relaxing only to strain once more.

There's something very wrong. I jog after her, wishing these dress shoes I'm in didn't make so much noise. As I round the bend, I see her, standing on the sidewalk looking ahead.

"Hey," I say.

She spins around, almost dropping her bag. My hand shoots out, steadying the bottom and helping her keep it in place. "You got it?" I ask.

She glances behind her. "What are you doing here?"

I shove my hands into my pockets, almost thinking I should lie. It sounds better than the truth right about now, except that's not what I'm about. "I followed you out."

Her eyes round. "Why?"

Yeah, this sounds worse than I thought. "I went to get coffee and saw you. You seemed anxious. I wanted to make sure you were all right." I chuckle, hoping to lighten the moment. "Sounds stupid, doesn't it?"

She doesn't answer, which makes me think she agrees.

I pinch the bridge of my nose. "I, ah, was worried something was wrong."

I wait for her to tell me she's fine. She doesn't, so either something is wrong, or I look worse than I feel. "*Is* something wrong?" I question.

She turns back. A crowd a people cross the intersection, headed in our direction. Most aren't close enough to make out their faces, but there's someone Luci appears to recognize.

A woman with a puffy yellow coat that's about four sizes too big pokes her head around the crowd. Three more women shuffle behind her, one pulling a small wire cart. But it's the two businessmen in front who catch my interest.

Both men hone in on Luci. I can't blame them, not when the breeze sends a strand of hair to curl around her beautiful face and not when the coat she's wearing lights up her tender gaze.

The man in the dark suit and coat smiles his approval. The one in gray perks up, pleased to see her.

"You're meeting someone," I answer for her. Her eyes widen. "That's it, isn't it?"

She trips over her words. "I know this doesn't look good," she says.

"Because you just had lunch with me or because I'm following you around like a lovesick puppy?"

She frowns. "What?"

"Never mind," I grind out. Jesus Christ, when am I going to learn? Here I am, once again giving my heart to someone who doesn't want it and worrying over a woman who isn't worth worrying about.

Anger burns through me, as well as humiliation. She told me this wasn't the best time for her. I guess now I know why. "If there was someone else, all you had to do was tell me and I would have walked away."

I start to turn, my blood boiling when Luci scrambles in front of me. "This isn't what you think," she insists.

I'm in no mood for more lies and I'm damned tired of playing the fool. "Then enlighten me. What was New Year's all about? You being lonely? Or you being lonely that one night?"

She clutches her bag, her gaze shifting behind me. He's here, that man in the gray or black coat.

My steely gaze turns to greet him, whoever *he* is. I shouldn't resent him or feel jealous. For all I know, Luci knew him long before she met me. I should stand down like any decent man would and walk away, pretending I don't know her like I do. But here I am, waiting to see who it is so I can finally accept there is no us and take it as another screw-up on my part.

As one, they both frown when they see me, looking quickly away from Luci and straight ahead. They don't stop to greet her and she doesn't seem to notice them. She's focused on someone else.

I turn expecting to see another man, my spine stiffening when a crowd of homeless people edge forward. The woman in the puffy coat is first in line, followed by the woman with the metal cart and another one wearing a dirty red coat. Two other men hang back, both strung out, but not too high that they don't know to keep their distance.

"Do you have any money?" the first woman asks.

Luci positions herself in front of me. "He doesn't have any money," she answers for me.

She places the large bag on a bench and steps out of her reach. "There's plenty for everyone," she tells them.

As she backs away, she clutches my arm and leads me toward the park. That's a good thing and a lot nicer than the punch to the nuts I deserve.

She hangs tight to me as we enter the park, glancing behind us every few feet to make sure we're not being followed. We pass a small garden where city workers have begun to dig up the soil for new plants and flowers. It's not until we reach another bend that she eases her hold and her arm slips away.

"I really wish you would say something," she tells me.

"Sorry, it's a little hard to speak with my foot rammed in my mouth."

She laughs, but keeps her attention ahead. When she doesn't say anything, I realize I need to. "You feed homeless people during your lunch break."

"Yes," she admits, her voice more quiet than usual.

"Why sneak around to do it?"

Her pace slows to a crawl. "There's a lot I don't want people to know about me," she replies.

"I can see that," I say. "But you feeding those who need it, it's a good thing."

I sigh when she when she doesn't respond. "Luci, I've seen a lot of suffering around the world. What I haven't seen is enough people willing to help." Her head lowers, like what I say makes her feel bad. "Why do you seem ashamed by it?"

I don't think that's the right word until I say it and realize how bad it stings. This time, I'm the one holding her. I lead her to the bench. There's a lot I want to do. For starters, apologize for being such an asshole. Instead, I keep my arms around her to offer the comfort I think she needs.

"Landon, I don't let many people into my life, and although I have friends, there's a lot they don't know about me and more things I feel I need to keep to myself." She swallows hard, like she's fighting not to cry. "It's nothing against you or anyone. I just don't want others to know what I do during my lunch hour."

I still don't understand. What I understand is that she's a private person, more than I gave her credit for. I won't push. Not now. Now, she needs my respect. "All right," I say.

Considering what a dick I was, I don't think I have a right to hold her. But I can't stop myself from touching her and gifting her with the kindness she's always shown me. I stroke her cheek, wishing I could make the hurt she's feeling disappear with each brush of my fingertips. "I thought you were meeting another lover."

"Another lover." Perhaps those aren't the best words to use. They assume too much, like that's what I am to her.

She adjusts her purse. I think she's going to leave, but then she lifts her chin to better see me. "Why would you think that?" she asks, not bothering to call me out.

"Because you're beautiful and smart and every man who meets you knows it."

She drops her gaze. "That's not why you followed me."

"No," I agree. "You seemed upset and worried. I guess I was upset and worried for you."

"Why?"

She still doesn't understand why I'm here. "I like you, Luci, and not just as a friend. I want to make sure I can help you if you need it."

I'm expecting her to glance away the way she often does when things grow uncomfortable. She doesn't, meeting my face with something that looks too much like hope. "You thought I was meeting another man," she repeats, like she can hardly believe it.

As embarrassed as I am, I don't bother denying it. "Yeah, I did."

"You were really angry," she points out.

"And jealous and humiliated," I add. "I wish I weren't, and I wish I'd given you the benefit of the doubt. I've just been burned in ways you can't imagine." My voice drifts when I catch the hurt and pain that lingers in her features. "I take it back, maybe you can imagine."

"Maybe," she agrees.

I reach for her hand, taking it gently in mine. "I'm sorry for how I acted and how I spoke to you. Believe it or not, I'm not such a bad guy."

"I don't think you're a bad guy."

It's what she claims, and at first I think she's about to tell me more. When only silence follows, I'm the one who speaks. "Good," I tell her, using care.

"You were *really* angry," she says after a moment.

"Well, yeah," I say, not bothering to argue.

"Why?"

"Because I thought there was someone else," I remind her.

My comment seems to confuse her, as if she can't understand how I'd think there could be someone else. I tell her why, even though, like her, there are things I don't want others to know about me. "My ex-wife had a pretty shit life." She looks up, stunned. "I didn't marry a socialite if that's what you thought. I married a woman I thought I could help."

"Help?" she asks.

"Yeah. She grew up surrounded by violence, a lot of addiction, and a father who cared more about boozing and snorting whatever drugs he could get his hands on than his own daughter."

Luci stops moving completely. It doesn't look like she's breathing. I think I'm doing a piss-poor job of explaining why I married Bernadette, so I try harder. "I thought I could save her and give her a better life, but I was never enough. It wasn't a good marriage. I know that now. But I wanted to make it work. It took her cheating on me to see we were done."

"I'm sorry," she says, her voice more of a stutter.

"I'm not," I say. "Not any more. As much as I like helping people, some aren't worth a damn."

Luci looks down, swallowing enough misery to fill an endless ocean. "Baby, why do you look so sad?" I ask.

I don't deserve to call her baby. But the word comes as easily as my need to feel close to her. Her gaze travels to where our hands are entwined. "There's no one else," she tells me, keeping her voice as tender as always. "I want you to know that."

I take a chance. "Do you mean there's no one at all, or no one besides me?"

A small breath escapes her mouth. This is what I've been waiting for, for her to stick me in the friend zone or to take us one step closer. "There's no one besides you."

She raises her chin.

I take another chance and kiss her.

The wheels of a squeaky stroller roll by and in the distance the laughter of children fills the air. But right now, all I think about is Luci, how good she feels in my arms and how much I don't want to stop kissing her.

Chapter Eighteen
Luci

I'm not having sex with Landon.

My hand vigorously whips the heavy cream and sugar in my large mixing bowl.

No, I'm not.

I search for my rubber spatula to scoop the whipped cream into a bowl. When I'm done, I seal it with clear plastic wrap and place it in the refrigerator beside another bowl piled with blueberries.

"I'm not having sex with Landon," I repeat. But good heavens, I really want to.

The day he followed me into the park could have been disastrous. He could have thought I was truly meeting another man and walked away, and I could have let him. It would have been an easy way to let him go. But as angry as he was, it was his hurt I couldn't see past. I didn't want him to walk away or to think I betrayed him. While we didn't promise each other anything, there was an unspoken bond between us from the first kiss we shared.

That bond and that moment almost made me tell him everything, including who Fernie really is. Until he told me about his ex-wife.

She was me in too many ways. Someone he thought he could save. When I think about how her life mimicked mine I cringe. I didn't want Landon to think I was another woman who needed saving or one he'd ultimately regret helping.

So I opened myself enough to let him know what he means to me, all while keeping Fernie tucked away.

Landon . . . likes me. The past few weeks we've shared have proven as much. And it all started out with that amazing kiss in the park.

"What are you doing for Valentine's Day?" he'd asked.

"Nothing," I answered cautiously.

"Neither am I," he explained. "So how about we do something together?"

It was our first real date, with flowers and dinner and lots of kissing. Yet it wasn't our last. Instead of rushing back into bed, I took him up on his original offer to get to know him first and allow the sex to come later.

He agreed and I love everything I'm getting to know.

"Love," I say quietly. I play with the spray of flowers on my small dining room table, flowers he brought to our last dinner date.

I'm in love with Landon. Totally, completely, and madly. I tried to deny it and push it aside, only to ultimately give in and feel everything that word allows.

I skip around my condo, arranging the throw pillows on my couch just right as my thoughts stay on this incredible man.

Some people don't know the exact moment they fall in love. I do and I'll never forget it.

It was at the company party for the staff. Mr. Bradley and Mr. Ballantyne had asked for volunteers to attend the function on behalf of the legal staff. I'd just finished dealing with a few last details when I walked into the reserved dining area and saw Landon speaking to a cluster of legal secretaries.

He immediately left them upon seeing me. If that wasn't enough to show those in attendance there's something between us, what followed was.

He reached for me, his hands falling to my hips and into the "boyfriend zone." "You look beautiful," he told me.

He only kissed my cheek, but the way he gazed at me and the way my face flushed, it seemed like so much more.

Even now, my body warms, remembering how he led me around the table and pulled out a chair for me. His arm found my shoulders, and that's where it stayed long after the partners arrived. Landon isn't afraid to show anyone who I am to him. And while we still have people glancing our way at the office, the reception has been positive.

I only wish I could be more open. Fernie remains my most guarded secret and I struggle with whether that's the right decision. I don't like hiding things from Landon, but I won't be his ex-wife, no matter how similar our lives. She used her past to get what she wanted. I refuse to use mine to keep him.

My doorbell rings, allowing me to push aside my guilt if only for a moment. I throw the door open. Almost immediately, Landon lifts me into his arms.

"Hi," he says, grinning as he breaks off our kiss.

"Hi, sweetie," I say, smoothing my palms down his chest.

He shrugs out of his jacket and removes his holster. It gave me pause the first time I actually saw his gun. It shouldn't have, since many of the other attorneys carry them. But I suppose I've always placed Landon in a class by himself. Now, I don't think twice about it. I only think about how good it is to be alone with him.

We walk into my kitchen. He pauses, closing his eyes. "Pot roast?" he guesses.

"And potatoes, spinach, and baby carrots." I point at him as he takes off his leather jacket, trying not to gape when I see how perfectly his gray T-shirt stretches across his chest. "Just don't compare my cooking to your mother's."

He flips on the water at the sink and washes his hands, laughing. "I won't. But I think you should know, I'm mad at you."

I lift the bowls of food from the oven and place them on the tray. "Why?" I ask.

"You know why," he tells me. He dries his hands and helps me by lifting the ceramic dish out of the slow cooker. "You wouldn't let me kiss you goodbye before I went to court."

He follows me into the dining room. After several dinners, we've established a routine. "That's not true."

"Yes, it is." He places the container on the chafing dish. "Ask anyone who was there."

"Oh," I say. "You mean all those people who were watching us when you tried to kiss me?"

He smirks. "You don't like an audience?"

I arrange the serving utensils closer to the food. "You do?"

Landon's arms curl around my waist while I'm still bending forward. "Not for more intimate moments." I involuntarily groan when he drags his tongue along the curve of my neck. "But a goodbye kiss is innocent enough," he adds, giving my earlobe a tug with his teeth.

"Not the way you kiss," I stammer.

The no sex thing doesn't exactly mean no contact. The way Landon's hand lifts to cup my breasts is a reminder of that. "No?" he asks, his fingers separating my blouse from my skirt. "Whatever do you mean?"

Okay. Landon and I *are* having sex.

The pads of his fingers skim along my stomach. I don't stop him. But when they pause beneath the swell, I do encourage him, craning my neck to meet his lips.

My heat-filled gaze meets his as I pull slightly away.

His jaw tenses. "Are you trying to tell me something?" he asks.

"Yes," I reply. My breath catches when his fingers trail down my waist, slipping beneath my skirt and stretching out against my pelvis, his touch mere centimeters from my throbbing skin.

If he's not certain what I mean, I slide my backside against his front, up and down, my speed increasing when his fingers slide further down and circle. He bites back a hiss, whipping me around and kissing me hard.

My legs leave the floor when he hoists me in his arms and carries me to the couch. I peel off his shirt when he falls on top of me. My blouse and bra follow, landing somewhere behind me.

I jerk when his hand disappears under my skirt and he pulls off my panties. "Are you still on the pill?" he asks.

"Yes," I groan, my hips swiveling.

He curses when his phone rings.

It's his work phone, the one he has to answer. He pulls off me, reaching for his phone. "Summers," he says. "What? . . . Wait, slow down."

I pull myself into a sitting position, knowing he's upset.

Landon shoves himself into his shoes, snagging his shirt from the floor. "No. I'm coming . . . Sweetheart, don't worry. I'll be there and take care of you and your momma."

He disconnects, placing the phone on the coffee table just long enough to pull on his shirt. "I'm sorry," he says, bending to kiss me. "ICE showed up at Dania's work and took her in. Her oldest found out when she didn't come home and she tracked down one of her coworkers."

That poor child. "Why did they arrest her? She has an attorney and a temporary stay."

"I don't know. But I have to take care of it." His gaze passes along my bare skin. "You know I wouldn't leave you otherwise."

I nod, but I can't seem to look at him then. "Okay."

"What's wrong?"

I shake my head. "I'm sorry. I just wish you could spend the night."

He stills. "If I can, I will. But I can't let this family down."

"Landon, I know. Please, don't think I'm asking you to choose. I'm just . . ."

"Just what?"

"I'm just sorry I didn't ask you before," I admit.

"Don't be," he tells. "I meant it when I said I want to know you in and out of bed." He presses a brief kiss to my lips. "I might be a while, but if I can, and if you want me to, I'll come back tonight."

My voice stays quiet as I realize how much of my heart I keep giving away. "I want you to."

"Then I will," he promises. "The only way I won't is if this takes all night." He huffs. "And it's possible it might."

Worry fills me. As passionate as Landon is in bed, that same passion extends to work. He's raring to fight anyone who mistreats the family he's representing, I can feel it. I just don't want him to lash out in a way that will cost him.

He kisses me again, but it doesn't last as long as I want.

I slip into my blouse and follow him to the door, locking it when he rushes out.

I stare at the door for the longest time. I don't want to screw things up with Landon. I suppose that's why I was so determined not to have sex with him.

Ideally, for a relationship to work you should take things slow and get to know the mind and heart, before you know the body. We worked in reverse, familiarizing ourselves with physical pleasure rather than opening our minds and heart. But after getting a wisp of his mind *and* heart at the party, I almost needed his body more.

I pull off my blouse, and return to my small living room in search of my bra. I want Landon to love me. I thought maybe he could start with the real me, and not the me who can't get enough of his touch. It's worked to a point, but his touch is irresistible and his heart is something altogether sexy.

My phone announces a text just as I locate my bra. I shouldn't be so shy, but still I press my blouse against my breasts when I check it.

Do you miss me yet?

I laugh a little. Landon never seems to lose points in the charming department.

Standing without out a blouse leaves me bare in many ways. Perhaps that's why I type what I do.

I always miss you, Landon.

The pause on the other line is so dramatic, I'm afraid I said too much. Until he replies in a way that assures me it was just enough.

Same.

I slip on my bra and blouse and return to my dining room. I was hungry prior to his arrival. Now, I simply miss him and I'm wondering what I should do with all this food.

I check my phone. It was warmer today, almost seventy. In contrast, tonight is supposed to be ridiculously cold with temperatures hovering close to twenty-nine degrees.

My attention returns to the feast I made for just us.

I send Landon a quick text.

Hey. Do you think you'll be back for dinner?

No.

I already know he's upset based on his response.

They're trying to move Dania and two others they arrested out of state and into a different holding facility.

My eyes widen.

Why? I ask.

Charlotte isn't prepared to enforce the new policy. Officials don't have any place to put immigrants besides jail. No way in fuck are they taking her out of state as far as I'm concerned.

I don't know Landon as much as I want to. But I know enough.

Don't get arrested, I reply.

Don't worry about me.

I always worry about you, I reply truthfully.

You're cute.

I'm serious! I write back, going as far as including an angry emoji.

I take it back, he responds. *You're hot.*

Landon, being Landon, always has to one up me, including a smiley emoji with the hearts bulging out of the eye sockets.

You're blushing. Aren't you?

I laugh. *Yes*, I admit.

Is your face all red? Maybe your body, too?

I cover my face as if he can somehow see me.

My body was red, too, right before I received that call.

I don't reply. Landon replies enough for the both of us, taking advantage of his voice to text feature in his car.

Maybe I was hot.

Maybe you were, too?

Maybe you were the one who made me hot.

Yeah. That makes more sense.

Could have been all the cooking you were doing.
It was pretty hot in that kitchen.
Never mind.
It was probably just you.
Your smile.
Your body.
Your heat.
Damn. And that personality.
I finally reply. *Personality?*
Oh, yeah. It's the best thing about you. Hey? Do you think you can slip a negligee over that personality sometime? I'd love to rip it off with my teeth.

I fall back on the couch, pressing the phone against my chest and wishing he was here.

Sorry, he writes. *I have to go. I'm here.*
It's okay. Just be careful, I type. *Oh, and one more thing.*
What, baby? He asks.
I work up my courage. *My personality only wears thongs.*
I hit send before I lose my nerve.

Landon doesn't text back, likely because he can't. He has more important things to do than flirt.

I adjust the straps on my bra and take in the feast laid out along the table. I return to my bedroom and change into a sweatshirt and a pair of jeans. It doesn't take me long to separate portions of food for me and Landon, with a larger portion for Fernie and whomever I find her with.

This past weekend, I purchased some inexpensive plastic containers with the hope of giving Fernie more than just sandwiches. I pack everything in a paper bag and head to my car, placing the items on the passenger side floor for easy access.

I don't usually search for Fernie at night, but I have so much food and she has so little. She's refused to go to the local church for meals, likely because the local church advocates their drug rehab program so fiercely. That doesn't mean she and her friends should go without a warm meal.

My body shivers from the cold. I don't bother with a coat since I don't intend to step out of my car. I also don't want anything that could impede my movements. Fernie . . . she's been a little better lately, speaking more, and maybe listening more, too. A counselor I was seeing told me that the majority of people with severe mental illness don't acquire the help they need, due to lack of family support, their own minds working against them, or dislike for how the medication makes them feel. But she did tell me that sometimes, they receive enough clarity to know they're in trouble and need help.

I want that day to come and I'm hoping maybe the time is finally here.

It doesn't take me long to reach downtown. I pass the office, my mind sorting through the tasks that await me in the morning, including meeting with the decorator now that the upper level is almost complete. Without meaning to, my mind also wanders to Landon. He was offered a new office on the new floor. He politely refused, in his own way.

"No, thank you, sir," he told Mr. Ballantyne. "I prefer the view down here," he said, tossing an unapologetic wink my way.

The warmth of the memory fades as I make a right toward the park. I don't bother to circle the perimeter. Instead, I proceed forward and two blocks down, straight toward the collection of apartments.

It's amazing how quickly the area changes in a span of a few blocks, from high-rise condos that cost more than mine, to more modest homes, and ultimately to lower income neighborhoods lined with small box-shaped houses.

I don't know where Fernie sleeps, if she squats in an abandoned apartment or someplace far worse. In many ways, I don't want to know. Those thoughts, along with who she spends those nights with, haunt me. I'm hoping things will change for the better. They have to for me, and more importantly, for her.

When I reach a less than desirable area, I make a "K" turn as fast as I can. There are a few kids playing in the street and older teens loitering along the sidewalks. I move fast, noting how they stop and stare.

It's not just my car that alerts them I don't live here. It's me. When I was young, I lived in a similar neighborhood. I belonged because I dressed and acted the part. As these children likely do, I also had family in the area. My uncle lived in the apartment below my grandmother's and several of my cousins lived on the street that ran behind ours.

There's a sense of neighborhood and belonging, where outsiders like me are perceived as a threat. I'm not panicked, per se, but I am aware, and I am respectful. People who look like me and drive the car I do only come in here because they made a wrong turn or because they're looking for drugs.

I just want to find my mother.

I drive back in the direction I came. I'm almost to the more middle-class area when I spot Fernie, huddled with her friends. There's a long stretch of empty parking spots leading to them. I slow my speed and coast, watching them closely as the two cars trailing me swerve around me.

The group tightens their circle, appearing eager. Disappointment fills me, trudging through my veins like tar. I don't know if Fernie is shooting up, or smoking something she shouldn't. In the shadows where she stands, she could be doing anything.

The man with the red beanie and perpetual glassy eyes perks up. He nudges the other man beside him. I hate the way they look at me. I'm ready to drive away when Fernie abandons the group.

She's limping and hurt. I slow to a stop, her attention fully on me as she walks across the street in front of my car. Against the beams of the light, her once deep olive skin appears horribly pale.

I crack my window as she reaches my side. "Are you all right?" I ask her.

"Do you have any money?" she asks.

Her voice is scraggly, that of a woman with more years than Fernie has.

"I need to know if you're all right," I say.

She doesn't answer, staring at me as if she doesn't understand. "I can take you to a doctor," I tell her, stealing a glance at the group to make sure they haven't moved. "He or she can help you feel better."

"Can he give me drugs?"

I try to focus her. "A doctor can give you medicine to treat your illness." She makes a face, appearing confused. "You're sick Fernie. Please, let me help you."

She doesn't answer, her attention lifting to the group of friends waiting for her on the sidewalk.

I'm not getting through to her and I don't like how those men keep looking at me. I have to leave, fast.

"I have food," I tell her. I rush and reach for the bag, pulling it onto my lap.

An arm reaches in, yanking me by the hair and slamming my head into the window. My foot slips off the accelerator, rolling my car forward.

Whoever has me isn't letting go. I fumble to grab the steering wheel and hit the button to close the window. The bag of food on my lap hinders my movements and I end up rolling the window all the way down.

A fist crashes into the side of my face, startling my fight or flight response into overdrive.

I stomp on the gas. Someone fumbles, falling hard. The cold air streams into my face as the hold to my hair releases. I barely avoid the oncoming car as I veer back into my lane, slamming on the brakes to keep from ramming the car at the light.

My hand smacks against the button to pull up my window, my motions jerky. In the rearview mirror, I catch sight of Fernie and another woman rising slowly to their feet from where they lay in the road.

The driver in front of me, the one I almost hit, throws his door open. I think he's angry with me, but his focus is on Fernie and her friend. He turns in my direction, his expression aghast.

"Are you all right, lady?" he asks.

I nod, my hand trembling as I swipe at my face.

"I saw what she did to you," he says.

I lift my hand, trying to assure him I'm all right and doing a horrible job. Pain rips through my scalp and my head is pounding.

The light turns green. Someone in his car calls to him. He stands there watching me, stunned. I put my car in reverse, then pull forward and around him just before the light changes. At the next street I cut a left, maneuvering through the city blocks, hoping he doesn't follow me, or report this, or . . .

I start crying as I lift the crumpled bag away from me. My jeans are soaked. In my struggle to get away, I either cracked one of the cheap containers or caused the lid to open. I don't care enough to know which. I'm so rattled I can barely drive.

I manage to make it home, stopping only to throw the bag of food in my dumpster. I can't stand to look at it or have it anywhere near me.

My hand shakes as I place the key into the slot and turn it. I want to think it wasn't Fernie who hit me. Maybe it was her friend and Fernie intervened to help me. I want to think all these good things about her. But good thoughts don't come with Fernie. They never have.

I start the water to my shower and assess my injuries. My eyes are swollen from crying and my left temple is swollen from whoever hit me. I pull away the strands of my hair and carefully examine my scalp. I lost some hair in the struggle, it feels thinner. I don't think anyone will notice.

Except maybe Landon.

I glance back at the mirror. He's coming back to me tonight. No matter how late, I know he'll be here.

I take a cold shower, worried that if I use warm water the swelling will increase. I'm freezing when I step out, but I still add a cold compress to the side of my face. I may be overdoing it, but I can't risk Landon knowing what happened.

More than once, I want to cry again. Not from the physical pain, but from all the pain that comes with having the mother I do.

About one in the morning, I surrender to my exhaustion and go to bed. It's almost three when I hear a faint knock at my door. I startle awake, my nerves keeping me alert and making me rush to the door.

"Who is it?" I ask.

No one answers. I look out through my peephole. "Hello?"

I can't see anyone and crack open the door, careful to keep the chain in place. I catch Landon's back disappearing down the walkway. "Landon?"

He whips around. I shut the door and remove the chain. When I open it again, he's standing in front of me, looing as exhausted as I feel.

"Hey," he says, bending to kiss me. He cocks his head before his lips quite reach mine. "You all right?"

I reach for his hand and lead him inside. "That's a question I should be asking you. What happened with Dania?"

He shrugs off his jacket and hangs it on the hook near the door, followed by his gun secured in its holster. "You know how I know people?"

"Powerful people?" I offer.

He chuckles and places his arm around me. "Yeah, them. I called a few tonight and was able to get Dania out."

Something in his tone shifts. "Is she home?"

"No." He stops in front of my living room. "Do you want to know?"

"I don't want to put you in a bad position."

He grins, his hands securing my hips. "I was thinking the same about you. She and her girls are in a new place, where they'll stay until I can sort things out."

A new place he probably secured for them. "I'm just glad they're safe," I say, my voice fading when he frowns.

"What happened?" His thumb passes along my temple. "Shit, you have quite a goose egg."

I try not to wince. "I fell on my way to the dumpster."

He lifts my hands, examining them and my forearms. "It doesn't look like you fell," he says.

"You mean it doesn't look like I caught myself," I add. I don't want to lie, but I don't want the questions or the tears to follow. "The only thing that tried to break my fall was my face since my arms were full."

I sound about as convincing as I feel. But Landon, as caring as he is, only focuses on my injury. His hands hold my face carefully, pressing a gentle kiss that melts my heart. The gesture and the tenderness he uses almost makes my cry. I hold back. Tears in his presence don't feel right. Only happiness does.

"Let's go to bed," he says.

I nod, although I'm no longer sure I can give him what we both wanted earlier.

I wrestle with how to tell him without coming across like a tease. Yet the moment he removes his shoes at the foot of my bed and pulls me beneath the warm sheets, I'm reminded this is Landon, and I don't have to worry.

He doesn't seek sex, he simply seeks my presence, curling into me, his voice and thoughts revealing the extent of his fatigue. "It's been a shit week," he says.

"Yes," I agree. "And it's only Tuesday."

He lifts his head enough to check my digital clock, then flops down, tucking me against him. "Technically it's Wednesday."

"This is a comfortable bed," he adds.

I snuggle closer to him. "It is," I agree, trying not to yawn.

"My bed in Kiawah is more comfortable," he reminds me.

I won't argue with that. Instead, I wait to hear what he'll say next. "I'll be out of the office the next two days."

"Out of the office, or out of state?"

His palm slides over my hip. "Both," he admits.

I guessed that's where he was headed. "Oh."

"I'll be back Friday morning, but plan to take the day off." He kisses my head. "Will you take it off with me so we can head to Kiawah and back to that comfy bed?"

"We don't have to do anything," he adds when I don't answer.

Despite my horrible night, I grin against his chest. It's the same thing he claimed when he tried to convince me to spend that first weekend with him. I know he means it, but I think we've gone long enough without doing more. "Do you think it will look bad if we both take off the same day?"

I can't see his face, but I sense his humor. "I don't care how it looks. This case, and the one I'm taking for that same sex couple who were denied a marriage license, are going to make Ballantyne and Bradley a global name. If they don't want that kind of attention, I'll take my clients and go." He laughs. "And maybe take their cute office manager with me."

"I couldn't leave them," I reply, even though I'm not entirely certain how serious he is.

"Not even for me," he murmurs.

The seduction in his voice curls my toes. I wiggle them, trying futilely to gain some semblance of control. "There's a lot I would do for you, but leaving Mr. Ballantyne isn't an option."

"No?"

"Not yet, not until he retires at least."

"What about crazy-ass Kee-Kee? I think she'd lose her mind if I stole you away."

I think about it. "It might upset her."

"Might? Damn, woman, she'd throat-punch me if she knew I was offering."

"So are you offering?" I ask.

He quiets. "Maybe one day," he says.

There's more to what he says. I can feel it, and I think he realizes it, too.

He clears his throat. "In the meantime, come with me to Kiawah. We could both use some time away."

He's right about that.

I adjust my body against his, feeling myself fade as I think through the projects that await me at work. "If I can finish my evaluations in the morning, we could leave around lunch."

"Yeah?"

I smile, ignoring the yawn that comes. "Yes. I want to be with you."

The muscles along his chest grow rigid. It's then I sense a trace of sadness, and maybe a little bit of hope, too. "I want to be with you, too, Luci."

I hope he means it. I want to give him everything, including what's left of my heart.

Chapter Nineteen
Landon

We roll into John's Island around five. It's slightly warmer here than in Charlotte. I crack the window and breathe deep. The minute that salty air wafts into my nose all the stress from the last few days leaves me and only peace floods my mind. Home. This is what it's like to be home.

I chuckle when Luci shudders. "Sorry," I say.

She gathers the travel blanket she brought around her, smiling. She's done that a lot, smile and laugh the whole way down. If I was worried things would be awkward, that changed when I cracked my first joke and her lovely laughter drifted in the cabin.

As close as we've become over the past month or so, we haven't been physically close. I've given her time like I promised, not that it's been easy. The other night, if it weren't for that call and dealing with ICE, I would have spent the night with my hips buried between her legs. At least, that's what I think she was giving me permission to do. But when I returned, that desire I all but felt clawing at my clothes was gone when she opened the door.

She banged her head pretty hard from the feel of it, and I kept checking on her during the night to make sure she was okay. I think anyone else would have blamed her injury for the change in her mood, and maybe I should have done just that. Except there was that familiar shield around her, keeping me from touching her and far away from her heart.

I wasn't sure what she'd say about coming to Kiawah with me, knowing that offer included my bed. I was prepared to tell her she could sleep in one of my spare bedrooms if it came down to it. Hell, I want her with me more than sex.

But then she said yes, both to the trip and my invitation for more.

"Are you planning to sleep outside?" I ask, motioning to her blanket.

"Only if you're bad," she counters.

I grin. "Does naughty count?"

Hey, she already knows I'm up to no good. Might as well make sure she wants to be up to no good with me.

She presses her lips together, trying not to smile and not quite managing. "When you say naughty, what do mean?"

I pretend to give it some thought. "Oh, I don't know, petroleum jelly on the toilet seat, taking pictures of my ass with your phone, or maybe grabbing yours." I give her a wink. "I guess we'll have to wait and find out."

She laughs. I do, too, loving the way the tone melds with hers.

"Why did you open the window?" she asks me, settling into her blanket.

"Smelling the salt."

She looks ahead. "You can smell it from here?" At my nod she asks, "Are we almost there?"

"To my place, we have a little less than an hour. Too far to see the ocean, but not so far I can't smell it."

"Oh," she says, perking up. Her attention stretches ahead, and I can feel her excitement build. It's one of the things I love about Luci. When she feels something, especially something as precious as joy, she feels it down to her bones. Like all that zest for life she carefully clutches releases at once.

"Love." I don't miss how that word digs its way into my brain more and more around her. The parts of me that were burnt to a crisp perpetually rap my knuckles with a ruler, reminding me the last time I used that word this soon, it didn't work. It went up in flames shot from a redheaded demon now known as my ex-wife.

Luci's hand falls to my lap, stroking me lightly. "What are you thinking about?"

"Crabs." *And the evil redhead demon.* But she doesn't need to know the latter.

"Excuse me?"

"You like crabs? There's this place called Gilligan's I'd like to take you to. But if you don't like seafood, there's a real nice place that serves steaks."

"We're not going straight to your place?"

I toss her a playful look. "Now, darlin'," I say. "I know you're just dying to take advantage of me and have your way in all the right ways, but I figured we'd better eat first or risk dying of starvation."

She turns her attention to the passenger side window, her face flushed red. "I thought you said we didn't have to do anything."

It's only because I catch her smile in the reflection that I say what I do. "We don't. You're the one taking us to Orgasm Mountain and staring out at the peaks and valleys."

"Landon!"

"How's the view from up there? Any sight of Pleasure Hill, Lake Orgy, or Highway 69?" I click my tongue. "And those valleys must be something, huh? Mind if I take a peek in between?"

She covers her face, muffling her laughter. "You really know how to make a woman blush."

I nod, thoughtfully. "I know how to make a woman do a lot of things, if you know what I mean."

"Landon," she warns.

I glance from the road back to her. "I'm sorry. Would you like me to explain?"

"*No.*"

It's what she says, but she can't stop laughing, and all that bashfulness is too cute to abandon this soon. "You see, I'm what some women consider attractive."

"Are you?" she asks, playing right along.

"And sexy," I add.

"Hmm," she says.

"Also dashing, with the right amount of rugged."

"Rugged?" she questions.

"Just a sprinkle for color and only enough to know it's there." I adjust my hand on the wheel. "There's also what some might describe as hotness."

"Is there?"

"Of course, you can't have attractive, sexy, and dashing without hotness."

"What happened to rugged?" she asks.

"Don't worry. That's there, too."

"You forgot modest," she points out.

"No, I left that out on purpose," I tell her. "Don't like to talk about myself much. It's bad for my attractive, sexy, rugged, and dashing persona." It's hard not to laugh when she giggles, but I push on since I'm on a roll. "Anyway, like I was saying, I know how to make women scream with pleasure, beg for more, and writhe in ecstasy." This time I do laugh. "Sorry, I forgot you've already seen that side."

"I have," she says. She's looking shy, and maybe she is. It doesn't stop her voice from growing husky or her from saying what she does. "It's why I'm surprised we're stopping for dinner."

I ease around a pothole in the road and another one that follows. "Did you think I just brought you out here for a toss and tumble and maybe a few licks?"

I mean it as a joke, but she's no longer laughing. "Didn't you?" she asks, her voice just above a whisper.

Shit, it's hot in here.

"No," I admit. "I want more."

She doesn't move, and if it weren't for me driving, I wouldn't move either. We're getting serious, me and Luci, whether we planned it or not.

At least, that's what I want.

I'm not talking a ring and forever. It's too soon even with feeling everything I am.

I am, however, promising as much as my heart will allow.

"Why did you come?"

"Maybe I want more, too," she admits.

"Maybe?"

Out of the corner of my eye, I catch her fussing with her hands. "I haven't had anyone in my life for a long time," she says carefully. "Not anyone who mattered, and even then, it wasn't like this."

"You mean like you and me?" I'm putting it back on her, not to be a prick, but more to show her where I'm coming from, and maybe where we're headed.

If I hadn't taken a moment to glance her way, I would have missed her nod. As it is, I barely hear her response. "Yes."

"It's been a while for me too, but the more I get away from it, the more I wish it hadn't happened."

"Did you love her?"

Her voice is quiet as it often is, gentle like she thinks she shouldn't be asking what she does. But she wants to know, and maybe needs to.

I owe it to her to tell her.

We pass one of those rusted old shacks along the road, and several others further down on the same side. I note a beaten down willow tree beside the next, its long, withered branches flowing close to a battered picnic table perched on the front lawn.

I used to be that tree not long ago, until Luci added the blooms, reminding me I'm still alive.

Maybe that's why it takes me a moment to answer, and a moment longer after that.

"I thought I did," I finally answer. "But I was wrong."

"How do you know?"

"That I was wrong?" I ask.

"Yes."

"Because love, the real kind, doesn't fade away." The thought used to tear me apart. But for the first time it doesn't. The only thing I sense is relief. That, and now hope.

I lift her hand and kiss it when I catch her softening features. The sun beams against her, highlighting her pretty face and somehow accentuating the gentleness of her spirit. Once more, I can't get over Luci. She ensnares me, making it hard to keep my attention on the road. I manage, more because I never want to risk hurting her.

"So what will it be, darlin'?" I ask, trying to keep my focus. "Someplace rustic or someplace elegant?"

"Let's go with rustic," she says. "I have a feeling that's where you're leaning."

Now I'm the one who quiets. "It is, but if steak is what you want, that's where we'll go. You've been without that smile I like for too long." She grins in the way that lights her eyes. "Yeah, that's the one," I say.

"Let's do seafood. If you'd like, we'll try the steakhouse tomorrow."

"Sounds good," I reply. "Besides, I like showing you off."

If you ask me, I can't think of a better woman to have on my arm. The more days that pass, the more I want to show the world how special she is to me.

The silence spreads between us as softly as that red blanket she tucks beneath her chin. As much as I welcomed all the laughs on the way down, I welcome that quiet with equal force. It's comfortable, easy. There's no underlying dread of what may come, what'll piss her off, or how she'll treat others around us. That's what my life used to be. I guess it took leaving to make me see how bad it was.

"Are you okay, Landon?"

I didn't realize she was looking at me. I grin, passing my thumb along the ridges of her knuckles. "I am," I admit.

I hold her hand the entire way to Gilligan's, even as I park. It makes it challenging, but I find it harder to let her go. It's only when I cut the engine that I finally release her. I wait for her to slip into her coat before I open the door and step out.

Luci isn't used to having a man do things for her. She doesn't wait for me to open the door. I don't argue with her. I simply reach for her when she comes around.

Gilligan's is a hardcore hole in the wall. Wide wood planks make up the siding and steps, and its high triangular roof is probably older than I am. Their food can't be beat and

Gilligan would shoot down from heaven itself to rough up anyone who said otherwise.

Ever since I was a kid, it's always been one of my favorite places to eat. I never really brought another woman here, unless you count my mother. It was below the standards of the women I dated, especially the one I married. But if I was going to bring any woman, I'm glad it's Luci.

Luci doesn't care about cloth napkins or waiters with fancy accents. Just the other week she was perfectly content eating a hotdog when I took her to the zoo. The zoo. I offered to take her anywhere she wanted and that's where she picked just so she could see their new baby gorilla.

She glances up, smiling. "This here is what we call a real Southern restaurant," she says, imitating my accent and speech.

"Yes, ma'am, it is," I agree.

The lack of windows gives the interior a very dark look, but the activity of the bustling waitresses, the loud voices of parents fussing over their children, and the booming laughter that never seems to fade is what gives Gilligan's life.

"Hey, y'all," the hostess says when she sees us.

Her name is Lashanda. She used to say, "Welcome to Gilligan's," when my folks and I first started coming here. It didn't take her long to figure out we were locals, so her greeting switched real quick.

"Evening, ma'am," I say. "Two for dinner, please."

"This way, sir."

I guide Luci ahead. The center tables are wide and long, and the ones in the booths are only slightly smaller. Every table sits a minimum of eight comfortably and every four place settings there's a large hole with a bucket underneath to dump garbage and shells.

There's barely enough room for one adult to walk through the aisles. But the atmosphere is friendly and the service is classic Southern charm.

Lashanda motions to one of the large booths. "Wow," Luci says, taking in the size.

"You want 'wow,' y'all have to check out the fresh oysters. It's our special tonight."

"Thank you," Luci says.

Luci scoots in first. I start to follow when I hear, "Landon? Is that you?"

Jesus, God help me.

I slowly turn. Trin, Callahan, and Cal, Jr., perched in his daddy's arms, are walking toward me . . . directly in front of my folks.

Oh, *shit*.

Trin reaches up to hug me, her lips pursed the same way they did when we were kids and she snagged me doing something I shouldn't be doing. "What are you doing here?"

She's asking me, but poking her head around me to see who I'm with.

"Ah, what are *you* doing here?" I reply, patting her back like a moron. I look ahead to my mother, whose eyebrows are almost to the ceiling and to my father who's narrowing his eyes. "I thought y'all were in Tennessee."

"Business concluded faster than expected, son," my father drawls. Like everyone else, his attention drifts to Luci. I clap Callahan on the shoulder. He looks at me, pretty much in the way any decent man would look at another about to be humiliated.

"Payback's a bitch," he whispers.

Never mind. Maybe he's just revving up to enjoy the show.

"Hi, Momma," I tell her, bending down to embrace her.

"Hi, baby," she says, barely glancing at me.

"Hey, Daddy," I say.

He shakes my hand, cocking a brow and tilting his head in the direction of the table. "I have a date," I begin.

"I can see that," he says.

"I'll get more menus," Lashanda offers.

"Thanks, Lashanda," I say, pinching the bridge of my nose.

So much for a romantic getaway.

I'm not embarrassed that Luci is with me. But as much as I like her and am ready for more, I'm not mentally prepared for her to meet my family. Don't get me wrong. My family is awesome. We're real tight and I consider them among the best people to every walk the earth.

The problem is, even the best people have their flaws, and if I'm right, they're preparing to wave those flaws like flags and poke me with the staffs.

Luci had scooted all the way in. It's darker than sin in here, but I can tell she's already blushing. With everyone honed in on her the way they are, I can't exactly blame her.

I chuckle. What the fuck else am I going to do? Knowing my family, that there is the first of many blushes to come. "Everyone, this is Luci. Luci, this here's my sister, Trinity, her husband, Callahan, and my parents, Owen and Silvie Summers."

She shifts timidly forward, managing to reach the end by the time I'm done with the introductions.

"Hello," Luci says, extending her hand to my mother first. "Nice to meet you, ma'am."

"Hello, dear," my mother says.

My father takes her hand gingerly. "Charmed," he says, eyeing her carefully.

Callahan nods cordially when Luci greets him, adjusting his hold over Cal. But as she turns her attention on my nephew, that smile gets a whole lot brighter. "Hello, little man," she says, rubbing my nephew's wrist with her finger. "What's your name?"

"That's Cal, Jr.," I say, watching the way she interacts with him. "You like kids?"

She doesn't even look at me when she answers, too fascinated with Cal, who's giving her a toothy grin. "Are you kidding? I *love* children," she says, beaming at him.

"Well, I'll be," Trinity says, a big shit-eating grin on her face. "You're the girl from Becca's party. The one who helped me with my crab cakes."

Luci tucks one of her long waves behind her ear, embarrassed. "I wasn't sure you'd remember."

"How could I forget? You were so sweet to help." Trin's words should put me at ease. But I know Trin and she's just getting started. She swivels around. "Becca's party was New Year's Eve," she reminds me *and* our parents.

"New Year's?" my father says. "And we're just meeting her now?"

Trin places her hands on her hips. "Funny you should say that, Daddy. I was thinking the same thing," she tells him.

My body stiffens. Of course, why would that discourage Trin?

"Now, Landon," she says, her thick accent turning up a notch as it often does when trouble isn't too far away. "Seeing as you've waited *so long* to properly introduce your lady friend here to your folks, I'm sure you'll agree this is the perfect opportunity for all of us to get to know each other."

More like the perfect opportunity to be bitch-slapped in public. Christ, I can practically hear the wheels in her head turn.

"Well?" she asks when I don't reply. "Aren't you going to invite us to join you?"

"He doesn't have to do that," Callahan says.

"Oh, yes, he does," Trin and Momma reply.

Callahan swipes at his mouth, trying not to laugh. He shrugs, assuring me he's done his best and that I might as well give in.

"I insist that you join us," I mutter through my teeth.

"You sure?" Trin asks. "Far be it for us to impose."

"Of course," Luci says. "Please, we just arrived."

She scoots back down to her seat. "Uh, uh," I say, hooking Trin's elbow when she tries to follow. "You, over there."

I point to the opposite side of the table and to the far end. That doesn't discourage her in the least. No, not my sister. "Even better," she says, moving quickly so she can sit facing Luci.

I place myself beside Luci. It's the least I can do, since Momma follows Trin and Daddy isn't too far behind.

"May I?" I ask Callahan, extending my arms to my nephew.

He laughs, knowing perfectly well I'm about to use his son as a human shield.

Cal, Jr., comes easily to me and takes even quicker to Luci. "Hang tight to the kid," I whisper, plopping him in her lap. "He's the only chance you have to make it out of here alive."

She lifts him so he's facing her and standing on her lap. "What?"

"Run away," I mumble.

She blinks back at me, puzzled. Poor, sweet, innocent Luci. She has no idea what she's in for. Instead of prepping herself for the worst, she gives Cal her full attention. "Hey, cutie," she says. "How are you doing, handsome boy?"

I don't think Cal, Jr., finishes his giggle before Trin and Momma start in. "Look, Momma," Trin says. "She's a real woman, with real parts."

"And no glitter," Momma points out, thanking Lashanda when she returns with a tray of waters.

"And no tassels, either," Trin murmurs.

"Mm-hmm," Momma says.

Luci stills in place, confusion as evident on her face as the glee on my sister's. Before I can give it much thought, I slip my arm around her. The baby doesn't seem like enough. Someone has to protect her from Hell's version of Steel Magnolias.

"Tassels?" Luci asks, probably thinking she misheard.

Trin folds her arms on the table and leans forward. "So, Luci. Do you have any hobbies?" she asks. "Scrap booking, horseback riding, or say, um, bedazzling unmentionables?"

"Trin," I warn.

"I like to read," Luci answers. "But I'm afraid I don't have a lot of time."

"She can read," Daddy says, sounding impressed.

"Oh, come on," I reply. "It wasn't *that* bad."

"Yes, it was," they all mutter, including Callahan.

Luci gapes back at me in the same way any sane person would. "Believe it or not, they're insulting me, not you," I assure her.

"I could learn to bedazzle," Luci says slowly.

"*No*," Daddy, Momma, and Trin say, holding out their hands.

"So, you've been together since New Year's?" Trin asks, ignoring the way Callahan cackles.

Luci and I exchange glances. "Not exactly," I admit. If she wasn't beside me, I might have said yes. God knows I haven't looked at another woman since I first laid eyes on her.

"We met that night," Luci says, her face growing more flushed with each breath. "But we didn't start dating right away."

"Is that a fact?" Trin asks, enjoying herself. "Ivy Lionelle told me she lost track of you, Landon, that you seemed to disappear and no one could find you."

"Did she?" I reply. Good ol' Ivy Lionelle never could keep her trap shut.

Trin's smile widens, ignoring my scowl. "Well, I suppose now we know why."

"*Trin*," I say again.

She taps her chin, giving it some thought. "And maybe, *just maybe*, that explains why you opted out of brunch on Saturday. Oh, and Sunday, too." She grins like the Cheshire cat after eating the damn rabbit. "Hmm. And why you seemed so tired when we finally did see you Monday."

I grin right back. "I'm going to kill you and bury your body right next to Blackbeard's."

"Do you think he might show me his booty?" she counters. "Or are you more concerned about showing Luci yours?"

"Trin," I warn again, like that's going to do anything.

"You like her," she says, as if I don't already know.

I look to Callahan. "Jesus, doesn't your woman ever shut up?"

"Nope," he answers, taking a sip of his water.

"You do like her," Momma agrees, her voice more careful. "And it seems to me, she really likes you."

The muscles in my neck are so stiff, it takes some doing to turn to look at Luci. For as red as her face is, she's smiling in a way I've never quite seen.

I'm not openly affectionate with women in front of my family. I don't know, it's not that they'd say anything. It's just never felt right around them.

It feels right now. My fingers skim down Luci's arm and I kiss her cheek. "Good," I say. "'Cause you're right about me liking her."

Luci lowers her chin, her shyness returning full force. When she glances up, her gratitude is as evident as the warmth in her eyes. I love her. I know it now, despite everything that warns me I shouldn't.

"Look at you," Momma says. "And you used to be so shy."

"When in the hell was this boy ever shy?" Daddy counters. "Don't you remember when he went through that naked stage? Every time we had some place to go he'd strip down to nothing and tear through the neighborhood climbing trees and pretending to be Tarzan."

"I was two!" I fire back.

"Five," my family reminds me.

"Christ," Callahan says, despite the way he's covering his mouth laughing.

"The wild boy of Kiawah, that's what they called him," Daddy says.

"He even made the paper," Momma, adds proudly.

"Thank God Trinity never pulled that," Daddy says, shaking his head like this is something I still do. "Worst thing she did was sit on the beach and eat sand."

"Well, yeah, she was always the sensible one," I agree.

Trinity pretends to scowl, but ends up laughing. "Did y'all come down for Spring break?" she asks, turning her attention back on Luci.

Luci seems hesitant to answer. She doesn't know Trinity, at least not well, but Trin has this gift for simultaneously busting balls and charming hearts. I hope Luci understands that despite her needling, she means no harm. Regardless, I try to shift the attention away from her. "We're just down for the weekend. Grant Parsons called me. This is a slow time of year for him and he told me he'd redo the kitchen for me at a sweet price." My voice grows serious. "I would have called, but you said you'd be away."

"Like I told you, son, we wrapped up business quick and came home," Daddy says. "Trin hasn't been feeling like herself."

I frown. "Everything all right?"

"It's great," Trin says. "We're going to have another baby."

Momma wipes her eyes, although she's trying not to let anyone see her. I scoot up to hug Trin and shake Callahan's hand. "That's the best news I've heard in a long while," I admit.

"Congratulations," Luci says. "You must be so excited."

Trin laughs when Callahan gives her a wink. "We are. We've always wanted lots of babies." She shrugs. "God willing, we'll keep having them."

"What about you, Luci?" Momma asks. "You think you might have children one day?"

Momma glances at me, but thankfully, Luci doesn't appear to notice. "I hope so," she answers, her attention wrapped around Cal, Jr. "I've always dreamed of a big family."

We've never talked about kids and have kept our talks about our future to a minimum, not that I mind what she has to say.

I ease my arm back around her shoulders when she quiets. "You all right?" I ask.

She surprises me by cuddling Cal, Jr., closer. Between the other patrons and my family, it's loud in here. But Cal is fading away, his eyes blinking fiercely as he fights to stay awake.

The way Luci holds him and the way he's so at ease against her gives me one hell of a pause. "You know what this reminds me of?" she asks, motioning around the table.

"The looney bin?" I offer.

She laughs along with my family. "No," she says. "It reminds me of the day you met Kee-Kee and the rest of the staff."

"Who's Kee-Kee?" Trin asks.

"One of the junior partners at the law firm where we work," Luci explains.

My father frowns. "You got Luci a job there?"

Here we go. "No. Luci has been working there for years. I . . . didn't know until my first day when I saw her."

They stare blankly at us, and while I'm not looking directly at Callahan, I can feel his stare, too.

"That there's fate if I ever saw it," Momma says.

I normally laugh off Momma's superstitions, but I don't laugh this time. Not with how I feel having Luci this close and not when she feels this perfect in my arms.

Chapter Twenty
Luci

Landon punches the code to his alarm, disarming the system protecting the house. The only lights on are the one on his front porch and the one in the foyer. The small amount of luggage we brought with us is swallowed by the expanse of the area. I'd forgotten how large his house is.

I bend to reach the handle of my travel bag, only to stop in place when his arms wrap around me. He kisses my shoulder. "I meant what I said about us not doing anything." His fingers splay along my belly. "But having you this close makes it damn hard."

A small groan of anticipation cuts through my throat. I turn around, intent on wrapping my arms around him. I manage one arm, but then I stop to stroke his face. He didn't shave today, and I think he skipped yesterday. It doesn't bother me. I love the way the small hairs skip along my fingertips and the way his gaze softens as he watches me.

"You miss the beard?" he asks.

"A little."

He turns his head to press a kiss along the fingers stroking him. "Why?"

I almost don't admit as much as I do. "It tickled."

"Oh, yeah?" His smile will be the death of me. "Where?" he asks.

I think my blush is enough of a response. "You like embarrassing me, don't you?" I ask.

His teeth nip me gently across my jaw. "I think 'embarrass' is too harsh a word."

"What would you call it?" I murmur, my hands sliding down his chest.

"Making you happy."

His words, combined with his serious tone, halt my movements and I swear I can't breathe. "I like you happy," he tells me. "And that's how I want to keep you."

He kisses me long and deep. I welcome him as I do each beat of my heart. Landon stirs a sense of security I've never felt. "Home," that's what he feels like, the place I've always needed and have spent a lifetime without, within a man who captured my heart.

My grandmother's small apartment always felt temporary. No matter how long I lived there and how much she welcomed me, I remained that little girl, waiting for my mother to return.

I give his hand an extra squeeze as he leads me down the hall, the lights automatically switching on as we pass.

I glance around. "Your house is so pretty," I say, worried I'm not saying enough.

"It's nice," he agrees, glancing back to wink at me. "But it's better with you in it."

"If you're trying to win me over, you already have."

"Yeah?" he asks, leading me to the deck. "Baby, I'm just getting started."

He releases me as he reaches the control panel. The buttons beep in a slow succession as he taps them. Almost at once, the blinds part, unveiling a view that's too beautiful to be real.

The moon hovers above the ocean, its magnificent glow turning the water a deep blue. "This is incredible," I say, so mesmerized I'm not certain I speak.

I almost crash into the glass, forgetting it's there. Landon hooks my waist, just in time. "Thank you," he says over my apology.

"For what?"

"For loving this view as much as I do," he quietly explains.

"I really do," I admit, taking in the millions of stars blanketing the sky. My hands fall over his forearms, sliding across them. In the distance the waves gently crash, matching the mood of the tranquil night.

"Let's go outside," he says. "There's something I've been dying to do with you." He opens the door. "After you."

I step out carefully, my heart thumping as my ankle length boots tap against the wooden deck.

There's a small part of me who's frightened, who isn't sure how this happened, and who fears it might all slip away. But most of me is so consumed by Landon's presence, the fear I sense is barely there. We have the entire weekend to spend together. I can't think of anything better.

The skirt of my dress slaps against my knees. I turn slowly only to jump when Ann Wilson's belts out, "Black on Black," from every direction.

Landon pokes his head out. "Sorry!" As I watch, he punches several buttons on his control pad. "Wrong song," he yells over the first verse.

I cover my mouth, laughing as he steps onto the deck. He reaches me as Eric Clapton's *Wonderful Tonight* begins to play. It's a soothing tune as hypnotic as the melody of the ocean waves.

He lifts my hand and kisses it, then places it around his waist. My head falls against his shoulder as we begin to sway to the music. If I could choose a super power, it would be to freeze time so I could hold onto this moment forever.

"I wasn't in a good mood the day you left," he tells me.

I smile, saying nothing and allowing him to speak.

"I came back out here and blasted the most rage-filled music I had to match what I was feeling."

My smile turns sad. "Why were you so angry?"

He edges away so I can see his face. "Because you were gone and I didn't do anything to stop you."

"I know," I say.

He grins. "Know what? That I should have stopped you?"

I shake my head. "I mean I wish I could have stopped it, too. I wasn't ready for our time to end."

He spins me around slowly, bringing me back just as smoothly as the breeze sweeping my hair above my shoulders. I dissolve against him, welcoming the heat from his body as he pulls me close. "We don't talk a lot about that weekend," he says quietly.

"No," I agree.

"Why do you think that is?" he asks.

I dig through my memory of that day until I find the right words. "Because it was too much like an end, rather than a beginning."

"The beginning of us?"

His hands trail lower to rest just above my backside. "The beginning of the best thing I've ever had," I confess.

A tightness builds in my chest, triggering pain I don't want to feel. Landon is the best part of my life. But there are parts of my life that cause me more sadness than I can bear.

He lifts my chin, his tone dropping. "If that's true, why do you look so sad?"

I blink back tears that don't belong with Landon so close. Regardless of how kind he is and all the smiles he brings, I remain that same woman who can fix everything at the office, but who can't fix the one person she needs to. "I just really like you," I say.

"I like you, too," he says, gathering me close. "But that should make you happy, not leave you with a broken heart."

A broken heart. Is that all I have to offer him?

I can't tell him everything, even though I think he needs to hear it all. My brain wrestles with what to say. I should distract him or share something else besides the truth. Instead the truth comes out before I can stop it. "This is just something I've never had."

Confusion deepens his frown. "You mean a decent relationship?" he asks.

The way he holds me is so shielding, it's as if he can sense those demons that constantly surround me, pointing out the ways I'm failing. Perhaps that's why more of the truth spills, no matter how hard I try and hold it in. "No, happiness."

Landon doesn't move and doesn't breathe. I'm ready to take it all back.

No, I'm ready to run.

He fastens his hold when I try to pull away. "Why haven't you been happy?"

Don't say it. "I've never met anyone like you."

Stop talking. "You're good to me."

Don't tell him. "And . . ." *Please don't tell him.* "I love you."

Landon releases me, his hands dropping to his sides.

A small embarrassed laugh escapes me as I wipe my eyes. "I'm sorry," I say. "I know it's too soon."

The song switches to Bon Jovi's *Always*. I can't see Landon's face. He's too busy drilling a hole into his deck with his gaze. "I really am sorry," I offer again.

"Don't be." He looks up at me, the devastation in his expression matching everything I'm feeling. "I'm sorry I can't say it back."

Misery pours over me. Sometimes, things are so beyond sad, you can't cry. But this feeling isn't for me and for what I don't have. It's for Landon and everything he lost.

I clutch his shoulders and lift up on my toes. My mouth seeks his, my tongue sweeping over his in a delicious tease.

He grasps my arms, pulling me away, his jaw clenched tight. "I want to be able to say it. Do you understand? I want to. I just can't right now."

I'm not trying to make him love me or force him into a corner where he feels he has to say something he's not ready for. What I do want is to show him what he means to me and how much I miss his touch.

"You don't have to," I tell him. "Please, just let me make you feel good."

My lips devour his, hunting for his passion. I don't want Landon to hurt or suffer. I've felt that pain too many times in my life.

He hauls me to him, permitting me in and returning my affections with primal desire. His large hands clench my hips. Mine shove between us, yanking his belt free and unzipping his fly.

I reach in. "*Fuck*," he grunts.

We stagger backward as I begin to rub, starting at the base and tightening as I reach his throbbing tip. My back hits the side of the house. I don't stop, too enraptured by how his body moves up and down against me, matching the glide of my hands.

Landon tries to reach beneath my skirt. I don't let him, falling into a crouch and taking him far into my mouth. The way I handle him isn't remotely tender. It's aggressive and deeply erotic, my desire to erase his pain shoving aside my timidity.

Landon's voice turns animalistic, his words low and throaty. He tells me how good it feels and how much he wants me.

I moan, my efforts and the heavy lust in his timbre turning me on and making me go faster.

His palms slap against the siding, the force vibrating against my spine with his release.

I told him I love him. I suppose I wanted to prove it, making this moment about him and the excitement he stirs within me.

His legs tremble as he finishes. I wait, taking everything. As his movements slow, I slip from beneath him, the change in position allowing Landon to take center stage.

He kicks out of his shoes and jeans, stalking toward me as I back into the house. I'm almost halfway across the living room when he peels out of his shirt, slamming the glass doors and setting the alarm.

I stop at the base of the stairs, watching as he marches across the room, his feral stare keeping me in place. "My turn," he says, wrenching me against him.

He rips my panties off, tearing the flimsy fabric from the side as his teeth find my neck. I grip his arms to keep from falling when his fingers find my folds. The delicate skin is already slick, pleasing Landon as he pushes his fingers in and out.

My knees buckle. He holds me in place, allowing me to enjoy my orgasm before ridding me of my dress.

"Take off your bra," he tells me, his hot breath and mouth over my nipple, sucking hard through the lace.

Ardor seers painfully through my veins, causing my thighs to clamp. Landon parts my legs, flicking and circling my center. I don't curse much. But I'm cursing now, close to screaming as I lose my mind.

He bites down on the center of my bra, pulling at the fabric. "Baby take it off," he begs me. "I want to taste you for real."

I pinch the band over the hooks, the fabric slipping between my fingers more than once before I finally unsnap my bra. I still have one strap dangling over my shoulder when Landon's mouth pulls in my nipple. He lowers me on the steps, hooking the back of my knees with his arms and spreading me open.

I kick out when his face disappears at the "V," my already tantalized skin pulsating with every flick of his tongue. My next orgasm comes hard, but it's the one that follows that has me screaming his name.

It's too much for Landon. He lifts me, placing me on all fours, my knees on the stairs, my hands a few feet up.

My eyes scrunch closed as he joins us. "You're so tight," he says, his voice pained.

I turn back to look at him, worried I'm somehow hurting him.

I'm not certain what catches in my expression. He freezes, not moving for what seems like too long. Slowly, he eases out of me.

"What's wrong?" I ask, certain I harmed him.

He cups my face carefully, the tenderness in his visage bringing me close to tears. "Not here," he says.

He sweeps me into his arms, slipping off my shoes as he carries me up the stairs. They fall and bounce to the bottom as we reach the second level.

My desire to numb Landon's torment made sex with him unbearably raw. But as he lowers me to his bed and climbs on top of me, the sex we have becomes something more.

It becomes the love I intend it to be.

Chapter Twenty-One
Landon

My phone rings. And rings. And Goddamn rings.

I ignore it. With Luci so warm and close beside me, it's easy. Sunlight streams through the large windows. In the distance, the sea's lyrics call out a good morning. Or afternoon. Can't really say I know what time it is. Can't really say I care.

Ever since we started seeing other, I've looked forward to waking up with Luci naked in my arms. I knew it would happen. We've grown so close. I just didn't expect it to mean as much as it does. But I suppose I didn't expect it to mean as much the first time.

Last night was different than the first time she came home with me. I like what she did and how hard she took me. Her aggression was a turn on, making me hot and surging my lust several degrees.

I wanted to return everything she gave me. But when I flipped her around and saw the look on her face, I couldn't do that to her.

She made herself vulnerable to me, in her actions and in what she claimed. I make her happy she'd said. It was amazing to hear what I want. But to then hear happiness was something she's never had was enough to tear me open.

The final blow came when she told me she loved me. I saw what it took for her to be so honest. I saw it in her gentle features and how it left her raw when she looked at me. Whether she planned it or not, Luci had exposed her soul. She wanted me, sure, but I wanted something better.

Lust is one thing.

Luci is something more.

My eyes close and I settle back against her, only to groan when the phone starts ringing again, and again, and *again*.

Luci stirs, the strands of her hair tickling my nose. "Babe?" she says.

God damn, she has the nicest way of saying, "Answer the fucking phone." I grin, although that ring has me ready to smash the phone to bits.

I flop over and away from where I'm curled against her, swearing when I knock my phone off the nightstand. I reach it as it stops ringing, noting two missed calls from Trin. I place it on the stand, guessing it will ring in five, four, three—

Ring. Damn. *Ring.*

"Hello?" I mumble.

"You still in bed?" Trin asks.

I mutter something that may or not have been polite. She laughs. "Why, Landon, what on earth are you still doing in bed at this hour?"

She's lucky I like her. "Did you need something or did you just call to piss me off?"

"My, you're cranky. What's wrong, couldn't sleep?"

"Trin," I mumble.

"Poor thing, were you up all night, tossing and turning, trying to get just right?"

"Trin!"

She sighs, ignoring me like usual. "I remember that feeling. The only difference is now when Callahan and I are up past ten it's because the baby's up, not because we're reliving the night of his conception. Although the other night, Cal, Jr. did go down early. We were able to sneak onto our deck. Have I mentioned how limber my man is—"

"I'm going to stop you right there," I say.

"Why? This is where the story gets good."

"I'm sure it does. Just as I'm sure I don't want to hear it," I tell her. "You want to talk about what you and your man do, call Becca. That's what she's there for."

"Oh, believe me, I do. Why just the other night I told her about the time me and Callahan were out in the woods and—"

"Trin," I beg, falling back against the mattress. "Knock it off."

Luci giggles beside me. I turn, sweeping back her hair to kiss her neck.

"Is that Luci I hear? Oh, what am I saying, of course she's there. How could she let a catch like you go? Lovely girl, just can't wait to see her or talk to her again. Put her on, will you?"

"You want to speak to Luci?" I say, lifting off her.

Luci adjusts what remains of the bedsheets around her, smiling as Trin yaps away.

"Why wouldn't I?" Trin asks. "She's all sorts of nice, pretty too. Are her eyes lavender? I thought they were. I haven't had a good look at them. But I'm sure you have all those times you've whispered sweet nothings in her ear, between praising your sugary sweet sister, I mean. You have praised your sugary sweet and intelligent sister, haven't you? What am I asking? Of course you have!"

"She can hear you," I say, when Luci laughs. "Not that it's hard."

Trin doesn't miss a beat. "Well in that case, put her on. I don't want her thinking I'm rude or that I'm talking about her instead of with her."

Luci holds out her hand. I stare at her palm as I continue to talk to Trin. "What are you up to?"

"Nothing," Trin says.

"Don't embarrass her," I warn. "And don't embarrass me."

"Now, why would I do a thing like that?" Trin asks.

"Because you're you and that's just what you do."

Despite my well-founded reservations, I concede and hand Luci the phone. "Hello?" she says.

"Luci, I'm so glad to find you there. Landon is such a good man, and I'm not saying that because I love him. He can be annoying, I know, like when he leaves the toilet seat up or squeezes the toothpaste from the center instead of from the bottom. But we all can't be perfect. Anyway, we're having dinner at my parents' house tonight and Momma and I would just love for you to join us."

Luci turns enough that the sheet falls away, revealing the swell of her breast. She seems hot, bless her heart. I do the right thing and pull the sheet the remainder of the way. She yanks it back up, narrowing her eyes and pointing at me.

But damn it she's hot. I don't want my woman to suffer.

"That's so nice of you to think of us," she says. *Stop it*, she mouths when I snatch the sheet away and toss the crumpled mess to the floor.

Stop being so damn sexy, she means.

"What would you like us to bring?" she asks, instead.

She squeaks when I pull her onto my lap, my fingers sliding over the round globes of her ass.

"Just yourselves," Trin says. "We're having crown roast."

"Sounds wonderful," she stammers. She points at me. *Behave*, she mouths.

To be honest, I don't know exactly what she said. She might have meant "more" or "don't stop" or something like "I can't live without you, you sexy beast. Kindly pleasure me with all your alpha might."

All I know is, Luci enjoys art. To be nice, I start painting the Mona Lisa across her breasts with my tongue.

"I'd love to bring something if I can," she manages, her body shuddering when my teeth graze the stiffening points of her breasts. "Would you like dessert?"

"Oh, yes, I would," I murmur between her breasts.

Poor thing is jerking so hard she screws up my perfect portrait and I have to start all over again.

I return to her nipple. That's probably what Mona would want.

"When would you like us to come?"

"The sooner the better," I whisper, dragging my tongue further down.

"What time can you get here?" Trin asks.

My fingers turn circles against her back. "Later, much later," I mutter.

"Six?" Luci asks, her lashes fluttering.

"Perfect," Trin says. "Tell Landon—"

I swipe the phone. "Goodbye, Trin," I say, and disconnect.

The phone slides across the mattress when I toss it. "You hung up on your sister," Luci accuses.

"And?" I say.

"And that was rude."

"No Rude would be saying no to dinner to make sweet love to you, instead." I think about it. "But my parents would understand if I opted for the lovemaking. They're good like that."

Her arms wrap around me. "You're trouble, mister. I knew it from the start."

"Then why didn't you run away screaming?" I tug on her bottom lip. "Instead of flashing me like you did."

She lifts a finger and drags it along my jaw. "I didn't flash anything but a smile."

"That's all you needed." I pull her into a bear hug. She melts against me, her soft hair cascading along my arms. "You could have said no to dinner."

I don't have to see her to know she's smiling. "I wouldn't do that. Your family is so welcoming. I'd never want them to think I'm keeping you from them."

Yet another thing that makes Luci so special. I trail my fingers down the sweep of her waist. "They would have understood. We came here for us, not them."

"Does this mean you don't want to have dinner with them?"

"No," I say, realizing how much time with Luci and my family would mean to me. "I just want to make sure you want it, too."

"I do." She kisses that delicate spot behind my ear. "They're sweet. Like their son."

"All right. We'll go, later. For now, let's just make it about us."

The taut centers of her nipples graze my chest. If I allowed it, I'd let them get me hard and we'd pick up where we left off earlier this morning. Except the more I think about last night, the more I realize too many things have gone unsaid.

"I'm sorry about what happened." I ease away from her slightly. "I mean what didn't happen."

I don't have to spell it out. By the way her hand passes along my cheek and the gentle way she speaks, she knows what I'm talking about. "I don't want you to tell me something you don't feel."

The problem is, I feel it. Fear can cripple a man, make him less than he is. Combine it with the heartache only betrayal can bring and it's enough to fire that final bullet into his heart.

"I want to tell you something about me, something that happened during my marriage that I never got over." I loosen my hold slightly. "Maybe then you'll understand why I hold back."

Her hands fall to hold mine, steeling herself for what she's about to hear. "She hurt you, didn't she?"

I nod slowly. As distant as that memory feels here with Luci this close to me, it's a vicious undercurrent threatening to pull me down. "I thought we were okay," I admit. "Not great, and definitely not perfect, but where we should be."

"And where was that?" she asks.

"Married," I say. But that's all I can say me and Bernadette were.

Luci waits, not quite understanding what I mean. I do my best to explain, as messed up as it sounds. "I'm not sure what I expected when I proposed. Maybe something better than what we had. I thought in showing her how committed I was, she would commit to our relationship and prove we did belong together."

"It sounds like you had problems even before," she says.

She's not judging. If anything, she seems concerned.

I straighten my legs, keeping Luci on my lap. She hangs on to me, afraid to let me go. "We did, but I wanted us to be good together. You saw my parents, right? How dedicated they are even after all these years and how much they genuinely like each other.”

“They’re wonderful together,” she agrees quietly. “Something I’ve always dreamed of having.”

She means what she says, which only makes me feel like more like an ass. “I never dreamed of it,” I confess. “Like a fool, I just assumed I’d have it.”

“What do you mean?”

It’s hard not to sound like an arrogant son of a bitch. I manage well enough. “My parents instilled a lot of confidence in me, praising me when I deserved it, all the while slapping me upside the head when they felt I deserved that, too. But since my achievements always seemed to outnumber my screw-ups, and because I honestly cared about the people around me, I thought I was a good man and that I would get some good back.”

“You are a good man,” she interrupts. “And you’ve earned everything you have.”

“Maybe. Maybe not,” I tell her, lifting my chin, although I hadn’t realized it dropped. “But I wasn’t a smart man, not when it came to Bernadette. My folks knew each other only a couple of months before my father fell on one knee and asked my mother to marry him. He told me he knew she was his forever.” I press my lips, not wanting to admit what I do. “I expected the same thing to happen to me. In my head, I did all the right things, worked hard, earned my degree, did right by others. Why would marriage be any different? Why wouldn’t I pick the right one?”

Luci listens as she always does. I only wish I didn’t have so much to say.

“I wanted to help her,” I tell her, even though I’ve told Luci as much before. “It should have been a good thing, but it ended up blinding me to all her faults. Call it a superhero complex, but it’s like I needed to swoop in and save her.”

Save her from those damn clear heels and all that techno shit she used to dance to is more like it.

Luci’s shoulders droop and she seems to struggle to speak. “You’re sweet.”

"Ah."

"And generous," she adds, because I'm not feeling like enough of a moron.

I turn toward the long setting of windows. It's better than looking at her and all the guilt stabbing my spine.

"Landon, why do you look so angry?"

"I picked the wrong woman to help. I thought she was a victim, with the household she grew up in and how fucked up her family was."

Luci falls perfectly still. I want to say guilt and shame clouds her gaze, but that doesn't seem right. It's not like she's done anything wrong. "Bernadette wasn't a victim," I say. "Not anymore. Be it life or just her, but she became the victimizer."

"Maybe she didn't mean to."

"What?" I ask, unsure why Luci feels the need to defend her.

"Maybe she was desperate or down on her luck."

"More like up on a pole," I mutter.

She tilts her head, appearing confused until realization smacks her awake. "She was a *stripper*?"

"Exotic dancer," I mumble.

She blinks back at me. It's better than shoving me away, which is what I was expecting. "I'd taken my friends to a gentleman's club."

"A gentleman's club," she repeats, like I couldn't possibly be this dumb. Except I was.

I clear my throat. "She caught my interest."

"I'll bet she did." She cuts herself off. "Is that what your sister meant about the tassels and, and, the glitter? Oh, God, and the bedazzling? Tell me you didn't marry a woman with a bejeweled vagina."

"Of course not!" I snap. She looks at me. "Okay, yeah."

"She was dancing to pay for her college," I offer. Hey, I already sound stupid, might as well keep going down the imbecile expressway.

"That's understandable," she says, nodding. "Most colleges take singles."

"I know how it sounds. Believe me. But some of those women are genuinely decent and trying to make a living. She just wasn't one of them." I swipe at my face. "I wanted to help her," I remind her. "But in spite of everything she did to me, it took me finding her blowing her manager in my kitchen to make me leave."

"What?"

Again, Luci stops moving. "I caught them together, saw everything she did to him. It shouldn't have taken so much, but it did. Like I said, I wanted it to work and would have done anything to make it happen."

Luci buries her face in her hands, her petite frame quivering.

"Are you laughing at me?" I ask. She doesn't answer, her body continuing to shake. "All right, fine. But believe it or not, I was trying to do the right thing. All I got was a shit ton of depression and more regret than I can stand."

I bite back a curse, all the anger that lingers finding its way out of me. "We had more blow-ups than I can count and too many moments where she humiliated me in front of my family and colleagues. Every fight, every harsh word, every time she pushed me away was bad, but it didn't compare to finding her with another man. She never intended to be mine, and she sure as hell didn't give a damn about me."

Luci's hands lower carefully, revealing the tiny tears glistening in her pretty eyes. The shimmer across her gaze and the gentleness she meets me with dissolves all the bitter memories and extinguishes my remaining anger.

She kisses me softly, as if I'm the one crying, not her. "I'm sorry she couldn't be your everything," she tells me.

Luci should be calling me out for being naïve. She should be leaving my arms and my bed for being such an idiot. Instead, here she is, allowing her heart to shatter because mine did.

"I'm sorry she hurt you," she whispers.

"I'm not," I say, sounding harsher than I intend. "Not anymore, not when that loss gave me you."

She cups her mouth, stunned.

I lower her hand, enclosing it with mine and placing it against my chest. "I may not be ready to tell you I love you," I say. "Not after everything I went through. That doesn't mean I don't feel it every time I look in your eyes."

Her head bows. "Don't say that just to placate me."

Her words and the way she says them reminds me how rough she's had it. I won't be another asshole who hurts her. But I also can't be the hero she needs. Not yet, even though I mean what I say.

"I'm not trying to placate you, Luci." In the tears filling her eyes, that final part of me finishes breaking, the one that stowed my happiness good and tight and made believe I'd never find it. My knuckles skim the curve of her spine. "I swear, I've never meant anything more."

A small tear escapes her eyes. Yet she smiles, conveying her tenderness and beauty and reminding me how much she means to me.

Tell her, I think. *Tell her you love her*.

Despite how my soul awakens, prepared to love her in return, I don't speak the words she needs to hear.

Instead, I show her, through the kiss I greet her with and everything that follows.

Chapter Twenty-Two
Landon

We roll to a stop in front of my parent's house at ten of six. "Never apologize for being early," my father always told me. "But be damn sure you're never late."

Luci was raised the same way and she would have been ready an hour early if I didn't keep stripping her out of her clothes every time she attempted to get dressed.

I step out of my dark blue Maserati, stretching as I breathe in the salty sea. My parent's house is a short walk from the water, but not on the beach like mine. They like the view from their bedroom and rooftop terrace, but prefer some distance from the water should a hurricane hit. I pause mid-stretch when I see Luci inch out, her gaze alternating between the large stretch of lawn where palms and magnolias spread out to create a picturesque garden straight out of a portrait, to the light brick house I grew up in.

"How you doing, baby?" I ask. I come to her side and lift the dish of rosemary potatoes out of her hands. She'd planned to bring dessert, but changed her mind when Momma texted to say she'd baked several pies.

"I'm all right," she says in a voice I don't quite believe. Her gaze lifts to the house. "This is beautiful," she says.

"Yeah, it is." I shut the passenger side door as she eases away. "Momma has a way with plants and gardening."

"She did this herself?" Luci asks.

I reach for her hand and lead her up the brick steps when she hesitates. "She did. It's been her passion forever and one of the many things she did to make this house a home."

"It's amazing," she says.

She means it, but I don't like how she seems to curl inward. My parent's place is larger than mine, and the property that much grander. That doesn't mean the kindness is any less, and my father proves as much when he opens the door. "Well, look who's here," he says.

The scrutiny he first met Luci with vanished four blushes into our first dinner. Now, only a big smile remains. "How y'all doing?"

"Good, sir," I reply, noting another blush from Luci and how that widens Daddy's grin.

"You have a lovely home—"

Daddy pulls her into a bear hug, cutting her off. "Silvie, *Silvie*. Landon and Luci are here!" he yells, placing his arm around her and leading her inside.

I walk beside them, trying not to chuckle at the way Luci takes in the foyer. A winding staircase leads to the second level where the bedrooms are, while another leads down to the basement bar, game room, and screening area. "Are we eating outside or in?"

"Outside," Trin calls, hurrying out to the kitchen.

"Pool or terrace?" I ask, stepping forward.

"Pool," Momma calls from the kitchen.

"Hey, Luci," Trin says. She gives her one of those cheeky kisses girls do. "Oh, what did y'all make? I told y'all you didn't have to bring anything."

"Herb potatoes, but that was all Luci," I answer.

"It was no trouble—"

Trin cuts her off. "Momma, Luci made herb potatoes," she yells. "Wasn't that sweet?"

"So sweet," Momma says. She rushes forward, her long white braid thrown over her shoulder and the floral apron she's had forever firmly in place.

"Hi, Luci," she says. "Don't you look, pretty. Hi, baby," she adds when she sees me.

"Hi, Momma." I bend down to give her a kiss, avoiding the large dish she's carrying. Once more, Luci tries to compliment their home, and once more she's denied. "Dinner is ready. Let's get downstairs. Becca will be here soon."

"Becca's coming?" I ask.

The excitement in Trin's smile fades. "She needs to," she says. She looks to Luci. "You don't mind, do you?"

"No, of course not," Luci says.

"Aw, honey," Trin says. "Thank you. But if you're going to be heard around here, you have to be louder than that." She ushers us toward the stairs. "We're right behind you, we just need to carry a few things down."

"Here, sugar, let me take that," Daddy says.

"Luci, do your potatoes need warming?" Momma asks.

"A little," Luci says. She smiles, though she seems overwhelmed.

"Landon, be a dear and use the downstairs oven," Momma says. "The two in the kitchen are full."

"Yes, ma'am."

We follow Daddy down to the outside dining area overlooking the pool. "You have a lovely home," Luci says.

Bless her heart, this time, someone hears her. "Thank you," Daddy says.

He turns to where Callahan is drying off his son. "Landon, Luci," Callahan says with a tilt of his chin.

"Hey," I say over Luci's quiet "hello."

I place the potatoes in the outside oven and crank the heat, bending down when Callahan sets my nephew on the floor. "Where's my buddy?"

Cal, Jr., grins and wobbles toward me, laughing when I swoop him into my arms. His attention turns to Luci, and like me, he appears to come alive when he catches her smile.

Momma and Trin make about three trips up and down the stairs and refuse help like always. "Becca says to start without her," Trin calls on her last trip.

I sit next to Luci and opposite Trin, Callahan, and Cal, Jr., in his high chair. Daddy and Momma sit at the heads of the table. We say grace like good Christians and start talking like bad ones the minute we begin to pass the food.

"Have y'all been skinny dipping at the lake yet?" Trin asks. "Callahan and I tried to go a few weeks ago, but it was still too cold."

Callahan swallows his first bite of roast like it pains him, because it actually does.

Luci pauses with a spoonful of creamed spinach hovering over her plate. Her face as red as the dress she's wearing.

Daddy frowns. "It's always cold at that lake. Why do you think we have a heated pool?" Daddy asks.

"So your grandson can swim in it all year?" Callahan asks, no, more like *begs* him to answer.

Momma nods thoughtfully. "Well, yes," she agrees. "But also so we can go skinny dipping."

"Momma," I say, covering my mouth with my napkin and trying not to crack up when I catch sight of Luci's slack jaw.

"Oh, I'm sorry, Landon," Momma says. "You didn't get any corn." She offers the dish to Luci. "Landon has always loved corn."

"Um," Luci says, or rather squeaks.

"You done with the spinach, Luci?" Daddy asks.

It's only then Luci lowers her spoon, passing the spinach along before lifting the dish filled with corn from my mother's grasp.

"I remember the first time Callahan and I went skinny-dipping," Trin says, because God forbid she lets the conversation go. "It was in Papua, New Guinea." She looks at Callahan, head down and shoveling food in his mouth for all he's worth. "Or was it Ecuador?" She holds out her hands, all excited like, right in the middle of spooning bits of sweet potatoes into Cal, Jr.'s, mouth. "No, I think it might have been in this very pool."

Daddy nods. "I can see that. Salt water is good for the skin."

Callahan looks up from his plate, his expression as heavy as any who've shared as many meals as he has with my family. "I'd like to say it gets better," he tells Luci. "It doesn't."

Trin rubs his back, smiling. "He's just shy, is all."

He pretends to narrow his eyes, but doesn't quite manage. Family full of crazy or not, he loves Trin and would marry her a hundred times over if he could. To prove my point, he hooks an arm around her shoulder and kisses her cheek, making her laugh. I look over at Luci, who's barely touched the small amount of food she served herself. I fork a piece of crown roast and add it to her plate.

"Eat," I say. "The night is still young and there are plenty more stories to come."

She doesn't quite take her first bite when Becca bounces down the steps. "Hey, y'all," she says.

She's as enthusiastic as always, but the hug she gives Trin lasts a little longer than it should and so does the embrace she gives Momma. Momma sweeps Becca's long hair over her shoulder. "You're going to be okay," Momma whispers.

Becca nods in that way women do when they don't quite believe what they hear, but know if they don't agree they'll just break down and cry. She composes herself quickly, greeting Callahan and Daddy. I try to catch her eye when I hug her, but she averts her gaze and smiles at Luci. "Well, hello there, Luci. Nice to see you, shug."

"Nice to see you, too, Becca," Luci says.

Becca scoots her chair forward. "What did I miss?" she asks, smiling when Momma passes the first of about twenty dishes she and Trin set out.

"Nothing, the usual, how much I love corn and where everyone skinny-dips," I offer. Hey, they're going to say it anyway, might as well beat them to the punch.

Becca frowns. "The lake still too cold this time of year?"

"It is," Trin says. "I don't remember it being this cold in high school."

"Me either," Daddy adds. "I remember my friends and I swimming in that thing as early as February one year."

"I think it's an age thing," Becca reasons. "Lord, once I hit twenty-six I couldn't tolerate water colder than eighty degrees."

My family mumbles in agreement, nodding like they can relate.

"How's the law office?" Becca asks, cutting the piece of roast she snagged.

"Good, busy," I reply. "I have a few immigration cases I'm trying to sort through. Each one is worse than the next."

"I'll bet," Becca says, making a face. "So much for 'give me your tired, your poor, your huddled masses.'"

My family and I nod, this time with less enthusiasm. "How's Mr. Ballantyne, Luci? I swear I haven't seen him and his wife in ages."

"He's fine," Luci replies slowly.

I lower my fork as I realize why Luci answers the way she does. But it's Trin who asks the question I'm suddenly dying to know. "Becks, how did you know Luci works with Landon?"

Becca wipes her mouth, but doesn't quite wipe off her grin. "You didn't," Trin tells her.

Becca smiles at me.

"No," I say, glancing from Luci's stunned expression back to Becca's all-too-knowing one.

She laughs. "Someone had to say something, Landon. Lord knows you'd all but given up."

"I don't believe you, Becca." That's not true. I do. I just can't believe I didn't figure it out before.

"Nine women, Landon," she reminds me. "I introduced you to nine women dying to meet you and where did your eyes go wandering off to? This young lady right here. You're welcome," she adds, pointing.

"You didn't see us," I argue, trying to make sense of it all.

"Oh, yes, I did," Becca fires back. "Mm, good roast, Momma."

"You left," I remind her over Momma's thank you.

"True, but I have security cameras for a reason."

"To spy on your guests?" I offer.

"Well, yeah," Becca says. "I don't want people stealing my shit."

Again, my family whole-heartedly agrees.

"I didn't see what happened when you went out there on the terrace, but I did see the footage of you leaving holding hands. Neither of you came back," Becca admits. "I also did some prying and talked to a few people."

"Ivy Lionelle?" Trin asks.

Hell, that's my guess, too.

"No, Darlene Sotta," Becca clarifies. "Ivy's always been too gossipy." She angles her head to better see Luci. "And Blythe, but she probably told you as much."

Luci shakes her head. "Wow, I . . . wow."

Becca laughs again. "When Mr. Ballantyne needed someone to make them look good, and you needed a job, Landon, I thought it was the perfect solution. Worst case scenario nothing happens, you go elsewhere, life goes on."

"And best?" Trin asks, glancing at Luci.

Becca's voice softens. "Landon gets the smile he went too long without."

The table becomes a buzz of conversation, about me and Luci, and Becca's involvement, Cal, Jr., and how Callahan and Daddy are going to start extending the house so they'll have more room when the baby comes. But my thoughts stay on Becca and the gift she handed me, wrapped in a sweet bow.

"What about you?" I ask Becca quietly. "How do we find your smile?"

I expect her to make a joke and laugh it off. When she doesn't, I realize she's worse off than I thought. She takes a sip of her water and carefully lowers it back down. "I don't know," she admits, her voice a little lighter and a lot less confident.

I shouldn't say what I do, but it comes all the same. "Do you think Hale might know where it is?"

That same glimpse of sadness she showed Momma makes an appearance. "If he does, I doubt he'd show me the way. That man stopped giving a damn about me a long time ago."

I look at Luci and give her hand a squeeze, practically melting when she meets me with her warm gaze.

"I don't agree," I tell Becca, lifting the hand carefully grasped in mine. "Sometimes, you just need the right chance."

Chapter Twenty-Three
Luci

Mr. Ballantyne storms forward, the anger in his face making those walking toward him escape into the row of cubicles. "Luci, what the hell is this about the new offices being painted red. It's a law firm, not a brothel!"

I snag Jillian, the new legal assistant, by the wrist when she tries to bolt. "Sir, the offices will be paneled in dark wood to give the floor a more classic look."

He rams the piece of paper he's holding forward. I lift it from his grasp and examine the image. "I see."

"A brothel?" he offers.

I try not to laugh. "The decorator's computer system contains more advanced graphics than our software. It makes the images appear a different color, rather than the tones they'll actually be." I return the paper to him and pull up the images on my iPad. "This is what the main reception area will look like. If you scroll through the other pictures, you'll see the rest of the floor plan in detail, in addition to the color palates for each office and common area."

He takes my iPad, scowling at it. As he flips through the pictures, his features soften. "This is . . . nice."

"Yes, sir."

"Better than I thought."

"She did a nice job," I agree.

He glances up, what's left of his frown still in place. "You're sure it's this." He lifts the hard copy. "And not this shit?"

"Yes, sir. The more advanced images are included digitally in the contract. I approved them and signed on your behalf, as per your instruction."

He nods. "Tell me this. Why doesn't our technology measure up to the decorator's?"

"Because we don't need the software she uses at Ballantyne and Bradley. If we did, or if we need anything close to it in the future, I'll be sure to research it and present it to you."

"All right."

He seems troubled as he hands me the iPad. I take a moment to forward the email. "I just sent you another copy of the pictures, including the contract. The images will appear better on your computer screen and you'll be able to look through all the specifics at your leisure."

"It's not necessary," he says. "But thank you."

He pauses before taking off. I watch him, wondering why he seems so upset. One of the new paralegals steps forward, waiting until Mr. Ballantyne disappears into his office before approaching me.

"Ah, Luci, is it?"

"Yes." I offer him my hand. "You're Dante, aren't you?"

He smiles, shaking it like he's afraid to break me. "That's me. I'm going to be helping Mr. Summers out. He told me to see you about getting an office next to him."

"Oh, yes, one moment please." I glance at the time, and pass the folders I'm carrying to Jillian. "I'd like you to distribute these to all the attorneys directly, except the senior partners. They're not to be disturbed, but you can give them to their assistants."

Jillian's hesitant gaze bounces from the pile back to me. "What if I see the partners?"

"You can explain you're dropping off the monthly reports with their assistants unless they prefer to view them directly."

"You can do it," I add when she doesn't move. "And it will help me out tremendously."

"All right," she says.

"Follow me, please," I say to Dante. I scroll through my iPad as I walk. "I won't be able to give you an office until the partners move upstairs. But if Landon wants you closer, I can certainly arrange that."

"Landon?" He trips over his words. "Sorry, I've only ever heard the higher ups call him by his first name."

"Oh," I say, noting how his comment makes me involuntarily smile.

Landon and I have spent the last few weekends travelling to Kiawah. Though our time often involves more work than play, him on his upcoming cases and me finishing the work I bring along, play time has brought us closer.

His family is eccentric, hilarious, and absurdly perfect. We have dinner with them every time we're down. But as close as we are, I still haven't told him about Fernie.

I thought in time I would. Yet after he explained how awful his ex-wife was and how "fucked up" her family is, I couldn't be another lover in his life with a dysfunctional past. I simply couldn't. He shouldn't have to deal with the baggage that I bring. If I could just help Fernie get clean, I wouldn't be another woman he feels compelled to save.

My concern is that I haven't seen Fernie since last Friday during my lunch hour. She averted her gaze and said nothing, even when I handed her a small bag of groceries.

"I take it you're friends?" Dante asks.

My fingers fly across my iPad when an urgent email pops up. "Yes, we're friends," I say. I reply to Jefferson's email, that no, he's not losing his insurance, rather we're changing providers to offer better coverage.

"All right," he says.

His tone is slightly off. I assume he picked up on more than I intended. I don't bother to clarify. He'll find out the truth soon enough.

People whisper about me and Landon. Thankfully, it's mostly positive. I suppose Landon won over the employees of Ballantyne and Bradley as easily as he did me.

Jefferson pops out of his office as Dante asks how soon the move will take place. "Luci, question," Jefferson says.

"One moment please," I tell him, turning to address Dante. "It might be a while. In the meantime, let me speak with Melinda about switching cubicles with you. She's physically closest to Landon, but she works directly with Desiree, the junior partner. The switch might work in both your favors."

"I can tell they're physically close," Dante mumbles.

"Excuse me?" I ask, stopping just in front of Jefferson.

He glances around. "I just meant Melinda and Mr. Summers seem tight. She's always hanging around him, offering to help."

"Dude," Jefferson says. "Don't be an asshole. Landon's with Luci, not Melinda."

Dante's face flushes red. "I'm sorry, I didn't know—"

"Now you do," Jefferson says.

"I'll let you know about the move as soon as I can make arrangements," I say, moving forward.

Jefferson trails me. I glance up from my iPad, trying to focus on anything but Dante's comment. As much support as we've received, I know there are a few ladies in the office who seek Landon out. That doesn't mean I'm thrilled about the reminder.

"How long do I have to enroll?" Jefferson asks.

I welcome the office talk more than he knows. "One more week. Fill out your information on the link I sent you. I'll take care of the rest."

"Can I add a dependent later on?"

My steps slow as I reach my office. I turn to look at him. "Are you anticipating having a dependent to add?"

Although I keep my voice soft, he glances around to see who might be listening. He hooks my elbow and leads me into my office, shutting the door.

His sullen expression says it all. "Who is she?" I ask.

He shakes his head. "Some woman I picked up at a bar."

I place my iPad on my desk and walk around it, giving him a moment.

Jefferson isn't a bad guy. He's smart, handsome, and a gifted litigator. But like many of the young attorneys who work here, he's allowed his accomplishments and the money he's accrued to give him a false sense of power and a belief he's untouchable.

I lower myself into my seat, motioning for him to take the chair in front of me. "You're not looking to put this woman on your plan, are you?"

"No."

My attention falls to my desk, wishing I could help, despite recognizing this burden is his to carry. "You're adding a child?" I ask, clarifying what I already know.

"She says I knocked her up. Maybe I did." He huffs. "We went out a few times. She told me she was on the pill. Like an idiot, I believed her."

I want to point out that these things happen even on birth control, but that's not what he wants to hear.

My hand slides across the skirt of my teal summer dress, the color bright despite the weak April sunlight streaming in through my window. It's the same dress I wore when I took a pregnancy test two weeks ago. I hadn't been feeling well, and my period was late. I stared at the stick on my vanity as I washed my hands, waiting for the results.

"Is there something I should know?" Landon asked.

I hadn't heard him walk in, too distracted by what I may or may not see. "I'm a little late," I admitted. "And I've been run down lately. I think I'm getting sick, but I need to make sure that's all it is."

He gathered me in his arms and kissed my cheek. "You've been working a lot," he reminded me.

"I know," I agreed.

"Maybe too much?"

"Maybe," I replied.

"How late are you?"

"Two weeks," I said. "But sometimes I skip a month."

I checked the time on my phone and sighed. "It's negative," I added, trying to reassure him and myself.

Landon stared at the stick and the single line it produced. "Are you sure?"

I couldn't blame him for having his doubts. We've had a lot of sex and there've been days when I didn't take my pill on time. "It's been ten minutes and it hasn't changed."

He hugged me close when I returned his embrace. I couldn't help thinking he was disappointed. And as worried as I was, I was disappointed, too.

"If you do get pregnant, I'll take care of you and our baby," he said, his voice thick with emotion. "I swear I will."

He meant it, which is why I love him.

"She's a waitress," Jefferson says, bringing me back to the moment. "She doesn't have insurance. I can cover her hospital costs if it comes down to it, but I will only add the baby to my plan."

"Your baby?" I ask.

"Looks that way." He shrugs as if it's no big deal and his life isn't imploding around him. "She's agreed to have a DNA test, but she's sure I'm the father."

"I fucked up, didn't I?" he adds.

"Take it one step at a time, Jefferson," I say. "That's all you can do."

He seems to be looking over my shoulder and toward the view of the neighboring building. I doubt he sees it or feels anything. I only hope when the time comes, he does the right thing. "This wasn't supposed to happen to me," he says. "Shit, it's not like I'm sixteen and naïve."

If he were anyone else, I could tell him a baby is a blessing and someone he'll grow to love and accept. But Jefferson never planned on a family. He's not one to commit. "If I can help, let me know."

"Thanks, Luci." He rises slowly, his worry weighing him down. "No one else knows. Keep it that way, okay?"

"You don't have to worry about that," I assure him.

He's almost to the door when Kee-Kee marches in. She frowns when he walks by without a word. "What the hell's wrong with him?"

"Rough case," I say.

"Fitzgerald vs Vitale?" She doesn't wait for me to answer. "That's because Andrew Fitzgerald is an absolute nutcase. If he didn't have the bills he does, no way would we represent that mess." She crosses her legs. "So, you and hotness."

"Pardon?"

She smirks. "You and Landon," she clarifies. "Still going strong?"

"He's good to me," I admit.

"Uh, huh." Her grin fades slightly. "Mr. Ballantyne is all up in arms, certain Landon is going to steal you away and that we're going to lose you."

I pause in the middle of logging on to my computer. "Why?"

"Luci, come on. Anyone here with half a brain can see how serious the two of you are."

I see it and feel it, but the guilt I have over Fernie keeps me from fully enjoying my relationship with Landon.

Fernie has been noticeably absent. So has her group of friends. If it weren't for me finding her the previous Friday, I would have opted out of going to Kiawah and searched the city for her.

"He's good to me," I repeat.

"A little too good, which is why Mr. Ballantyne is worried he'll lose you."

"I'll talk to him," I say, reaching for the phone when it rings. "Luci Diaz."

"Miss Diaz, this is Nestor from security. You have a visitor."

I scroll through my planner, thinking it's business related. "I wasn't expecting anyone," I add, skimming through my list. "Is he or she a representative of—"

"She's not a representative," he says, his tone cementing me in place. "She says her name is Fernie. She won't give me a last name, but she says you know who she is."

My stomach bottoms out. "I'll be right down."

"You don't want her up, right?"

He's not really asking me. He's pretty much telling me she doesn't belong in the building. "I'm on my way," I say, trying to keep my face neutral.

"You all right?" Kee-Kee asks, standing with me.

"I just have to meet someone downstairs," I say.

Kee-Kee watches me as I reach for my purse. "I'll come with you."

"That's not necessary," I say, trying to smile. "I'll be back." I stop in the doorway. "I'm sorry, Kee, was there something you needed?"

"It's nothing urgent. I'll catch you when you get back." She cocks her head. "Are you sure you're all right?"

"Yes, let's have lunch tomorrow. Okay?" I force another smile when she nods, then walk quickly away.

I hate leaving Kee-Kee, especially when she appears to need my assistance. But I have to make certain Fernie is safe. I dig through my purse and pull out my wallet, thumbing through the bills as I step inside the elevator.

It's a busy time of day and people are still trailing in from lunch. Whoever is lingering in the foyer will see me. But I can't miss an opportunity to help Fernie.

The doors part as I shove my wallet back into my purse and tuck the bills in my hand. I avoid showing cash around Fernie, but I avoid having my wallet visible even more. The last thing I want is to tempt her and cause a scene.

I hurry across the foyer, quietly greeting a few of the legal associates returning from court.

"Hey, Luci."

"Hi, Luci."

"Your man *killed it* in court," Duncan tells me.

"That's wonderful, thank you," I say, my smile lifting slightly.

The new attorneys are carefully scrutinized in action by the senior partners to ensure they've hired the right candidates, and by their peers as a way of gauging their competition. If they don't live up to Ballantyne and Bradley standards, they're usually asked to leave within the first year, sometimes as early as a few months. I don't worry about Landon leaving. I know how talented he is and how hard he works.

I want to do something special to honor his achievements, especially his latest one that secured Dania a work visa and allowed her family to stay. For now, though, Fernie comes first.

My steps slow as I look around. I catch sight of her near the far end of the walkway, her small stature overpowered by the two immense security guards looming over her. I frown, wishing they'd treat her with more respect. Yet as I reach them, I see why they're concerned.

Fernie appears emaciated, her eyes wide and glassy.

Her long greasy hair is matted in clumps around her face. It's almost eighty degrees outside, but the worn yellow coat she wore all winter still shrouds her delicate frame. I don't have to guess she's strung out. Her appearance and how she sways in place is telling enough.

"Hi, Fernie," I say.

I haven't seen her this inebriated in a long time. For a moment, I don't think she hears or sees me, until her focus trails to my closed fist where the nineteen dollars I have waits in my grip.

"Why don't we get you something to eat?" I offer.

"She's not allowed inside the offices," Nestor says. "The owners wouldn't like that."

"I realize," I say, bothered. He wouldn't say that about someone who wasn't homeless. I motion to the coffee stand. "Fernie, are you hungry? Let's get some food for you and your friends."

I edge back, hoping she'll follow. I sigh when she does. I keep her in my line of sight, noting how closely the security guards shadow us. "I'm just getting her something to eat," I tell them.

I'm prepared to argue and perhaps they know. They exchange glances and give us space, watching carefully as we reach the stand. Miss Belinda hones in on Fernie with as much enthusiasm as the security guards.

"Hi, Miss Belinda," I say, trying to maintain my composure. "May I have two waters—"

"Four," Fernie says, her expression deadpan.

"Four," I clarify. "And I'll take four breakfast sandwiches, please."

Belinda and one of her workers start filling my order, watching Fernie as they place the items in a bag.

"You always say you don't have money," Fernie tells me, her expression changing from deadpan to angry when I pay Belinda.

Panic sets in, although my voice stays firm. "I only have money for food."

"You're a liar," she says, her voice loud and harsh.

The woman in line behind us steps away. Belinda carefully places my order on the counter, worry stiffening her posture.

"Fernie, I'm trying to help you," I say.

"Liars can't help me," she says. "You're a liar!"

I turn as the security guards march forward. Fernie takes off, slipping in her too worn loafers as she nears the door. She lands hard and despite her condition stands just as fast, racing through the doors.

Whatever she's taken has altered her mood and made her frantic.

I reach for the bag, freezing when Belinda grasps my arm. "Stay away from her," she tells me. "You can't help someone like that."

My face reveals my frustration and fear, despite everything I do to hide it.

"*Niña*," she says, releasing me slowly.

I clutch my bag and back away. Does she know Fernie is my mother? In that simple moment, could she see how much I love her?

My emotions push me forward, morphing my quick steps into a run.

"Miss Luci," Nestor calls to me. "We can't help you if you leave the property."

And they won't help Fernie if she stays. I'm ready to scream. All I want to do is help her. It's *all* I've ever wanted.

I see Fernie further down the street, doing my best to keep pace despite the heels I'm wearing.

"Fernie, wait," I yell. "*Fernie!*"

The people walking toward me pause, their attention skipping from me to the direction I'm looking. She cuts between a woman carrying a heavy shopping bag and a young teen talking on her phone.

Air burns through my lungs and my leg muscles throb, begging me to slow. I ground to a halt near the crosswalk, my heart beating out of control. I'd just missed the light. Fernie didn't. She cuts a left, taking the sidewalk that runs parallel to the park.

For a brief moment she pauses, meeting my face, but then it's like she can't run fast enough.

If I don't reach her, she'll head down the street and in the direction of the lower income buildings. I'm not following her down there, not even during the day. I need to catch her while she's still in the better part of town.

The minute the light changes, I hurry across. I'm gassed out and doing my best to keep a somewhat decent pace. There's an event at the park. A few blow-up bouncy houses have been set up and there's a man making balloon animals for the children who have gathered.

From what I can tell, the local prep school has started a preschool program and is looking to recruit students. It's smart to come here. The park caters to young families.

"Daddy, look!" A little girl with long dark braids proudly displays her balloon flower. Her father pretends to smell it, making a big fuss.

"That's the best flower I think I've ever smelled," he tells her.

The women beside him laugh. I adjust the hold on my bag. It may seem over the top to some, but it's what the little girl needs.

I can picture Landon doing the same thing. It's exactly how he is with nephew, telling Cal, Jr., what he needs to feel loved.

Except Landon isn't here and I need to find Fernie. I force myself to move faster, my speed kicking up when I spot her.

Across the street, near one of the newer buildings, I see Fernie. She takes off her coat and heads into the small alleyway leading to the underground garage for the tenants.

I stop in the mouth of the alleyway, watching her pass the first of two dumpsters pressed against the wall.

"Fernie, don't go," I yell. "Please, take this food."

The alleyway is barren, free of debris and cars. Sunlight streams between the neighboring buildings. It looks safe on the surface, but something doesn't feel right.

I start to turn back to the park when Fernie looks over her shoulder.

I realize too late she's not looking at me.

My mouth is covered and I'm hauled backward. I barely catch sight of the man with the red beanie when my purse and bag are ripped from me. I can't see the man who has me.

All I see is the man in front of me, and the way his greedy stare drags down my body.

Chapter Twenty-Four
Luci

I rake my heel down the shin of the man holding me. He curses against my ear, his foul breath wafting into my nose as I lash out, kicking my heels and writhing violently.

His hold loosens. I start to break free when the man with the red beanie punches me in the stomach. The force he uses and the pain it causes shoots into my chest, curling me forward.

Acid roils my stomach and burns my esophagus, making me choke and silencing my scream. "Grab her legs," the other man orders.

I'm gagging, sick, my head spinning from lack of oxygen as the other man clamps his hand tighter over my mouth. They drag me toward the dumpsters. I buck, fighting as hard as I can, knowing what they'll do to me if they take me there.

Fear threatens to detonate my racing heart as the dumpsters close in. I'm thrashing, cold sweat pouring down my face and blinding me. I try to scream, but all that does is steal my last breath. I start to black out when I'm abruptly dropped on the ground.

I land hard, momentarily disoriented.

"Mother*fucker*!"

The man with the red beanie crashes next to me, blood gushing from his mouth. I push up on my side, my hands shaking against the asphalt. I start to lift my head when Landon hauls me to my feet and drags me behind him.

I barely keep from falling over, confused and trying to make sense of what happened. The man with the red beanie staggers to his feet, his eyes wide as he backs away and toward a larger man I don't recognize. It's only when I see the gun Landon is holding that I realize why both men have their hands up.

I can't control my breathing or the nausea twisting my gut. Landon is deadly calm, his hand steady and his aim trained on the larger man.

The man with the red beanie attempts to edge forward, freezing at the sound of Landon's booming voice. "Get anywhere near her and I'll *fucking* kill you."

"*Freeze*, drop your weapon. *Drop your weapon, now!*"

Landon drops his gun near his feet, kicking it toward the police and away from the other men. Several uniformed officers rush forward, securing Landon's weapon and wrenching him back.

Knowing Landon is in trouble immediately snaps me out of my terror induced fog. "Wait, don't," I say. "He didn't do anything—he was protecting me."

He's pushed against the wall with his hands out and frisked.

"He didn't do anything!" I scream, ignoring the female cop who steps in front of me, telling me to calm down.

"Luci, it's okay," Landon says. He keeps still, allowing the police officer to check him for additional weapons. "Officer, I have my license to carry in my wallet, as well as a permit for the gun I used. I pulled my weapon when I found these men attacking my girlfriend."

The police already have the two men who attacked me in cuffs when another female officer pulls Landon's permits and I.D. out of his wallet. Landon keeps his glare trained on them as he's led down the alley for questioning.

"Ma'am, you need to come with me."

I barely hear the police officer's voice, too focused on Landon as he's led further away.

"Ma'am, can you hear me?"

I nod, but even that seems like too much of an effort, my ears pounding from the residual adrenaline rush. The police officer motions me to the side. "Are you all right, miss?" he asks me.

"Yes," I reply. With how hard my voice quakes, I don't sound remotely convincing.

"Miley, call an EMT."

"Please don't," I say, looking back toward Landon. "That's Landon Summers, an attorney at Ballantyne and Bradley. He's my boyfriend. He was helping me. I-I-I was attacked."

My voice cuts off when I realize this is the same police officer who patrols the area, the one I've seen at the park several times, and the same man who warned me not to be out here at night.

"It's all right, ma'am. You're safe now," he says. "Just tell me what happened and we can get you out of here."

I do, knowing I have to help Landon.

It seems to take forever and more than once it feels like I'm answering the same set of questions. When I finish, the men who assaulted me are read their rights and driven away in separate patrol cars.

Once it's clear the investigator is done photographing the scene, Landon makes his way to me. The front buttons of his suit jacket are missing. I catch sight of one near the spilled contents of my purse and the demolished bag of food.

I shove my feet into my discarded shoes, then bend to retrieve my belongings. My cell phone screen is cracked, and the display doesn't appear to be working. I shove it, my wallet, and keys back inside my purse.

Landon lifts a pack of tissues and a lipstick from the ground. "You want these?" he asks, his voice gruff.

"No," I reply. He's angry. I know he is. Mostly, I'm just numb.

He tosses the remaining items in the dumpster. I look away from it, realizing what could have happened to me if he hadn't arrived and sick over what could have happened to him if he hadn't been able to defend himself.

We walk out of the alleyway. He doesn't touch me, but stays close.

"My car's up here," he says. He huffs when I look at him. "One of the security guards called Kee-Kee, saying you went after some homeless woman, trying to give her food. He told her she didn't look right. Kee-Kee called me as I was driving back from court. I circled around the park, figuring you went there. I wasn't sure I'd find you. But I did."

He hits the key fob to his car, causing the young teens who stopped to admire it to step away. Landon opens the passenger door for me, his features hard and menacing. I slip inside and snap my seatbelt in place.

Landon falls into the driver's seat, slamming his door shut before pulling on his seatbelt and peeling away from the curb.

I'm not surprised when he passes our building and keeps going. I'm not certain what I look like, but most of my hair is in my face and I can taste blood when I swallow.

"There was a woman passing by when I saw those men dragging you into the alley," he bites out. "I told her to call for help and ran after you."

His chest rises and falls with purpose, his fury building with each second that passes. "What in the *hell* were you thinking, Luci?"

I press my lips together.

"Anything could have happened to you," he snaps. "You know that, right? When the police checked, the one with the hat had a knife and a syringe filled with some kind of shit." He slams his hand against the wheel. "God damn it, I could have lost you!"

His voice cuts off when he sees how bad I'm trembling. "Christ," he mutters. He slings his arm around me, pulling me against him when I break down. "I'm sorry, baby. I'm sorry."

Landon doesn't say anything else, he simply holds me, letting me cry every bit of fear I felt and appearing afraid to let me go.

We reach my condo complex several long minutes later. He pulls into the lot and parks in front of my house. When I moved in, I was assigned two spots. I never thought I'd have a use for the second one until I met Landon and he showed me just how empty my life had been.

"Don't get out without me," he tells me.

Like I could move if I tried.

He comes to my side, helping me out and lifting the purse from my trembling grasp. As soon as he shuts the door, he places his arm around me and guides me to the front door.

Landon uses his key to unlock the door. The familiar surroundings and the aroma of bread I baked this morning offers me comfort, but not as much as the man who holds me.

His cologne, the one I like and sprayed into the lining of my clutch that morning I thought I was leaving him forever, drifts into my nose, mixing with a masculine scent triggered by his adrenaline. He may have feared losing me, but I could have lost him, too.

He leads me into my bathroom, lowering me to the edge of my tub before starting the water to the shower.

"I-I have to call work," I stammer.

He kisses my head. "You don't have to do anything. I'll take care of it."

The hot water from the shower mists the air in his absence. When he returns, it's more like heavy fog. He doesn't complain, nor does he ask why I haven't moved. Perhaps he knows that I can't. I'm physically exhausted and emotionally battered by what happened.

Landon flips on the exhaust fan and kneels in front of me, helping me out of my shoes. "I'm okay," I say.

He shakes his head. "No, you're not, baby."

With gentle grace, he threads his fingers through my hands and helps me to my feet. It's not much of an effort on his part. I allow him to undress me, relishing those large hands and his tender touch to soothe me further.

My dress falls at my feet. He pulls me to him, encouraging me to step out of it.

"Jesus," he says.

I glance down at the ugly bruise forming around my stomach and the scratches along my skin from my fall.

"He hit you?" he asks, his voice barely registering.

I don't want to upset him further, but there's no point in denying it. "Yes."

He turns me around, examining me closely. "We should get you to the hospital. You could be in shock, have internal bleeding, or . . ."

"I'm all right," I say, although it's clear that I'm not. The bruises will fade. So will the lacerations. The emotional trauma is a different story.

I try to remember where I placed the contact information of the therapist I was seeing. I know I'll have to start attending counseling again. Not just because of this incident, but for everything that's happened since the last time we spoke.

I ease away from Landon and adjust the temperature in the shower. I step inside, thinking I'm ready to move on and not simply wait for my body to regain its composure.

For a long time, all I do is stand beneath the water, allowing it to bathe me and wash the filth and memories keeping me immobile.

The door rattles as Landon opens it. He pulls me to him, gathering me close. "I would have done anything to stop this," he says.

And I would have done anything to spare him from danger.

My arms feel heavy as I embrace his bare form. I start to cry again without meaning to, but with Landon it's okay to feel even the not-so-good feelings.

He washes my hair, my body, using care around the bruises and even more care when he dries and moisturizes my skin. I don't mean to be so pathetic, but I know what's coming and that I can no longer tuck my secrets away.

We slip into my bed naked. It's just as well. I would have felt the same way with clothes. Water gathers along the ends of my towel-dried hair, trickling drops against my back. Along the busy street behind my house, a truck barrels down the road. Aside from that, only quiet lingers.

If we were in Kiawah, we'd hear the lull of the ocean, tempting us outside to watch its soothing waves spill across the endless beaches. I wish we were there, far from the city and the memory of the day. But we're too close to everything that transpired and mere moments away from the truth.

I watch the way his chest rises and falls, not knowing where to start, my heart heavy with the words preparing to spill from my lips.

Landon strokes my face. "She led you to them," he says. "That woman you go to the park to feed gave you to those men." His voice sharpens, despite how he's fighting to keep it gentle. "It was her, wasn't it? The one who always wears that yellow coat."

My first instinct is to deny it or make excuses that could explain Fernie's actions away. It's what I've done all my life and something my grandmother conditioned me to do. Mamita was like that, always defending Fernie until she died and I stepped up to take Mamita's place.

"I know you want to help her, Luci. And God knows, she needs to be helped. But not by you, not anymore. Not when she cares more about her next fix than your safety."

I don't respond, listening and waiting for the right moment, and wishing I didn't have to say what I do.

"You can't help her," he says. "She's beyond what you're capable of."

"I have to find a way." My voice cracks, revealing the traces of my splintered soul.

"Why?" he asks. "Look, I'm the first person to help someone who needs it, but not at the expense of my life—"

"She's my mother."

Landon doesn't move, horror claiming his features in a way I wish they wouldn't.

"Her name's Fernie," I add.

There are a million things I could have said. As it is, I barely managed as much as I did.

"Why . . ." He swallows hard. "Why didn't you tell me?"

My eyes sting, although I don't want the tears to come. "It's not something you tell anyone."

"Ever," I want to say. But that's not true. Not anymore.

I use the sheet to wipe my eyes. "I don't have the kind of mother you do, Landon. But your mother is the kind I always wanted." Thinking of Landon's mother and how much they adore each other makes everything so much harder to say. "Fernie started using marijuana young, in middle school from what I understand. By the time she reached high school, she was experimenting with heavier drugs. My grandmother told me she stopped when she became pregnant with me, and for a long time, she didn't use anything. But then she did." I try to steady my voice, but simply can't. "As sick as she was, she realized she could no longer take care of me."

"Is that why you were raised by your grandmother?"

"Fernie was young," I reply. "Only fifteen when she had me. She promised Mamita she could do better and be better, and sometimes she could. But her addiction was always stronger than she was."

I give myself a moment, and maybe give Landon one, too. He had been waiting for me to tell him more about my past. I can tell by the sense of compassion lighting his brown eyes.

"What about your father?" he asks. "Where was he?"

Yet another strike against me. "I don't know who he is," I say, shame finding its way into each syllable. "I never met him."

Landon waits, guessing there's more to say. He's right. "There was speculation about a young man who lived close by. But no one was completely sure. I don't think Fernie knew either. The lifestyle she fell into was one of promiscuity and men who didn't care much about consent." I try to pull the sheet closer to my chin, feeling exposed. But it's already as high as it will go. "I saw him a few times and he always looked at me when I walked by. He never approached though, and I never felt right approaching him."

Landon rubs his eyes, the way he does when he's stressed. I almost expect him to stand and pace. Instead he drops his hand away, unveiling the sympathy claiming his features. "Is Fernie the reason you left New Jersey?" he asks. "I get the feeling she made her way down here first."

I nod, thinking back. "Mamita died unexpectedly my sophomore year of high school. No one could locate Fernie to tell her, and no one knew where she was. It wasn't until she called one of my uncles asking for money that we realized she was in Charlotte. I finished the few weeks of school that remained, took the G.E.D., then left to find her."

"By yourself?" Landon asks. "You were just a kid."

"I was sixteen," I explain. "Already a year older than Fernie was when she had me."

"But still just a kid," Landon repeats. "Didn't anyone—your uncle, another relative, shit, *anyone* try and stop you?"

"They did," I agree. "But they had their own problems and it wasn't uncommon for kids to drop out of school where I grew up." I shrug. "I didn't have a choice. Someone had to take care of her."

Landon's voice takes a reflective tone, trying to process everything I said and likely envisioning it, as well. I expect a firestorm of questions. Instead, he summarizes everything in a few simple words. "All this time, you've been taking care of her."

"She wasn't so bad at first and she tried to get help on her own. She followed a friend down south and was in and out of rehab. But she couldn't stay clean and her mental state deteriorated the more drugs she used." I look up at him. "She was better than this, I swear she was."

I stop speaking when anger flashes across his features. "Does she hit you?"

He mutters a curse when I don't answer. "The other week, you didn't fall, did you? You went to her after I left and she attacked you."

I'd planned to tell him. This just wasn't the way I intended. "I'm not sure."

"You're not sure? Luci, what does that even mean?" He sits up, digging his fingers through his hair. "I . . . you have to come clean with me."

He's right, but it doesn't lessen the blow. I sit up, gathering the blanket at the foot of the bed around us. "We had a lot of food that night. I couldn't stand the thought of her not having any. I found her with another woman and . . ."

"And what?"

My muscles stiffen as I remember. "Someone grabbed my hair when I tried to pass a bag of leftovers from my car. I didn't see who it was. It could have been the other woman."

He angles his chin to face me. "I don't believe you. Not because I think you're lying," he adds quickly. "But because I think you believe in her too much. So let me ask you again, has she ever laid her hands on you?"

"You don't understand," I say.

"Then help me. Tell me if she's ever hurt you."

Some things aren't as easy as a yes or no. "She wasn't always like this," I say.

I'm certain he's going to lose it. Instead he pulls me to him, that same way he did in the alley when his body shielded mine. "You sound like an abused woman and I fucking hate it," he bites out. "You have to know you deserve better than this."

"*She* deserves better than this," I counter, curling into his chest. "Fernie was the smart one, Mamita always said. The one who would make something of herself and leave a neighborhood no one else could." My fingers trail down his skin. "She believed that this young woman who loved animals and fed the pigeons in the park, who worked hard in school, and who all the little girls wanted to be was still in there, and that I could help her." My eyes scrunch closed when tears stream down my eyes. "I'm not stupid, Landon. I just want to help her. It's all I've ever wanted to do."

Landon pulls away, his hands firm along my shoulders. "Not like this. Not by giving her food and chasing after her."

"I know," I say, ignoring the latter. "But feeding her and giving her clothes is as much as she'll let me do." I wipe my cheeks. "That coat she wears, I gave it to her. I'm the only one she trusts."

"That's what you think. But she's not capable of trusting anyone. If anything, you're the one who trusts her, and today, she used it against you," he tells me. "She lured you into that alley, Luci. She risked your life to get what she needed from those men.”

I think about the way she glanced back at me right before those men grabbed me. She saw what happened and did nothing to help me.

“I know,” I agree. “But I can’t give up on her, not yet.”

“Even after today and what it almost cost you?”

“No,” I reply, my voice breaking. “No matter what, she’s still my mother.”

It’s hard for Landon to see where I’m coming from. His mother and father have always provided for him and loved him. And regardless of what she feels, I still love Fernie, the beautiful young woman my grandmother never stopped believing in.

I leave Landon to his thoughts as all those stories my grandmother would tell me flood my mind.

“She had pretty hair,” Mamita would say as she braided mine. “Just like you. And a smile as bright as the sun.”

I don’t know when that smile faded. I only know my grandmother would have given anything to see it again.

“The police are looking for her,” Landon says after a moment. “If they charge her, and if I can prove she was an accomplice, I can make a plea for drug testing and counseling.”

“You want to help her?” I ask.

“No, I want to help you.”

My gaze melds into his as his thumb swipes away the last remaining tear. Traces of his anger don’t lie far from the surface, yet here he is, offering to help in a way no one else has.

“There’re a lot of ‘ifs’,” I say. “What if we can’t manage it?”

“Then we’ll try something else.” His expression grows sad. “I’m not going to keep you from helping your momma. But I swear to Christ, I’m going to keep her from hurting you.”

It’s what he said and I believed him. If anyone could help me, it was Landon.

But we never had the chance.

Fernie was found dead from an overdose the next day, in an alley a few blocks from the last place I saw her. Landon went with me to identify the body. He did a lot of things, including holding me close when the coroner pulled away the sheet covering her face.

The woman lying on the metal stretcher had deep set wrinkles that didn't belong on someone so young and bruises that clustered along her withering shoulders, each injury painting a picture of the hardships she'd endured in her short life.

She'd laid in the cold rain overnight, the exposure discoloring her skin and leaving the hair that resembled mine in matted clumps.

But she was still Fernie.

She was still my mother.

Dying was the last thing she did to hurt me.

I'll admit, it hurt more than the rest.

Chapter Twenty-Five
Landon

I meant to help.

I meant to fix everything.

I learned a long time ago that some things can't be fixed and some people can't be helped.

That didn't mean I didn't want to make it right for the right woman and under the right circumstances.

I stare at the steaks I placed on the grill, giving the one to my right a hard poke before my attention drifts over the terrace and to the sand below. Luci is kneeling beside Cal, Jr. Her hair skims along her elbows as her hand stretches out to show my nephew the shells she found.

He tosses his bucket aside, and as if handling something precious, carefully lifts one from her palm. I can hear his giggle from here, even over the harsh waves following last night's storm. His entire face lights up as he presses the shell between his tiny fingers to show her that indeed, she made a great find.

I can't tell if Luci is returning his grin, not from the position she's kneeling in. I only hope she is.

God, I miss that smile.

"Here," Daddy says, motioning to the grill. "I can do that. You go be with Luci."

I hand him the long grill fork, not bothering to argue. "Thank you, sir," I tell him, edging around Callahan when he appears with a plate stacked with shrimp kabobs.

The weight of his worry pelts me as I pass him. Like Daddy, he's concerned and wants Luci and me to be okay. They're not alone.

Trin and my mother pause from where they're laying out the rest of the food along the table. I walk past them, my steps sluggish despite my desire to be at Luci's side.

I never thought I'd have a use for a dining set this soon. But every weekend since the first time I asked, Luci and I have headed down to Kiawah. The first few, Trin and Momma took turns having us over for dinner. Luci didn't want them fussing so much, not over her. But that's Luci, never wanting to receive more than she gave.

"We should have them over here," Luci suggested.

She was right. They belonged with us at our place.

No, our "home".

I rub my jaw as my bare feet smack against the stone steps leading down to the sand. It's been a hard few weeks filled with too much work and too much stress. But nothing I felt compares to what Luci has been through.

When people love and try as hard as she did, it's supposed to work out. Whatever "it" is, it's supposed to push aside all the bad, allowing the good in. It's only right. It's only fair. Mostly, it's what someone as kind as Luci deserves.

Thing is, right and fair are attributes that don't always come in life, no matter how much you pray you'll receive them.

My feet hit the sand as I hop off the last step, the familiar feel of soft grains sliding between my toes giving me some reprieve. I wish I could share that reprieve and gift it to the one person who needs it most.

The wind picks up, cooling my legs as I stop to watch Luci. If she's cold, she doesn't show it, so focused on little Cal and the pebble he bends to lift.

It damn well broke my heart to see what Fernie's death did to Luci. I couldn't help her like I wanted to, nor could I give

Fernie that chance people in her condition need. So I did what I could. I honored her in death.

The service was nice. Trin and Momma helped put it together. Becca helped too, reaching out to that cheerleader Luci knew. Blythe wasn't much of a friend to Luci. But I suppose she was one when it counted, rounding up a few friends to attend the memorial.

I stayed by Luci's side, holding her hand when Mr. Ballantyne, Kee-Kee, and hell, even Jefferson and Duncan whispered their condolences. Mr. Ballantyne is a good man and offered to split the costs with me. I allowed it only because I know how much Luci means to him, and maybe how much Luci means to everyone, including the family she left behind in New Jersey.

They all flew down, permitting me to put them up at the Hilton. No one mentioned how Fernie died. But they spoke of how she lived, back when she was young and still had a chance to live a good life. It meant a lot to me and even more to Luci, giving her better memories than the ones that continue to haunt her.

Luci picks up the pail Cal, Jr., abandoned, following behind him when something else catches his attention.

She bends to look at what he found. The breeze sweeps in, fanning out the edge of her tunic and giving me a peek of her flat stomach and bra covering her breasts. We made love this morning, and we'll likely make more tonight. It's the one constant we've had, allowing me to feel close to her.

"Hey," I say when I reach her side.

She places the pail beside Cal, Jr., straightening as I wind my arm around her and clutch her hip. "Hey, sweetie," she says.

I motion with my chin as Cal, Jr., hurries forward, his chubby little legs wide to help him balance through the sand. "The kid likes you."

She laughs. The first time I think since Fernie's death. I try not to react, but it's hard. I miss her laugh as much as her smiles. "I like him, too," she says.

"But he likes me more," I whisper in her ear. I shrug when she looks at me. "I'm not trying to rub it in, just stating a fact."

I hold out my hand and little Cal gives me a high-five. He laughs. I do, too.

"See?" I tell Luci.

"It's not a competition, honey."

It's what she says, but she still scoops him up in her arms. Cal, Jr.'s, smile is probably as big as mine. He reaches out, tugging Luci's hair. "He still likes me more," I murmur.

I hold out my hands, catching him when he launches himself from Luci's arms into mine. "Ready to fly?" I ask.

Cal, Jr., flaps his arms out, knowing what I mean. I throw him up in the air, each time higher, each time drawing out more giggles than the rest. Luci pokes his belly when he lands in my arms, the three of us laughing together.

Cal, Jr., abruptly stops, turning to the side when he sees someone approach. Callahan stands a few feet away, smiling, hands on his hips. "His momma wants him to eat," he tells us. "She's going to try to put him down before supper."

Between Callahan's presence and the word "momma," me and Luci don't stand a chance. The moment I put Cal, Jr., down, he takes off like a wobbly little rocket, his arms outstretched to meet his father.

"Hey, partner," Callahan says, lifting his son and cuddling him close.

"I think he likes him best," Luci whispers.

"Can't say that I blame him," I say. I'm not the jealous type. I am a little now. But for once it's a good thing, giving me the spark I need to say what comes next.

I take Luci's hands in mine, watching the way my thumbs slide over her knuckles. "I want that for us," I confess.

She falls perfectly still. "You want what for us?" she asks.

I think she knows what I mean, not that I mind telling her. "Children. I want to make lots of babies with you."

Her lips part slowly, revealing her shock and amplifying the warmth spreading along my chest. Goddamn it, how did I go my whole life without her?

I motion ahead, to where the waves have started to settle and the clean scent of salty air escalates with the next crest that forms. "What I feel, I'm always going feel for you. It's eternal, like this ocean, something that's always going to be."

"And what do you feel?" she says, sounding afraid to ask.

I don't want her scared, not when it comes to us. "That I love you," I explain. "You're my world, Luci, my ocean, and the eternity that I've waited for."

All I say is maybe too much too soon, given Fernie's death happened just shy of a month ago. But the day Luci was attacked was a reminder that love isn't something you take for granted, ever. Not when it's real, and not when it's something that means more than your own life.

I could have lost her that day. I swear to Christ, nothing has ever scared me more. She could have died, this sweet little thing I hold could have left this world without knowing my heart and soul have belonged to her from the first moment I saw her.

Between the baby talk and my words, I'm certain she'll bolt. Instead, that smile, the one she first showed me when she told me her name lights up her gaze and casts a shimmer along the most beautiful face I've ever dared laid eyes on. "I love you, too, Landon. *Always.*"

Love heals all wounds, the bitter ones filled with distrust and resentment and all the ones caused by those you try to save, but can't. As I draw Luci to me and kiss her, and promise her forever in that kiss, I allow it to heal the last of our wounds.

Epilogue
Luci

The sun sets along a horizon painted in swirls of lavender and orange. I huddle closer to Landon as he pulls me tighter. Even from this distance, I can hear the band Becca hired blasting away.

It's New Year's Eve. I can't believe it. And what a year it's been.

For my birthday at the end of May, Landon gave me an envelope with a check and an opportunity to start a foundation. I hesitated for only a day or so, like he knew I would. Then together, we started a foundation that caters to the homeless scattered along the streets of Charlotte.

It's still in the bare bones planning phase and there's a great deal left to do. But if we receive the permits and licenses we need, a mobile unit staffed with drug counselors will start its first route late summer.

I look down the long stretch of beach. "Is that the same band she hired last year?" I ask.

Landon shrugs. "Sounds it."

I grin as we walk along the sand, shoving him toward the shore when he tries to lead my feet into the water. "Behave," I tell him.

"I am," he says. "You still have your clothes on, don't you?"

My cheeks warm despite the cold. We've had our share of sex on the beach, and if Landon has his way, we'll have a little more before the night ends. I won't complain. I welcome his touch as easily as I welcome waking up to him in the morning.

"You sure you want to go to this thing?" he says, motioning ahead when what sounds like *Shape of You* begins to play.

"It was nice of her to invite us. I don't want to be rude."

"I guess," he mumbles. "I'd just rather spend it with you."

I feel the same way, but it's nice to relive the night we met, and how that chance meeting completely changed my life. With Landon, life doesn't simply pass me by, it pauses, allowing me to live and love in return.

"One drink," I say, thinking back to how those few words changed my world. "Just one and we can leave if you'd like."

"Fine," he says, snatching me into his arms.

"Landon," I say, laughing when he palms my butt. "Be good."

"E.T. and Elliot good? Or naughty good?" He gives me a squeeze. "I'm going to go with naughty good."

"You're impossible," I say, my voice trailing when he frowns. "What's wrong?"

"What the hell is that?"

I follow behind him, slowing my steps when I see where he's headed. Between a thick row of trees, a long white blanket has been placed on the sand, white votive candles encasing the perimeter in an arc.

"You coming?" he asks when I stop. "Looks like there's free booze."

I walk carefully toward him, cupping my mouth when he points to the champagne bottle sticking out of the sand and the two flutes placed on a silver platter beside it.

"Landon," I gush. "You're so romantic."

"You think this is romantic?" he asks.

I clutch my heart. "Of course I do."

"Humph." He crosses his arms. "More romantic than our trip to Scotland?"

I scan the beautiful display and how the candles dance in the breeze. "Yes," I agree, barely managing the word.

He quiets, his warm brown eyes glistening as he takes me in. "Well, in that case . . ."

I gasp when he takes my hand and falls to one knee. From the break in the trees a small group of people with acoustic guitars appear. My tears start to fall as the first cords of *Love on the Brain* begin to play.

"By the way," he says. "These here are the Three Amigos. All five of them," he adds with a wink.

My jaw falls open. "It's the first song we danced to," he reminds me. "But it wasn't the last. For that, and everything you've given me, I'm thankful."

He bows his head, taking a deep breath and letting it out slowly. When he lifts his chin, all traces of humor are gone, his warm gaze cementing where I stand.

"I think I have a hero complex," he begins. "But I've never wanted to be a hero more than the moment I met you. I love you, Luci . . . will you marry me?"

Just like the first night we met and he asked me to go home with him, there's no hesitation. There never will be when it comes to Landon.

"*Yes,*" I whisper.

I watch him slide the ring across my finger, squealing when he lifts me in the air for a kiss. He lowers me, holding me close as we dance to the rest of the song.

I catch sight of Becca as the music fades, leading the musicians down the beach, her eyes glistening with what I hope are happy tears.

Landon and I continue to hold each other as she turns in the direction of her house. I want to thank her, and maybe Landon does, too, but then she abruptly stops.

I don't know why until I see Hale step forward, a bottle of champagne tightly clutched in his hand.

I smile, wiping my eyes. I'm getting my chance at forever.

And maybe Becca will, too . . .

This book contains excerpts from *Inseverable* from the Carolina Beach series, as well as excerpts from *Let Me*, *Feel Me*, and *Crave Me* from the O'Brien Family novels by Cecy Robson. The excerpts have been set for this edition only and may not reflect the final content of the final novels.

Inseverable

A Carolina Beach

Novel

by Cecy Robson

Prologue

Callahan

Three days.

That's all I have left until this shit ends.

Three days shouldn't feel like forever, not compared to the eight years I've bled to the Army. Thing is, good men have been killed in less time. In as quick as a blink, a squeeze of a trigger, or a small breath right before a grenade blows is all the time it takes to shove someone right out of life and well into death.

That's what makes three days as long as it is. Three days is plenty of time to die.

My eyes tear when the wind picks up and shoots grime through the small hole of my lookout point. This blown out piece of cinderblock is only big enough to allow me a view of the street below, but not so small I don't get smacked in the face with more filth. The tarp flaps above me as I spit out another layer of the dirt-sand mix spackling my teeth. Christ Almighty, I need a swig of the water resting near my elbow. But my thirst, like everything else has to wait.

I have a job to do.

I adjust my hips against the cracked cement of my bed, bathroom, and home all rolled into one, thankful that the agonizing ache stretching over the lower half of my body has settled into a now familiar numbness.

Out of all the points I'd scouted, and all the accumulated years spent in this position, I should be used to it. And in a strange way, it should almost be home. Yet nothing ever has been home.

But in three days, maybe something finally will be . . .

I shove my thoughts away and breathe as my fellow Rangers stalk along the street. It's then I see them, a mother and daughter walking straight toward my team. Less than one city block separates them from the men counting on me to keep them alive.

The hell? How did they get past the other sniper unreported? Rogers is new on watch. But the quick paces these two are taking should have clued him in that something's up. I train my scope on their faces; their expressions are blank, unreadable. 'Cept that's not what keeps my attention.

The little girl can't be more than five. So why the fuck isn't her mother holding her hand? I lift my radio and bark a warning, dropping it beside me as I lock my scope dead center on the woman's head.

The radio crackles and Modreski chimes in, yelling at his team to hold their positions. He asks me what my plan is, knowing if something's caused the short-hairs on my neck to rise, he and the boys damn well need to listen. But I don't hear him, with a breath and a squeeze of the trigger, I leave a kid without a mother.

Just beneath the sleeve of her *abayah*—the dress completely covering her body—I see it, a detonator that would trigger the explosives likely strapped to her chest. A few Rangers I know—Simons and Boreman, rush forward. I start to mutter a curse, pissed at her for making me shoot her in front of her kid. But the curse lodges in my throat when I see the kid isn't looking at her mother lying next to her dead.

She's watching my advancing team as she lifts the detonator clasped tight in her hand.

Let Me

An O'Brien Family

Novel

by Cecy Robson

CHAPTER 1

Finn

I see the strike coming at me a split second before it connects with my skull. My head snaps back from the force, the crowds' hollers resonating like a muffled cry in the distance. It was a good punch—lightning quick with enough impact to knock most guys on their asses. But I'm not most guys.

You hit me, I'm only going to hit you harder.

My right hand shoots up, blocking and smacking away the kick gunning for my ribs. I pivot out of the way, again, and again, and again, avoiding Easton's arms and legs as they come at me. He's fast, strong, with a six inch reach advantage. But he's too eager to take me out and not pacing himself like he should. Already he's breathing hard and it's just the start of the second round.

I take my time to figure him out, planning each move, searching for that opening I need. Do I take a few bashes because of it? Sure. It's part of the job. But believe it or not, it's part of the job I look forward to.

Those punches and kicks remind me that I still *feel*, that I'm still human. And that for now, I'm still alive.

"Oh!" some drunk behind me yells when my uppercut finds Easton's chin.

He staggers back, swiping the blood oozing from his lip,

yet he keeps his grin. He's trying to make like it was a lucky shot. That it won't happen again.

Like me, Easton needs to win this match. And if he does, he'll move up to the top ten, making him a contender for the UFC Lightweight title.

Talent aside, the guy's a raging asshole, and so are the idiots in his training camp. They've been trash-talking since the moment I agreed to this match. I didn't really care and laughed most of it off until they got personal and took it a step too far.

Again he nails me in the head. It's not as hard as it was last time which tells me he's getting tired. Does it hurt? I guess.

But let's say I'm a guy who's used to pain.

Easton grins. He thinks I'm afraid of him. He thinks he has me where he wants me. But fear is an emotion I don't allow myself to entertain. Fear gets you hurt and rips you apart till you think there's nothing left.

I dodge out of reach. He scowls and takes another swing. This one gets close enough to my jaw to create a breeze that whips across my skin.

"Finn," my brother Killian barks from the side. "Take him out *now*."

He's worried about me. So is my family. But now's not the time to think about them. I keep my hands up as I edge away, letting Easton think I'm backing down, that I'm tired and need to catch my breath.

I sidestep when he lunges forward, avoiding his next swing and use the momentum to drop my head and nail him in the temple with a roundhouse kick.

Like I said, Easton's fast.

Too bad for him I'm a little bit faster.

The kick is my signature move, as natural for me as the next breath. He goes down like I planned. But in the Octagon you don't stop just because your opponent collapses like timber. You charge forward. You show him what you're made of. And you prove just how tough you really are.

That muffled screaming, isn't so muffled anymore. The crowd loses their shit as I pounce, my blows nailing Easton in the face until the ref's arms hook beneath mine as he hauls me off. I back away, my fists up because I already know I won.

I should do a back flip or some crazy shit to incite the crowd. This is it. My time has come to own it. But the good things aren't as great as they can be. Not with the memories that haunt me. And not with the anger they stir.

Killian rushes in as the medic wipes down my face. I'm bleeding from the punch Easton caught me with at the beginning of the round. I didn't think it was that bad, but the way the ringside medic is pressing the towel against my head clues me in the gash isn't closing like it should.

"I'm going to have to stitch you up, Fury," he mumbles.

"I figured," I tell him.

Kill pats my back. "Good job," he says.

Maybe he believes it, but I don't miss the concern in his voice. He thinks I took too many unnecessary hits. I can't really argue, seeing how it's true.

He doesn't understand that I don't feel those strikes the way I should. Hell, I don't think I've felt anything the way I should in a long time. Not like I used to. I try to tell myself that maybe that' a good thing. That numbness is better than pain. But I'm not so convinced anymore, and neither is my family. I try to shrug it off like I'm fine. Except given the way they've been eyeing me, I'm not fooling anyone.

I'm scaring everyone around me. And it sucks. Not only because I don't want them scared, but mostly because I don't know how to stop it.

"The referee has called a stop to this match at two-minutes and forty-nine seconds into the second round," the announcer begins. "The winner by TKO, Finn 'The Fury' O'Brien."

The crowd screams and pumps their fists in the air when my hand is raised. I take the few seconds I need to thank my sponsors, my camp, and my brother, because that's what I'm supposed to do despite the fog clouding my senses. I wish that disconnect had something to do with all the hits I took, but deep down I know that it doesn't.

I'm back in the locker room before I know it getting stitched up, too many people talking at once. God, I barely hear their questions or my responses. But they're there and somehow I make it through.

"I'm worried about you, Finnie," Kill says when everyone piles out.

"Don't. I'm not drinking tonight. I'm headed home," I assure him.

"That's not what I mean," he says. He's sitting in a fold out chair, his arms resting against his muscular legs. "I think you need to talk to someone."

I stretch out my arms. By now they're so tight, they pull against the bones. "I am. I'm talking to you."

I don't have to see him to know he's shaking his head, or that he's looking sad, disappointed, and maybe something else, too. "I'm not who you should be speaking to," he says. "Not for what's going on in your head."

"You're enough," I say, even though I know it's no longer true.

"Finn," he begins.

I don't wait for him to finish, leaving the changing area and heading toward the showers. "Go find Sofia and Wren," I call over my shoulder as I strip out my shirt. "See if they're up for some dinner."

I don't remember peeling the rest of my clothes off. That numbness I've been feeling too much lately claiming me like a mist until it fully engulfs me. Fuck. It's like I've stopped living even though for the most part I think I'm still alive.

I lean against the tile with my arms spread, allowing the water to beat against my back. It's too hot. I should turn it down, but I don't bother. Eventually, like everything else, the sensation fades.

I'm not sure how long I'm in that position. A few seconds? A few minutes? But then Easton and his trainer Yefim are suddenly there. "You got lucky, O'Brien," Yefim calls out, taunting me with his thick eastern European accent.

Shit. Like all the trash talk before the fight wasn't enough.

"Did you hear me, you pussy?" he fires back when I don't answer. "Did you hear me, you goddamn coward?"

Coward? Fuck you. It's what I think, but not what I say, focusing instead on the streams of water that gather along my feet before they swirl into the drain.

It doesn't help. The rage that's building, the one I only manage to barely keep in? It stirs in my gut like a heavy pot filled with hate, sin, and all the curses my Ma would still beat my ass for saying.

"What're you doing?" Yefim asks.

His voice is closer, he's drawing near. It doesn't matter that I'm standing here naked. He wants to be next to me. I shudder, that feeling I keep buried drilling its way up.

"I know about you," Yefim says, not bothering to keep his voice low. "But everyone knows, don't they? Even if you don't want them to."

My body shakes a little more, but it's not from the cooling water. It's from his words and all that anger they trigger. *Don't do it. Don't go there.*

"You like to keep it a secret. Don't you, pussy?"

Yefim laughs when I keep my trap shut. He thinks I'm backing down, just like Easton did before his face met the mat. "He's crying," he calls out to Easton. "What? Not so tough now?"

That's where he's dead wrong. Every muscle I've conditioned serves a purpose—to take down those who fuck with me. And right now, Yefim is seriously fucking with me.

"You like to pretend that it's girls you like, don't you?" he says. "But that's not true, is it? Oh, no, that's not true at all . . ."

I raise my chin, knowing that someone's not leaving without bleeding, and I've bled enough tonight.

Yefim kicks at my calf. "What? Nothing to say? Can't speak without your boyfriend here?"

"Boyfriend?" Easton asks, laughing. "No fucking way."

"Yes. Way," Yefim insists. "Didn't you know this little pussy takes it up the ass—"

I punch him so hard, I feel his teeth crack against my knuckles. For someone with decades of boxing experience he never saw me coming. But I see Easton flying at me out of the corner of my eye. I toss him over my shoulder, slamming him hard onto the ceramic tile floor. Like in the octagon, I throw myself on top of him, my fists colliding against his skin.

Voices rush forward, telling me to stop. A woman screams, but I don't stop fighting off the bodies trying to grab me, breaking through the arms wrenching me back. I need to hit him—I need to feel my fists meeting his face—I need to feel *something*.

God damn it. I need to feel alive.

I don't want the pain.

I don't want the terror.

But once more, it's all I feel.

Feel Me

An O'Brien Family Novel

by Cecy Robson

CHAPTER 1

Melissa

I stare at the nameplate perched on my father's desk: *District Attorney Miles Fenske*. It proclaims his position, allowing those who read it a glimpse of what he's accomplished. Yet it's only a glimpse. It's not a true representation of all he is, or all he means to me. The nameplate is cheap, unlike the generous soul who stares back at me with the same loving expression he's held since the first moment I saw him.

What are you thinking, Melissa? He signs to me, moving his hands in beautifully fluid motions.

We're alone in his office. He doesn't need to sign to keep our conversation private. He could whisper, and I would still be able to read his lips. But he knows I'm more comfortable communicating with my hands, probably because American Sign Language is one of the many things we learned together. As a child I considered it our very own secret language, something he and I could share away from the hearing world.

That you're making a mistake, I sign back.

My comment earns me a smile, but I can see his concern, despite the crinkles around his eyes that deepen when he grins. "You're going to have to trust me," he says aloud.

I let out a breath. He knows I trust him. How could I not?

I was brought to the Lehigh Valley District Attorney's

office when I was about six years old, after my biological mother had attempted to sell me in exchange for drugs. My mother probably thought it was a brilliant plan. Being born with profound hearing loss, I couldn't speak, couldn't communicate, and couldn't understand. Which meant, I couldn't tell anyone what was about to take place.

My primal instincts ordered me to run, that I was in danger, so I did—thank God I did. I kicked and fought, dodging the hands trying to grab me, and scurrying out of my window.

To this day, I remember the way the cold metal grating of the fire escape felt against my bare feet, and the way my mouth struggled to form what I thought were words as I banged on my elderly neighbor's window. Miss Lena, the lady with too many cats and twice as many grandchildren, yanked me into her apartment when she saw me. She called the police, but by the time they arrived, my mother was gone. I never saw her again.

Not that I regret it.

I was placed in foster care, confused and frightened about what was happening and certain I'd eventually return "home". Instead, I was brought before the young Assistant D.A Miles Fenske. He was supposed to handle my case, dispose of it, and move on. He was never supposed to welcome me into his heart. Yet that's exactly what he did.

"Melissa," he says. His words aren't clear—not as clear as they can be, my hearing aids can only do so much, but I hear enough to sense the emotion in the way he speaks my name. "Why are you so sad?"

I raise my chin. "Declan O'Brien will never be the man you are. He's not the right D.A. for this position." I shake my head. "He belongs in the Trial Unit, Arson, Fugitive, anywhere else but where you've placed him."

"I know you don't like him . . ."

I raise my brows.

". . and that your first encounter wasn't a positive one .. ."

"That's because he was an asshole," I mumble.

He chuckles. "I assure you he deeply regrets what he said. But Declan is smart, quick, and kind."

I don't agree. Not completely. Is Declan intelligent?

Brilliantly so, and absurdly astute in court. With short wavy blond hair and a dashing grin that lights his blue eyes, he's also gorgeous, and he knows it. But is he kind? I'm not so sure that he is. "He'll never be the man you are," I repeat.

"I'm not asking him to be. I simply want the best person for the job, someone who will help the victims who need him most."

"That's what you claim. But he doesn't have experience handling delicate cases where offenders often inflict irreparable trauma."

"No, but as the head of Victim Services, you do," he offers with a knowing gleam.

My nails dig into the wooden armrests. "If you're trying to hook us up, I'm going to be seriously mad at you."

The edges of his mouth curve. "I'm only asking you to help Declan as he transitions into his new role. This new assignment won't be easy on him."

"Because he doesn't want it. He wants to be the head of Homicide." I stand with my hands out, pleading. "Daddy, please reassign him. The Sexual Assault and Child Abuse Unit is not where someone who seeks glory belongs."

My voice trails as I catch a glimmer of his pain. "Daddy?"

At once, his face scrunches, flushing red only to grow alarmingly pale. I race around his desk, clutching his shoulders to keep him upright as he grips his side and beads of sweat gather along his receding hairline.

It's only because he lifts his bowed head and a healthier shade of pink returns to his cheeks that I'm not screaming for help and dialing 911. "Daddy?"

He offers me a weak smile and pats my arm. "I'm all right," he says, leaning back in his chair.

"No, you're not," I say, my eyes stinging. His light blue dress shirt clings with sweat along his arms and plump midsection. He's not well. My father is . . . *sick*. "What aren't you telling me?"

His hand slowly eases away from his side. For a moment his eyes search my face, as they've done a thousand times throughout my life. "The doctors discovered new tumors along my colon," he finally says. "They're planning to resection my bowel and dispose of the affected area with the hope of avoiding chemo this time around."

Very carefully, I straighten, despite that my heart has all but stopped beating. My father was diagnosed with colon cancer years ago and barely survived the aggressive treatment. If it's returned, now that he's older, and not as healthy . . .

"When were you going to tell me?" I ask, struggling to keep my voice clear as it shakes, my fear likely worsening my speech impediment.

He sighs. "Friday, over dinner."

To give me the weekend to absorb it, no doubt. "And your surgery? When is that?"

"A few weeks." He frowns as if debating what to say. "I'll be out of commission for a while. In my absence, Declan will lead the office as acting District Attorney." He looks at me then. "And I ask that you help him, regardless of your feelings toward him."

Declan

"This isn't where I fucking belong." I'm beyond pissed, and started typing my resignation letter at least six times today only to delete it. Yet for as much as I don't want to head the Sexual Assault and Child Abuse Unit, I'm not a quitter. "Fuck," I mumble, dragging my hand along my face. "*Fuck.*"

My brother Curran crosses his arms over his chest, not caring how it creases the shirt of his Philly PD uniform. But then Curran doesn't care about shit like that. "It's still a promotion, Deck," he says. "You got this D.A. spot straight out of law school and have made more of a name for yourself than most douche-bag attorneys ever will." He holds out a hand. "No offense to the douche-bag attorneys of the world."

"That's my point. After all I've accomplished, I should be the one leading the Homicide unit."

I shove away from my desk and pace. When Miles gave me these new digs, I thought it was just the start of all the good things coming my way. When he assigned me a county car and a personal secretary, it only reinforced that my hard work had paid off. I was on my way …until I wasn't.

"I spent months dismantling a mafia empire, Curran."

"I know," he says. "I was there."

"I brought down a major crime boss—and his second in command, and his third."

"Yup. Saw that, too," he agrees.

"I received international attention—the trial of the century, the media called it—and for what? To be shoved someplace I don't belong."

"Why don't you think you belong there?"

Out of all my five brothers, Curran is probably one of the biggest ball busters. But he's not messing with me now. He's being serious.

"Do you want to hear about babies and women being hurt? Day in and day out?" I ask. "These are the cases I'm going to be dealing with."

"Someone has to do it, Deck. It's the right thing."

"I'm not saying it isn't. I'm only saying I may not be the man for the job. This shit's disgusting, what these low-life assholes are capable of."

"Is this about Finnie?" He huffs when I straighten and don't answer. "Christ," he mutters.

As easy as that, my brother nails it on the head. For all he sometimes pisses me off, my brother isn't stupid. "Finnie didn't deserve what happened to him," I say, feeling my anger burn down to my gut.

"Of course he didn't," Curran snaps. "No one does. But as his brother, you owe it to him to put monsters like the guy who hurt him away."

I sit back in my chair and rub my jaw. "I don't know if I can."

Our youngest brother was sexually assaulted by a neighbor when he was ten. It screwed with his mind. What he doesn't realize is we've all suffered, too—not like he has—of course, not like he has. That doesn't mean we don't hurt for him or haven't spent sleepless nights worried about him.

Nothing bad was supposed to happen to Finnie. He was the baby. The one who counted on us. The one we were all supposed to keep safe.

With this new assignment—hearing stories like Finnie's on a regular basis?—God *damn* it. "I don't think I can do this," I say yet again.

"Deck, you have to, man."

A knock on the door interrupts us. I know who it is before I even ask. "Come in," I say, assuming my attorney pose because for now, I have to. For now, I'm a professional. Even though all the Philly boy in me wants to do is rage.

My boss, Miles Fenske walks in, followed by his daughter Melissa. Miles smiles warmly, nodding my way.

Mel? What can I say? She's the one person who's never been taken by my charm. Today's no different. Unlike the other females who work here, from interns to attorneys, she doesn't meet me with a grin, doesn't flash me a little leg, and doesn't pretend to flirt. Brown hair, brown eyes, creamy skin, with a steel-hard exterior, she walks in with her hips swinging, her bright red dress hugging her hourglass figure, her full lips pressed into a firm line, and her unyielding stare meeting mine.

She doesn't like me. Not that I blame her. Too bad this is the one woman I can't seem to get out of my damn mind . . .

Crave Me

An O'Brien Family

Novel

by Cecy Robson

CHAPTER 1

Wren

I drop the keys in Mr. Esposito's hand and smile. He stares at them in his open palm like a precious gift, because to someone like him who's worked hard all his life, it very much is.

"Thank you, Wren," he says, meeting my smile. "I never thought I'd own a new car. Let alone be able to give one to my son as a gift."

"You deserve it, Mr. Esposito," I tell him, shaking his hand. "And so does your son for getting into Drexel. Tell Antonio, hi for me—Oh, and be sure to have someone take his picture when you hand him the keys." I motion to my office behind me. "I want to add it to my memory wall."

"I will." He presses his lips tight as if considering what to say. "Your father would be proud of you," he tells me. His soft brown eyes take in the massive dealership, fixing on the sales board displaying my current rank at number one. "Very proud."

I hold onto my smile as he walks toward the brand new candy apple red F-150 hugging the curb, ignoring the brutal January wind that sweeps in when the doors to the lot zip open. Mr. Esposito pauses when he opens the driver's side door. I had the boys in the back place a bow on dash like I do for all my customers. I think it's a nice touch, and a way to thank them for their business. Mr. Esposito tosses me a grin over his shoulder. Maybe it's the wind slapping against his face, or maybe it's because he's just that touched, but I catch his eyes glistening with tears.

Slowly he slips inside and grips the wheel, his widening smile lifting his deeply worn features.

The moment he pulls away, my smile vanishes. "Your father would be proud of you," he'd said. He meant it as a compliment. Mr. Esposito has always been nice like that. But instead of giving me the warm fuzzies, that familiar pang tugs at my insides.

My heels click against the bleached white tile as I cross the showroom. The phones ringing off the hook have me turning toward the finance department. It's been a nasty winter with all the snow we've been hit with, but I can't say it's been bad for business. One of the secretaries waves to me as she hurries to answer the phone. I wave back, not that she seems to notice. She starts writing as she takes the first call. Yeah, it's going to be a busy week. But busy means work, and that's something I've always been good at.

My eyes narrow when they fix on Oscar looming over Penny. Penny is smart, and an overall good person. She's young, and hasn't been here long, but she's trying, and I know she has it in her to succeed. Too bad Oscar is stomping on her success, luring customers away from her every chance he gets.

"You snooze, you lose," he tells her, pegging her with one of his more sleazy grins.

Penny was making headway with the guy who walked in, until Oscar shoved his way between them and baited him away, making Penny look like she didn't know what she was talking about. If I hadn't been busy with Mr. Esposito, I would have stepped in. Nothing gets me more than men who target those they think are weak.

"Wren!" Suze calls from behind the counter. "You have a call."

"Okay. Send it through to my office," I yell. I rush across the last few feet of the showroom, but not before I make sure Oscar steps far away from Penny.

The phone rings one, twice, before I slam the door behind me with my foot and reach across my desk and put the call on speaker. "Erin O'Brien," I say.

There's a brief pause before I hear, "Hi, Wren."

Shit. My stomach twists the way it always does when I hear his voice. "What do you want, Bryant?" I ask, digging out my cell phone from my desk drawer.

"I miss you," he says.

"Do you miss hitting me, too?" I fire back.

I'm talking tough. It's what I do. Too bad I don't feel so tough right now. Not when it comes to Bryant. A familiar sense of dread sends a chill down my spine, reminding me what happened the last time I pissed him off. I hit the record icon on my cell phone, hoping to catch him saying something I can use against him. But the damn thing beeps, and for all Bryant is an asshole, he's not stupid.

"Are you recording me, pretty girl?" He laughs when I don't answer. "Now, why would you do a thing like that?"

"Because I don't trust you, because you hit me—oh, and because you're an asshole."

"I don't know what you're talking about," he says, keeping his voice easy. "I'm just returning your call. You keep calling me so—"

"That's a lie," I say, my face heating with anger. He knows I'm recording him and trying to switch things around. "Don't call me again. I want nothing to do with you."

I hang up the phone. It's been months since I last saw him, months since he last put his hands on me. But just when I think I'm rid of him, he reminds me he's still there.

I could call the police. The problem is, he is the police. . .

Evan

My Jaguar skids, again, again, and again, fighting to keep pace with the other drivers insane enough to travel the Blue Route in this weather. Chunks of wet snow smack against my windshield. My wipers squeak against the glass as they race to keep my line of sight clear when another vehicle cuts me off, pelting my windshield with more ice. My current struggle with life and death does not evidently discourage Ashleigh from barking messages over my Blue Tooth.

"Yodel called again, Evan. They want you to reconsider."

"No," I reply, cutting my steering wheel toward the left when my car veers right. "We're representing Mellon, their biggest competitor. It's a conflict of interest to supply both companies with the same technology."

I mutter a curse when the minivan in front of me slams on their brakes and I narrowly miss ramming the bumper. And I suppose, because we're in Philadelphia, the City of Brotherly love, the woman rolls down the window, permitting snow into her vehicle just to wave an irate middle finger at me.

"Rich Bitch loser," she cries out.

I rub my face. Bloody hell, why am I here again? Before I can finish the thought, Ashleigh reminds me.

"Evan, we're at risk for financial collapse. The company needs the revenue."

"Not at the expense of our ethics," I counter.

True, my company is at risk. But it's due to poor business practices, such as the ones Ashleigh suggests I entertain. I understand she learned these tactics from my predecessor, but he was a conniving snake—which is why he's currently serving time for embezzlement and I had to leave London to rebuild my father's dying empire.

"What about your eleven a.m. with the V.P. of County General?"

"Have Anne and Clifton start straight away. I emailed them the presentation last night—"

"Do you really think they're qualified?" she interrupts.

I open my mouth to insist that they are and to remind her I'm her superior, not the other way around. But I'm not oblivious to what she tells me. Anne and Clifton are fairly new and not at the level I'd prefer them to be. Nevertheless, they're learning fast under my tutelage and the only ones from the original staff I trust.

"Evan," she presses.

"Ashleigh, Anne and Clifton will handle it. That's my final word." I disconnect, swearing as I take the ramp and practically slide down sideways.

Another proud Pennsylvanian sticks his head out the window. "Get a real car, fucker," he hollers.

I rub my face again, tired and frustrated. I didn't arrive home until three this morning. It wouldn't have taken as long had I been driving a vehicle capable of enduring this ungodly weather.

I glance up, releasing a tense breath when the sign for the Ford dealership I researched comes into view. Saving iCronos will take me time. Time I can't spare driving a Jaguar on roads better maneuvered via dogsled.

My car slows to a stop in front of the massive dealership. The combination of the vehicle I'm driving, along with the expensive suit and coat I'm wearing, command attention. The moment I step inside, a young woman with dark spiky hair hurries over. "Good morning, sir. I'm Penny," she says. "Welcome to Ford Nation. Are you interested in acquiring a new vehicle?"

She seems young, but eager, a respectable attribute. Yet no sooner does she finish speaking than a man about my age steps in front of her, adjusting the jacket of his gray suit. "I got this, P," he tells her. "Get us some coffee, will you?" He holds out his hand. "Hello. I'm Oscar Nelson. Welcome to Ford Nation."

My frown bounces from his hand to the young woman whose face is now bright red with humiliation and possibly more. "Are you his assistant?" I ask her.

"No," she answers. "I'm a car sales representative—"

Oscar speaks over her, but it's the sound of quickly approaching footsteps that causes me to turn. A woman with a pinstripe jacket and matching skirt hurries forward, the quick motions of her long legs causing the edge of her skirt to brush above her knees and swing her hips seductively. Long hair flutters like streams of ebony smoke, revealing a staggeringly beautiful face better suited for my wildest fantasies.

I spent the first five years following the completion of my doctorate in either a lab or boardroom packed with men in alternating stages of balding, and these last nine months trapped in a building working a minimum of eighteen hour days. I haven't had the opportunity or time to meet women. But if I'd known she was out here, I'd have spared a moment.

Good . . . God.

I don't realize I'm staring until she stops directly in front of us and juts out her chin. "Problem?" she asks Oscar.

Oscar straightens to his full height. "No. I was just showing Mr. . . . ." He motions to me. "My apologies, what's your name, sir?"

"Jonah," I say, returning my attention to the stunning young woman. I offer her my hand. "Evan Jonah."

Full pink lips lift into a dazzling smile that resonates in her deep blue eyes and lights her creamy white skin.

"I'm Erin O'Brien, but I go by Wren," she says. She shakes my hand with a firm grip, releasing me to guide the smaller woman forward. "How can Penny and I help you today, sir?"

"I'm afraid my vehicle isn't equipped for this weather and I am seeking a better alternative, possibly a truck or SUV," I reply, doing all in my power to keep my focus on her face.

"Then you've come to the right place. Penny, will you show Mr. Jonah—"

"Evan," I interrupt, mentally kicking myself for morphing into a fourteen year old boy the moment my eyes locked on this woman.

"Okay, Evan," she says. "Penny, please show Evan the latest members of the Ford family."

"Of course, this way, sir," Penny answers with a grin.

I reluctantly follow behind Penny. But as we reach a black Explorer my gaze trails back to Wren. She and Oscar have moved away from the showroom and closer to the rear offices. Yet it does little to muffle their exchange.

"What the fuck was that?" Oscar snaps.

My spine stiffens. I storm forward, ready to demand he apologize for using such foul language in the presence of a lady.

"You being a raging asshole," Wren replies.

I'll admit, her response gives me pause. And she doesn't stop there. "Look, I know you have to compensate for your less than average-sized dick. But that doesn't give you the right to mistreat Penny or pounce on every client she approaches. That's bullshit and you know it."

"Um, perhaps a truck will be more to your needs," Penny says, motioning to the opposite side of the dealership and away from the heated conversation.

I don't typically involve myself in affairs that don't concern me, nor do I interact with women who speak in such a manner. But it's not simply Wren's colorful vocabulary that captivates me, it's her strength and desire to defend her small friend.

"Where the fuck did you hear that?" Oscar responds. "I don't have a small dick."

Of all his possible retorts, this is the one he chooses?

"Suze," Wren calls over her shoulder in the direction of the finance counter. "What was it you said about that night you went out with Oscar?"

The woman behind the counter scowls and holds up her pinky. Wren smirks. "Looks to me like you should have called her back." She pats his shoulder. "My condolences to your man parts."

She starts to walk away, stopping when she realizes I witnessed their encounter. Instead of making a quick escape or pretending I didn't hear them, she walks toward me with her head raised. "Sorry about that, Mr. Jonah—"

"Evan," I clarify as she reaches me.

Her smile stirs one of my own. "Evan," she repeats, lifting a hand toward her friend. "I see Penny is taking good care of you."

"Um, maybe you can take over," Penny says. She edges away, aware how taken I am with Wren.

Wren tilts her head. "I don't want to step all over your pitch," she says.

"You're not," she responds. "I'll take the next one. Honest."

Wren waits for Penny to leave before turning to face me. She considers me a moment, but then motions back to the Explorer. "This is the latest model in Ford luxury," she begins. "Comfortable, secure, capable of meeting all your commuting needs, and packed with plenty of toys."

I follow her as she leads me around the vehicle. The ease of her speech and relaxed posture demonstrate a confident woman who knows her job well. I question her about the vehicle's basics first: mileage, warranty, and safety features, before testing her intelligence further. She doesn't disappoint, explaining everything in detail down to the engine's construction, adding to my growing attraction.

"Would you like to take her for a ride?" she asks. She punches my arm affectionately, the motion only briefly luring my attention away from her delicate features. "This way you can see how smoothly she handles the road and ask, 'Wren, how did I ever survive without a Ford?'"

"I'd like that," I answer, my deep voice quieting. This woman who appears more elite model than sales representative knows exactly what she's doing. "Very much."

"Good," she says, pointing at me. "You'll wonder how you ever got along without her."

As I watch her walk away, I start to wonder that myself.

Photo by Kate Gledhill of Kate Gledhill Photography

Cecy Robson is an author of contemporary romance, young adult adventure, and award-winning urban fantasy. A double RITA® 2016 finalist for Once Pure and Once Kissed, and a published author of more than sixteen titles, you can typically find her on her laptop writing her stories or stumbling blindly in search of caffeine.

For more, visit my Website:

www.cecyrobson.com

For exclusive information and more, join my Newsletter:

http://eepurl.com/4ASmj